To Lillian,
Enjoy the
journey!
Holly Kelly

RISING

Holly Kelly

Clean Teen Publishing

Rising

Clean Teen Publishing
PO Box 561326
The Colony, TX 75056

www.CleanTeenPublishing.com

For more information about our content disclosure, please utilize the QR code above with your smart phone or visit us at www.CleanTeenPublishing.com

My eternal thanks to my parents who told me I could be anything I wanted to be and to my husband and children who supported me enough to make it possible.

PROLOGUE

Kim grimaced as she gulped down the last of her stale diet coke. The lukewarm fluid slid down her throat like sweet, caffeinated dishwater. She glanced up at the clock and smiled. Only ten minutes left on her shift. A gut-wrenching cry echoed off the walls of room 121. It sounded like Nicole Taylor was making progress—either that or she had a really low threshold for pain.

"Drugs!" Nicole shrieked. "I need drugs!" Kim stepped under the muted lights of the plush room. Well, it was plush for a hospital anyway.

Nicole lay in a hospital bed, writhing in pain. Kim approached her, frowning. "Now Nicole, we talked about this. We are perfectly willing to provide an epidural. But it'll cost you more."

"I don't care if I have to sell my soul!" she snarled. "I need drugs, now!" Sweat dripped down her forehead. Her face contorted and scowled so deeply that even a girl as pretty as this one had lost her girlish appeal in the throes of pain.

"Well," Kim said, "before we call the anesthesiologist, let's see where you're at." She snapped on a pair of sterile gloves and checked to see how far Nicole was dilated.

"Nicole, sweetie," Kim gave a sympathetic smile. "I have good news and bad news. The good news is your pain will soon be over. The bad news is we don't have time to give you an epidural. Your baby's coming now."

"*What?* But I..." Whatever she was about to say was lost in another groan that quickly turned to a roar of pain.

The nurse stepped into the hall, picked up the phone receiver, and punched a series of numbers.

"Hello," a warm male voice answered. "This is Dr. Bloomberg."

"Doctor, this is Kim in maternity. I have a patient that's fully dilated and ready to start pushing."

"And you couldn't have told me sooner?"

"I'm sorry, she progressed faster than we expected."

He sighed heavily. "I've almost forgotten what hot food tastes like."

"You and me both."

His chuckle filled the phone. "Comes with the job, I suppose. I'll be right there."

Kim was about to walk back to the room when Amanda stepped off the elevator. "Anything interesting happen tonight?" she asked in way of a greeting.

Kim shrugged. "Oh, you know. The usual. Room 121 is where the action is right now. A nineteen-year-old patient is fully dilated and ready to push. Dr. Bloomberg is on his way and I was just about to go in, but if you don't mind...."

"No problem." Amanda smiled and hurried to assist the patient, who was once again screaming.

Kim stepped behind the nurse's station and snatched her purse.

"Kim!"

Kim dropped her purse. "I'm coming."

When Kim stepped through the door, she could see immediately what the issue was. The baby's head bulged out—slick, shiny, and ready to pop into the world.

The patient growled, her face crimson red.

"No, no, don't push yet," Amanda screeched and then looked desperately toward Kim.

Kim sighed. "Relax, Amanda,"

"Where's Dr. Bloomberg?" she whispered.

"He's on his way, but until he gets here, we are it."

"I've never actually delivered a baby before..."

"Hello ladies." Dr. Bloomberg smiled as he lumbered through the door. He looked at the patient. "Well, well, you weren't kidding when you said she was about to deliver."

He quickly snapped on gloves, slipped on a gown, and approached the soon-to-be mother, who was huffing and puffing. "Hello Nicole, I'm Dr. Bloomberg." He spoke as if he had all the time in the world. "I see you've already done most of the work. Now just relax until the next contraction starts, okay? Then you can push as hard as you can."

Nicole nodded vigorously.

Kim used this opportunity to leave. With Dr. Bloomberg there, Nicole Smith was in good hands.

Kim gathered her purse, picked up a handheld mirror at the nurse's station, and cringed at her reflection. She ran her fingers through her hair and pulled out her keys. A loud, audible gasp and noisy thump stopped her in her tracks. *What in the world?*

She was already sprinting toward the room when Dr. Bloomberg called, "Kim! We need you in here."

Amanda lay in a heap on the floor. Kim rushed to her side, dropped to her knees, and felt for a pulse—strong and a little fast. "What was wrong with...?"

"She's fine," Dr. Bloomberg interrupted. "She just had a shock. Now, I don't want you to panic either." He turned toward her, holding a tiny, squirming bundle in his hands. The squeaky cries of a newborn came from under the blanket. "And I need you to do everything I say, exactly as I say it, okay?"

This was weird. "Okay," she answered tentatively.

"I have to take care of the mother, so I'll need you to take the baby. Now listen to me closely." He narrowed his eyes, looking very serious—intent. "Go to the nursery, put the baby in a bassinet, and then, once she's safely lying down, you can open the blanket to care for her. Is that clear?"

Kim's heart sank. There was something seriously

wrong with this infant. She nodded, looked at the tiny, squirming bundle, and took it in her arms. When the baby was safely cradled against her chest, she looked up at the doctor, desperate for reassurance. His back was already to her as he worked on the mother. As she left the room, she could hear the mother sobbing.

Kim looked down at the bundle. She could do this. She'd been a nurse for ten years. There wasn't much she hadn't seen. Her heart pounded as she neared the nursery. She wondered what she'd find under the blue and pink folds. Well, whatever the problem was, it must not be life threatening or the doctor wouldn't have told her to take it to the nursery.

She stepped into the room; the braying cries of other newborns surrounded her. The nearest empty bassinet was pink. Was this baby a boy or girl? Did the doctor say? She couldn't remember.

She lay the bundle in the bed and let the baby squirm as she worked up the nerve to open the blanket. Would the baby have a severely deformed face? She'd seen a baby born with no facial features, only holes for a nose and mouth. That'd been pretty shocking.

Perhaps this was something she'd never seen. Maybe this was an oddly conjoined twin—like one head with two faces. Good grief, her imagination was running away from her. This baby couldn't be as bad as that.

She gently pulled the blanket so it slid away from the baby's face. A pudgy cheek immerged followed by two beautiful blue eyes and shaggy black hair. A perfect little face looked up at her. She sighed in relief. Okay, this was the face of a normal little baby. The problem must be with the body.

Perhaps the babe was born with sirenomelia—legs fused together. That would be shocking to see.

This time Kim decided to just pull the blanket away quickly—get it over with. She tugged the blanket back, expecting to be surprised. Instead, she sighed in relief.

Thank heavens.

She smiled—proud she'd predicted the problem. This baby *was* born with sirenomelia. What were the odds in guessing that right? Maybe she should take a trip to Vegas.

Her eyes popped open wide and her heart stopped when the baby once again squirmed. Dots swam in her vision as she sank to the floor. She had to be seeing things. It couldn't be.

She took two deep breaths and steeled herself. She was a nurse. She was not allowed to get woozy at an unusual malformation. It was, wasn't it? She looked again and doubt filled her mind. This was not simply two legs fused together. Legs, fused or not, do not move like that. But it *had* to be a deformity. Of that, she was certain. One fact blared in her mind, proving her right. And that fact was this... *There are no such things as mermaids.*

ONE

~Deep in the Mediterranean Sea—
Twenty Years Later~

Xanthus could taste the blood of a human in the seawater. He clenched his fists and swam faster, determined to reach his destination in time. His powerful tailfin drove him forward as he speared a path through the water.

Beams of sunlight danced over the ancient, stone road—the glow slightly dimmer than moments before. Nightfall approached. The high walls of deep ravine towered above and lined the path. Darkness seeped from the jagged rocks in the cliff walls, filling crevasses with blackness as shadows stretched across the highway. The stones on the path peaked from under the sand and silt, showing Xanthus the way to Atlantis.

Atlantis was the road's destination, not his.

The gorge widened, opening into a clearing as the rocky walls disappeared into the darkness. Silt swirled, clouding the seawater. The sharp, mineral taste of human blood washed over his tongue—stronger and thicker. A hum of voices signaled he'd reached his destination. As he moved forward, the voices rose in volume. A roar of outrage ignited other angry voices churning in the water. Through the haze, a mob came into view.

Rising

A snarling voice pierced the sea. "Gut the human and let it watch as we feed its entrails to the sharks!"

Xanthus headed straight into the crowd, shoving his way through a sea of grey tailfins and muscled arms.

Another voice raged. "Tear it apart, piece by piece. We all deserve a souvenir. I want its scalp."

From a distance, another voice said, "I want its heart."

Xanthus pushed two fellow Dagonians apart and came face to face with one of the most fearsome and deadliest soldiers in the sea—Kyros Dionysius.

"Xanthus, thank the gods you're here," Kyros said. "Your brother's crossed the line this time."

"Gael? What did Gael do?"

"He pulled a human off a dock. It wasn't even *in* the water!"

"I'd heard rumors..." Xanthus shook his head. "I didn't want to believe them."

Xanthus looked at the crowd. His older brother knew the punishment for this act—imprisonment. At least it used to be. In reality, Xanthus doubted his brother would ever see the inside of a prison cell. After the recent slaughter of Dagonians in the South Pacific, Gael would likely be hailed as a hero for this act. It didn't matter to the Dagonians that the humans didn't know what they'd done. The humans had no idea they even existed.

Xanthus caught sight of the air-filled sphere holding the prisoner. It rocked back and forth by the chaotic movements of the Dagonians swimming around it. Six strong soldiers held on to the ropes tethering it down and about twenty other soldiers kept the crowd at bay.

The sphere was smaller than Xanthus had expected. Dirt and blood smeared the inside, making it difficult to see in. As he moved closer, his stomach sickened when he got a look at the human. A small woman cowered in the center of her prison; tear-smeared dirt caked her battered face.

One Dagonian rushed between the solders, bared his teeth, and roared. The soldiers pulled him back as the woman screamed and scrambled against the far side of the chamber. To say she was frightened would be a gross understatement. A Dagonian mother seeing her only child in the jaws of a kraken couldn't have been more terrified.

"Ah ha, the Nightmare of the Deep has arrived." Gael smiled as he approached Xanthus. "So glad you could join us. Are you ready to live up to your name, brother?"

Xanthus pounded his fists against Gael's chest, shoving him back. "What are you doing?"

"What do you *think* I'm doing?" Gael snarled and pushed back. "I'm dealing out justice."

"Justice? Why? What did *this* human do?"

"You dare ask that question while the flesh of three thousand Dagonians rot in the South Pacific?"

"Yes, I dare."

Gael looked at Xanthus, disgust oozing off him. "The humans are a plague. They've overrun the planet. They've poisoned our seas. We can no longer stay down here and pretend they don't exist."

"There are better ways to handle this. Torturing and killing this woman will accomplish nothing."

"Wrong!" Gael shouted. "This is the *best* preparation I can give my men for the war to come. I can't have them hesitate to kill *any* human—man, woman, or child. I chose this human because she's a female, she's beautiful, and she made the mistake of throwing her trash into our sea. And that's what every human has done—you can't deny it. They've dumped so much garbage down here they've poisoned our homes. We are forced to swim in their filth. She's as guilty as the rest and she's going to suffer sorely for her transgression." Gael neared the sphere and sneered. "There'll be no quick and easy death for this wretched creature."

Xanthus continued to scowl at his brother, saying nothing.

Gael turned back to Xanthus. "So what do *you* think I should do? Petition the gods?"

"That's exactly what I've done," Xanthus said. "I sent a message to the Guardian. I have every intention of ending this war before it begins."

Gael laughed. "Triton? What a waste. He hates us. Even if he does answer you, it will mean your death. You're such a fool." Gael turned from his brother, raised his fists to the crowd, and shouted out as the mob cheered him.

Xanthus looked back on the woman with pity. She was not supposed to die. Only humans who presented a threat for Dagonian discovery were marked for imprisonment or execution. Xanthus had captured and executed many humans himself over the years. Those kills had been justified—this death was not. At least it *hadn't* been. This woman just happened to be in the wrong place at the wrong time. But now that she was here, Xanthus could do nothing for her.

Her eyes locked on his. *"Please help me,"* she said. *"Don't let them hurt me."*

This human seemed smart enough to recognize pity. Xanthus didn't answer her. For him to nurture hope would be futile. He could give her no hope.

"This has to be a nightmare," she said. *"Mermaids are supposed to sing songs, sit on rocks, and comb their hair. You're all just monsters."*

Thank the gods the Dagonians surrounding her didn't understand her language. Xanthus was one of only a few Dagonians in the sea that *could*. It was a good thing for this human. If there was anything a Dagonian hated more than a human, it was a Mer.

"Don't kill her," a voice shouted. "Make her suffer. Make her suffer until she begs for death, and then make her suffer more."

"Yes! Make her suffer," they all echoed.

Gael shouted, "She will suffer! I will see to it she suffers a much as any being *can* without causing death.

Once she's given us all the satisfaction her misery can bring, then and only then, we will kill her. And her death will be the first of many."

"Death to the humans!" a voice called out. A wave of voices caught the wake of that plea—the whole crowd shouting and shaking their fists. "Death to the humans, death to the humans, death to the humans..."

Xanthus's jaw clenched and his lips curled in disgust. They *were* acting like monsters. He looked back to the woman. She sat, wrapped her arms around herself, and sobbed.

As Xanthus approached her, she crawled up onto her knees and pressed her bloodied hands against the sphere. With desperation dripping from her quivering lips, she mouthed the words, "*Help me, please.*"

And so he did.

He released her. The sphere shattered and dissolved into the sea. The incoming seawater slammed into her body, the incredible force crushing her. She died instantly—her eyes forever open, forever pleading, and now forever void of life.

Xanthus turned away as the mob rushed in toward her.

"They're not going to like what you just did," Kyros said, coming up from behind him. "We need to get you out of here."

"Just where do you think you're going?" Gael shouted.

Xanthus turned and drew his sword. Gael and his

soldiers were at Xanthus's back, their weapons drawn.

"You have no right to detain us, Gael. *We're* not the ones who committed a crime here," Xanthus said.

"That's not how I see it. You've interfered with my capture..."

"Your illegal capture," Xanthus interrupted.

"That's up for debate. Even now the counsel is arguing on whether they should allow us to kill all humans who venture into the sea."

"That's insanity," Xanthus said.

"No. Insanity is letting the humans poison us as we die one by one, settlement after settlement." Gael clenched his fists so tight, his knuckles shone white. His chest heaved and his face burned red. "I'm through arguing with you. If you've chosen not to side with your fellow Dagonians, then you've chosen to side with the humans. And you deserve to die."

"You'd kill your own brother?" Kyros asked.

Gael snapped his head in Kyros's direction. "If he's aligned himself with the humans, he's no brother to me."

"I've not sided with the humans," Xanthus said. "I've sided against *you.*"

"Same thing," Gael answered. He turned to his men. "Kill them. Leave their bodies for the sharks."

Kyros moved in next to Xanthus, ready to fight. At twenty-six against two, the odds weren't good. He and Kyros were infinitely more skilled than any one of Gael's men. But coming at them all at once? They might have a problem on their hands.

The sea began to spin and stir around them, forming a whirlpool. Gael's men backed away, shouting in confusion. A loud clap, like the snapping jaws of a giant shark, pulsed through the water. Then light flashed.

A man stood before them on the dry sea floor in a column of air. The water rotated around him like a funnel. The man was well muscled, his eyes piercing, and his body glowed with unspeakable power. The winged sandals were a dead giveaway to his identity. This was Hermes, messenger of the gods. And the god's eyes fell on Xanthus.

"Xanthus Dimitriou?"

"Yes," Xanthus answered.

"I have a message for you." Hermes eyed the soldiers. He then looked back to Xanthus, smirked, and shook his head. "You are to report immediately to Triton's palace."

Hermes didn't wait around for Xanthus's answer, but disappeared in a flash of light as the sea slapped back together with a deafening crack.

Xanthus didn't move—stunned by what just happened. True, he had petitioned Triton. But he never truly expected an answer. Triton hadn't spoken to a Dagonian since they'd slaughtered the last of his merchildren two thousand years ago. Still, as newly appointed Guardian of the Sea, Triton should be informed of a gathering threat of war.

Fear fluttered in Xanthus's chest when he wondered if his brother was right. Would this meeting mean his death?

Xanthus looked back to the soldiers who, just a moment ago, were ready to massacre them. They looked just as astonished as he felt. When Xanthus and Kyros moved forward, the soldiers didn't utter a word of protest, but cast their eyes down and parted. One threat of death averted, on to another.

When they were a fair distance away, Kyros spoke. "Is there something you haven't told me?"

"I didn't think it worth telling."

"You summoned a *god* and didn't think it worth telling your best friend?"

"I didn't summon him, I petitioned him. There's a difference."

"Not *much* difference. Summoning Triton would have gotten you killed immediately. Petitioning him will buy you another hour or so before he strikes you down."

"He won't strike me down."

"Oh really. And why not?"

"Because my cause is just."

A short, hard laugh burst from Kyros just before a scowl settled on his face and he shook his head. "You may be older than me, but those years didn't do much to add to your wisdom."

"I'm not ignorant of Triton's hatred toward us, but he's also honorable. His position demands he listen to me. I'm going to offer to appeal to the humans. They must be reasoned with. They must stop their attack on our seas. It's the only way to save them."

"So you want to save the humans?" Kyros asked. "Even after they polluted our seas and killed over three thousand Dagonians?"

"It's not only the humans I'm worried about. A war won't solve anything. There are six billion people living on the surface. Our numbers aren't even close to matching that. "

"Perhaps. But physically, *we* have the advantage." Kyros flexed his impressive muscles.

"True, but how many of us will die? Thousands? Millions? They've already killed three thousand of us, and they didn't even know they'd done it."

"Well, you do what you need to do to stop this war. I, for one, will be spending more time at the training fields. Still, if you can convince Triton to join your side, anything's possible. Just be careful. Gods are rarely reasonable and quick to strike."

"I'll be fine," Xanthus said.

Kyros turned and opened his mouth to argue. Instead, he pursed his lips together and gave a quick nod.

Two

The Castle of Triton rose in the distance—a colossal fortress with many tall turrets, arched buttresses, and massive windows. Hundreds of sharks circled above and around the castle, guarding their master inside.

As Xanthus neared, five of the larger sharks broke rank and charged toward him. Their gaping mouths sneered, ridged with sharp, dagger-like teeth. Xanthus's steel muscles clenched, prepared for battle.

The sharks stopped just out of striking distance, effectively blocking his approach to the castle. Their eyes pierced him, oozing a deep and loathing hatred. The most frightening shark hovered in the middle, flanked by the others. Half his face was missing. The horrific injury had healed, leaving pink and grey flesh knitted together, knarled and misshapen. *How could he have survived such a severe injury?*

A thundering concussion pounded through the water. The rumbling sound formed words. "Let the Dagonian pass." A shudder went through Xanthus at that menacing voice.

The sharks hesitated a moment before parting.

Still, they continued to glare at him. Xanthus readied himself to respond in case any of the guards decided to attack. An assault would be unlikely; given it must have been Triton who had ordered them to back off. But with so much anger and vicious hatred directed at him, Xanthus held his defensive posture as he approached the castle.

A massive, grey leviathan clung to the side of the building. His mountainous bulk and countless tentacles snaked over the surface. Xanthus searched for the castle door. He circled the entire building but still couldn't see any sign of an entrance. Finally, he puzzled it out. The leviathan had to be covering it. He scowled at that realization. Surely, he wasn't expected to fight the thing. The creature might look soft, but inside that gelatinous body lurked a razor-sharp beak so large and powerful it could snap him in two. Xanthus might be able to slice off a tentacle or two during the fight, but in the end he'd still be dead and the injured leviathan's tentacles would grow back in a matter of months.

The monster's great eyes fixed on him as he moved toward the creature. When Xanthus swam close enough to touch him, the tentacles slithered back, revealing a gigantic door. One thick tentacle pushed the door open, generating a low, thundering rumble. Xanthus focused on the door as he tried to ignore the monstrous, fleshy archway he passed under.

Darkness enveloped him as he swam into an immense hall. A kaleidoscope of faintly luminescent stone framed great tapestries along the walls. He swam above an intricate mosaic map of all the oceans and seas. It covered the entire floor of the vast room. Near the back of the hall, high branches of black coral cradled an enormous throne. His eyes widened at what looked like fire-lit torches—something he'd seen pictured in a book of human lore.

Double doors slammed open at the back. A figure entered wearing a hard, stony glare. Firelight glinted across roped muscles and a mighty tail. His blond hair and trimmed beard swaying in the water did nothing to soften his scowl.

There was no doubt that King Triton had entered the room.

Xanthus's eyes widened in shock. Triton looked like a Dagonian.

"Xanthus Dimitriou?" Triton's deep voice rumbled.

"I'm at your command, Sire." Xanthus bowed before he neared the throne, careful to maintain a respectful distance.

"Before I give you *any* command, you will answer me this one question. Are you courageous or stupid?" The god's furious blue eyes reflected the fire of the torches. Xanthus felt as if he were staring into the burning pit of Tartarus. His first impression couldn't have been more wrong. Triton was nothing like a Dagonian. With the tail of a tiger shark, fiery eyes as blue as the sea, and the temperament of a raging typhoon, Triton's presence oozed powerful, menacing god.

Still, Xanthus answered without hesitation. "I am courageous, Majesty."

"Do you not know the hatred I bear toward you Dagonians? You slaughtered my children, my grandchildren—all my beloved merchildren!" Triton's voice boomed.

"Yes, Sire. I know." Xanthus wanted to say that he had not been part of the slaughter and the Dagonians had had no choice but to act on Poseidon's command but Xanthus felt Triton's unspoken demand that the Dagonians shoulder the blame for the destruction of his children. Xanthus bowed his head, astonished to see Triton's rage still fresh and fierce, even after two thousand years.

Xanthus steadied his breath and forced the fear bubbling inside to melt away. He could not forget his reason for coming. His mission was more important than the life of one Dagonian. And regardless of how fierce Triton acted or the fact he could kill Xanthus with a single glance, Triton was also honorable. Xanthus just needed to appeal to that side of the god and do it before Triton struck him dead.

"Yet," Triton continued, "you come to *me*, your enemy, to request permission to venture among the humans and appeal to their good natures. Not only that, but you expect me to impart some of my own power to make this travel possible?"

"Yes, Sire," Xanthus spoke firmly.

"You expect much, Dagonian." He paused, eyeing Xanthus. "Answer me this. How many souls have you sent to Hades?"

Xanthus tensed. What reason did Triton have to ask this question? "Over a hundred Dagonians, Sire, not including the ones I sent to Panthon prison and have since died there."

"And the humans?"

"Twenty-six... No wait, after today, twenty-seven."

Triton narrowed his eyes. "Do you think to redeem your soul from Tartarus by this journey?"

"No, Sire, I have nothing to redeem myself from. Those I sent to Hades were predators preying on the innocent. And the humans were... necessary."

Triton pondered in silence for several long moments. "So now you want to save them both— Dagonians and humankind alike. Do you truly think one man can make a difference? You think you can convince the entire human race to stop poisoning our seas?"

"I think it's worth trying, Majesty," Xanthus answered, his voice ringing with conviction.

Triton narrowed his eyes as he studied Xanthus. The god's scowl loosened slightly. "You're nothing like your father." Triton let that statement settle for a moment before he spoke again. "You remind me of Elsia."

Xanthus's brows furrowed. Who was Elsia?

"You were never told about her, were you?" Triton sighed, his eyes saddened by the burden of old memories.

"Elsia was my daughter, twenty-seventh child born to me three-thousand four-hundred and fifty-seven years ago. She was unique among my children—sweet, loving, and very strong willed. She decided to show all the Mer that the Dagonians were good, loving beings at heart. My daughter was a foolish mermaid. She even married a Dagonian and had a daughter named Xanthippe."

Xanthus's eyes widened. "My grandmother?"

Triton nodded. "Merblood flows strong in your veins." He closed his eyes and sighed. "I can feel it."

Triton took a deep breath, straightened his spine, and spoke the next words with authority. "I'll grant you your request—under one condition. First, you'll travel to the surface and find the human criminals responsible for poisoning the Dagonian South Pacific settlements of Calysos and Thebora. The city of Honolulu, Hawaii seems to be either the origin or place of transfer for the poisons. When you find the guilty humans, you will stop them from further dumping their poisons. Then you will send the guilty to me—alive if possible."

"Yes, of course, Sire."

"If you are successful, I will allow you one more year to do as you will. Convince the humans, if you can. But I wish to emphasize two very important rules you must understand and always abide by. First, do not let the humans discover what you are. If they do, you must see that they cannot betray our secret to others. Second, do not meddle in their lives unless their actions affect you or the creatures of the sea directly. Otherwise, leave them to their fate."

"Yes, Sire."

"I give you a month to prepare." Triton said. "It's a short time for such a task, and you have much to do before you're ready to walk among the humans. Study them, prepare your affairs, and make necessary arrangements. I will do what I can to help. You will return here in one week and stay to train for the remainder of your time. But before you leave today, I have a gift for you." Triton rose. "Come closer."

Xanthus approached the god with trepidation. Being this close to so much power intimidated and overwhelmed him. Triton laid his heavy hands on Xanthus's head. Xanthus felt heat building under the god's palms until white-hot waves of pain washed from his head down to the end of his tail. He nearly jerked away, but held still and absorbed the searing pain in agony. It lasted only a minute and then, to his relief, the pain faded. Despite the incredible agony he'd endured only a moment before, Xanthus felt strong and alert.

Triton removed his hands. "There. Now you have the power you'll need."

Xanthus wondered—confused at what power he'd been given. Regretfully, Triton didn't feel compelled to enlighten him.

Xanthus bowed. "Yes, Sire, thank you. And I will honor all your wishes, Majesty."

"I don't doubt it. Now go and prepare. I'll send for you in a week's time."

Xanthus bowed again and left.

As Xanthus put distance between himself and the castle, he felt as if a weight were being lifted off his shoulders. The cool current washed away the stifling sorrow. Triton was one seriously tormented god.

Xanthus wondered what further training he would need in order to prepare for this assignment. After all, he'd been preparing for this his whole life. He'd read every human book he could get his hands on, interviewed countless humans at Panthon prison, even volunteered on every human capture that came his way. The only other Dagonian that had as much experience with humans was his brother, Gael.

Gael wanted to destroy them. Xanthus wanted the Dagonians and humans to respect each other's right to exist peacefully. His job seemed impossible, given that he had to convince the humans to stop polluting the seas without revealing the existence of the Dagonians. But then, things of great importance never come easy.

Xanthus spotted Kyros just outside the castle perimeter.

Kyros rushed forward. Laughing, he slapped Xanthus on the back. "You made it out alive."

"Barely."

"So you're going to live with the humans?"

"For at least a year. I leave in a month's time."

Kyros shook his head in disbelief. "I've never understood your fascination with them. They are horrible, disgusting creatures."

"What you know about humans comes from Nereid tales, not facts."

"Well, you do what you need to do." Kyros scratched behind his ear. "I'm just glad it's not me having to live with them. I don't think I could stomach it."

"They're really not so bad. I shouldn't have much trouble as long as I can blend in. My biggest problem may be my size. Triton might be able to give me legs, but Dagonians are larger than humans."

"And you're larger than the average Dagonian," Kyros said.

"Right." Xanthus nodded. "I also need to consider human male fashion. From what I've learned, the clothing they wear indicates status."

"Their males have fashion? That's ridiculous. Covering the body is for females, although I think that it would be better if our females didn't cover themselves. I'd have an even greater appreciation for the dance of the Dagonian maidens."

Xanthus laughed.

"Speaking of maidens..." Kyros swished to a stop. "Mmm. Nothing smells better than a fertile female." His eyes glazed over as a smile pursed his lips.

Xanthus shook his head as his friend drifted toward a modest stone home. Two large warriors positioned themselves at the entrance in order to discourage unwelcome suitors.

"Too bad females are only fertile once a year." Kyros breathed in the alluring smell.

Xanthus never understood how males could lose their minds around a female at her time. He'd guarded more females than he could count and he'd never had a problem resisting. Not that it didn't affect him, but his control remained firmly in place at all times.

Kyros continued to drift toward the enticing scent. Xanthus put out his hand to stop him. "If you want to keep your male parts, I wouldn't move any closer."

Kyros jerked, shocked out of his stupor. The guards stared him down. "Sorry fellows," he mumbled. "I was just uh... you know, passing by."

Xanthus and Kyros remained silent until they were out of earshot of the guards. "You've got to learn to control your hormones," Xanthus said. "Those warriors were more tolerant than I would have been. I'd have had my blade at your throat in a heartbeat."

"Yeah, well, you see. That's how we're different. I'm a lover, you're a fighter."

"You're a soldier, but you'll end up a eunuch if you can't control yourself."

"I'm a soldier by trade, a lover by heart." Kyros pressed his hand to his heart and gave a sigh. Xanthus smiled and shook his head. His friend obviously still felt the effects of the pheromones. Xanthus knew Kyros would be appalled by his behavior later.

They soon reached the outskirts of Corin. In the distance, a massive air dome shimmered, nearly two leagues wide. Xanthus smiled, his mind filled with memories of his time at the academy. He'd been a master of air games.

"How about a race?" he asked Kyros.

"I don't know," Kyros said. "I'd hate to be the Dagonian who caused the Nightmare to lose his confidence."

"You act as if you have a chance of beating me."

"You may be bigger and stronger, my friend, but I'm faster."

"I hate to be the bearer of bad news, but I'm not only bigger and stronger—I'm also faster."

They approached the shimmering wall, reached out their fingertips to just a hair's width from the air, curled up their tails, and prepared to spring.

"You count us down," Xanthus said. "I don't want any excuses from you when I win."

"Being in denial is just going to make losing worse. Okay, you ready?"

Xanthus nodded.

"Three, two, one..."

Like harpoons, they both pierced the air pocket and flew. Xanthus and Kyros raced neck and neck over the dry sand, the wall of water closing in just ahead. In a few short seconds, Xanthus expected to celebrate a victory while rubbing it in his best friend's face.

Pain hit him like an explosion. He roared as his body dove down, hitting the sandy floor. He flipped, somersaulted, skidded over the surface, and finally stopped, sprawled on the dry ground just inches from the water. The crash itself had been very painful, but

Xanthus didn't pay it even a passing thought as he writhed from the pain emanating from his tail. As he lay there, every muscle in his fin burned. His tail felt as if it were being ripped in two. Xanthus let out a roar as the pain peaked and then suddenly vanished.

"Xanthus, what happened to you?" Kyros rushed over. His eyes widened as his face drained of all color. "Oh Hades, I think I'm going to be sick." Kyros slapped his hand over his mouth as he turned away, repulsed.

Xanthus shook with terror. He truly expected to find his tail ripped to bloody shreds. Reluctantly, he looked down.

Great gods of the underworld, he had human legs. They were ugly, bulging, hairy appendages. He didn't blame Kyros for his reaction. His own stomach twisted and churned at the sight. He didn't know if it was the aftereffects of so much pain that caused it, or seeing the hideous legs that had replaced his magnificent tail. Then he thought about the power needed to accomplish this change.

"Triton amazes me," Xanthus said. "I must remember to thank him."

Kyros turned toward him. "Thank him?"

"Of course. You think I should ignore the importance of this gift given by the Guardian of the Sea? I'm lucky he's even taken notice of me, much less given me this opportunity to breach the boundaries of our world and venture onto the surface."

"Well, when you put it that way..." Kyros's white

face had a tinge of green and he avoided looking just below Xanthus's waist. Xanthus avoided looking there too. Was he supposed to look like that?

Xanthus removed the gold bands from around his biceps—the bands that kept him aloft when out of the water. He wanted to stand on these new feet of his. He struggled to raise his body off the ground. It couldn't be too hard. If a human could do it, so could he. He placed his feet under his body, raised himself over his bent legs, and used all his strength to straighten them. His body shot up. He smiled, standing on his own two feet. His smile disappeared as he tipped over, crashing into the silt. Determined not to get discouraged, he tried again. This time, he swayed for about a second before he hit the sand. About a dozen tries later, he grumbled, "Hades, Kyros. This is harder than it looks." Xanthus breathed heavily as he nursed his sand-burned palms and elbows.

"Well, you have a month to learn to walk on those hideous things before you travel to the surface, and from the looks of it, a month's not enough time."

Xanthus growled. "I sure hope you're wrong."

THREE

~Hawaii—Six Months Later~

A fine mist of rain slicked over Sara, dampening her clothes as the wind plastered her hair against her face. With both hands occupied pushing her wheelchair, there wasn't a thing she could do about it. She pursed her lips to keep her hair from getting into her mouth.

Why oh why didn't I notice how late it was? Grasping the cold metal rings on her wheelchair, she bumped over the buckled surface of the darkened parking lot.

She focused on the dilapidated building ahead. The dark shape loomed tall. Light flickered from a pole, high above. It cast knarled shadows on the already menacing building below, making the image worthy of any horror movie she'd ever seen.

Sara scowled and grumbled. "Home sweet home."

She hated being out after dark, especially in her neighborhood. All around Oahu shined pristine neighborhoods—places where tourists poured out their money. But if one looked deeper, they'd find pockets of poverty. Sara lived deep in one of those pockets. Her tiny shoebox apartment gleamed as the one clean spot in her grimy, run-down building. She'd worked hard scrubbing the filth away as soon as she moved in two months ago.

Cleaning her apartment was quite the reveal. It started out looking brown and grey, but after a thorough cleaning, she was left with oranges, greens, browns, and dirty yellows—compliments of the 60s.

She didn't have the luxury of being choosy about decor. She'd rented this apartment because it was the only place she could afford. Her meager earnings didn't provide much in the ways of clean, modern style along with the privacy she required.

She felt better if she thought about how bad it could be. A year ago, she'd lived with her mother. Anywhere was better than living with *her*.

Sara bumped over the curb onto the sidewalk. The blanket covering her chair billowed in the cool breeze. No worries there. It would take a hurricane to tear it loose. Her embarrassing deformity would remain hidden from the world.

A creepy, crawly feeling tickled her spine.

Someone's eyes were on her.

Sara's looked around. She held her head still, careful not to turn it. She didn't want whoever it was to know she was aware of their presence. She couldn't see anything but the outline of cars behind a curtain of misted rain. Still, she started to freak.

She jerked her wheelchair to a stop at the front door and yanked out her keys. Her hands were shaking so hard that they couldn't move fast enough to settle her frantic mind.

Rising

She almost dropped her keys as tires screeched in the street. A dark SUV had stopped in the middle of the road for no apparent reason—probably a drive-by shooter taking aim. *Please, just let me get into my apartment and I'll be safe.*

"Sara, I'm surprised to see you out this late." A voice emerged from the darkness.

Sara squeaked out a cry as her heart catapulted against her chest wall. She breathed a sigh of relief as her friend stepped up beside her. "Oh, Gretchen, it's you. You scared the life out of me."

"I'm sorry, sweetie." Gretchen didn't look at all surprised that she'd scared her—probably because she knew her so well.

Sara finally got the key in the lock and turned it. As Gretchen pushed the door open for her, Sara glanced up. Gretchen stood as calm as a mountain lake on a windless night—her normal demeanor. At a very unformidable height of five feet with a model-thin frame, Gretchen's confidence must come from inside.

Sara's insecurities came mostly from her mother, who reinforced them on a daily basis. Now her mother was just a negative voice in Sara's mind. Yeah, she'd tried to banish her from there, too, but it had been harder than expected.

A year earlier, Sara had left her mother to live on her own. A lot can happen in a year. Now Sara had her own place, a small, web-design business, and twenty-seven dollars in her checking account that needed to last for a little more than a week.

"I don't know why you don't just room with me," Gretchen offered for the hundredth time. "I'm rarely home, you could work from there just as well as you work from here, and you wouldn't have to deal with the scumbags."

As if on cue, Sara saw her neighbor Slink slither out of his apartment. She had no idea what his real name was. Maybe his mother took one look at his face and decided the name fit. With his emaciated body and greasy black hair, it sure fit him now.

Slink gave Sara a creepy smile and a once-over that made her anxious for a shower and scrub brush. Yeah, she wished she didn't have to deal with the scumbags.

"Gretchen." Sara used her I-don't-want-to-hear-it tone.

"I know, I know. You and your space." Gretchen followed Sara down the dark, narrow hallway. Sara held her breath as Slink passed her. She'd made the mistake of breathing in the putrid air from his wake once and had never forgotten it.

"Sara, look, I think you ought to see Dr. Yauney. He's very good. And he is completely discreet."

Sara suppressed the urge to roll her eyes. "Is this about my legs or my mental health?"

"Um, he's the psychiatrist," Gretchen answered softly, taking a quick glance at Slink's retreating figure.

Sara opened the door to her apartment and, of

course, Gretchen followed her inside without being invited in. Did no one teach this girl manners?

"Dr. Yauney excels in treating phobias. You don't have to work on all of them at once. Just pick one to start. You have a lot to choose from. Let's see, you have a fear of water, doctors, strangers, a fear of people seeing your body, and... oh yeah, a relationship fear."

"Relationship fear?" Sara raised one eyebrow. This one was new.

Gretchen picked up a handful of pretzels from a glass jar on the counter and popped one into her mouth. "Yes, relationship fear. When was the last time you went out on a date?"

Never, thank goodness. But of course, Sara didn't say that out loud.

"I know you get plenty of men checking you out," Gretchen said. "You're one gorgeous woman and *completely* oblivious to the attention you get from the opposite sex. You just need to flirt a bit. I think you should start with Ron Hathaway."

Sara raised her eyebrows.

"I saw you checking him out," Gretchen said. "He is quite delectable."

"You think half the men on the island are delectable. Besides, I'm happy with my life the way it is. I don't need a boyfriend messing that up." Sure, deep down, she wanted one, but a relationship was out of the question.

"You're happy?" Gretchen looked doubtful.

"Yes, I'm happy." Sara put on her best smile.

"You could've fooled me."

Sara's smile vanished. "Listen, my life has never been better. My web-design business is booming. Before long, I'll be able to afford to rent a better place." *In a year or two or ten.* She kept that part to herself. "I just wish you'd stop trying to fix me. There's no fixing me."

"As long as you keep believing that..."

"It's true. So stop trying."

Sara wheeled toward the refrigerator and grabbed a plate of leftover lasagna. She refused to offer Gretchen any. She didn't even want her here. Well, okay, maybe she did after the scare in the parking lot, but she certainly didn't want Gretchen hassling her.

Gretchen continued to munch on pretzels as she spoke between bites. "I can't stop trying to help. You're my best friend. Listen, I know you had a rough childhood, but that doesn't have to damage you for life. With help, I know you can find a way to move beyond it. And whatever your legs look like, it can't be as bad as you make them out to be. Good grief, you won't even let a doctor see your legs."

"I should have never told you that."

"Well, you did and you can't take it back."

"I don't need anyone's help. I can take care of myself. Listen Gretchen, I'm really tired. I'm going to turn in early. So..."

"Yeah, all right." Gretchen shrugged away from the counter and stepped toward the door. "I'll see you

Tuesday. Remember, you promised to help me sew the drapes for my bedroom."

"I remember. Don't worry, I'll be there."

Gretchen glanced back. Disappointment showed in her smile as she slipped out the door.

Sara sighed at the blessed silence.

Less than an hour later, blanketed in darkness, she buried her face in her pillow and cried herself to sleep.

FOUR

anthus gripped the steering wheel of his SUV so tightly that the leather squeaked and steel bent under the pressure. His nostrils flared at the scent in the air. It was unmistakable.

It was impossible.

His eyes darted around the dark, decaying neighborhood. Rain battered against crumbling buildings and piled-up garbage. Across a narrow parking lot sat a small figure in a wheelchair—a woman. Another woman strolled up behind her and startled her. They wasted no time before entering the building.

It couldn't be. He had to be mistaken. He may have been living here five months now but he could never forget or mistake that scent. A female Dagonian's ripe fertility saturated the air.

What the Hades was she doing here? Did she come here on her own? Of course she did.

A horn blasted his eardrums. He cursed when he realized he sat parked in the middle of the street. He eased his SUV next to the curb and let the car pass.

He had to find out what this little female was doing here. Actually, her reasons were irrelevant. There was no good reason she'd be here. He turned off his engine, opened his door, and stalked into the night.

He approached the front door. Should he simply enter the building and knock? No, the other woman was there. He didn't want any collateral damage. The human might be innocent, even if this particular Dagonian female wasn't.

He circled around the darkened building and found the female's window within minutes. Her scent blew through a gap in the old, splintered window frame. Sudden need hit him like a blow to the stomach. Her scent billowed thick in the air and it smelled different from what he'd expected. It had a sweet, earthy smell to it and it appealed to him much more powerfully than he remembered. In fact, despite his years of training, he had to make an effort to keep his attention on the task at hand.

He approached the window and attempted to peer inside. Heavy draperies made it impossible to see in. Resigned to the fact that he could not see her at this point, he pressed himself close to the window to listen in on the conversation.

"Sara. Listen, I know you had a really rough childhood..." The human spoke. Her voice grated the way human voices do.

"I should have never told you that." Xanthus almost smiled when he first heard the musical lilt of the female. His near smile turned to a scowl as he realized the effect her voice had on him. He forced himself into predator mode, analyzing the criminal, looking for weaknesses.

Her voice rose and fell in a quiet, singsong way. The Dagonian sounded young, like a female who had just emerged into womanhood, yet she had an amazing command of the language. Xanthus listened further. She had no distinguishable accent. In fact, she spoke better than he did and he'd been studying English for years. How long had she been here?

Xanthus heard the door shut as the human left.

He followed the Dagonian's appealing scent as she moved to another room. He found it wafting from another window. That window proved just as visually impenetrable as the first one. She guarded well against prying eyes.

He heard her rummaging about the room for several long minutes, and then heard running water. It almost drowned out the heartbreaking sound of her weeping.

Almost.

Whatever her reasons for being here, she sounded miserable.

He knew what he had to do, what he'd done countless times before. As a trained soldier, he had a sacred duty to protect his people, guard their secret, and uphold the law. This female's presence here was not only a criminal act, but it also presented an imminent threat. And because of that, his course was clear.

He had to kill her.

His plan lay clearly before him. Blanketed in the shadows, he'd enter her apartment window. Moving silently, he'd strike fast. Before she could cry out for help, he'd have her throat slit wide open. With her blood flowing swiftly, she'd be dead in mere seconds. The fact that she bathed at this time added to the ease of the execution. Clean up would be simple. Before the night ended, it would be as if she'd never existed. The Dagonian threat of exposure would be wiped clean from the human world.

Xanthus stood, his feet rooted in place under her window. Her sweet scent surrounded him as he listened to her pitiful sobs. Then, in that moment, he did the most shameful thing he'd ever done in his life.

He hesitated.

No, he didn't merely hesitate. He halted. Fingering his blade in his holster, he willed his feet to move, but they seemed unwilling to obey. Then his mind latched onto a thought. It was no crime to wait for a more opportune time or a more secluded place to strike. He didn't need to act rashly. True, finding her here in the human world shocked him, but he needed to be clear-headed and sure when he killed her.

He made his way back to his vehicle and climbed behind the wheel. He leaned his head back against the seat, closed his eyes, and attempted to clear his head.

He'd be back and she would die. She deserved to die. She may have the voice of an angel, but that was a lie. She was a traitor, a threat to their people. No other explanation made sense.

He felt someone near just before a fist rapped on the glass. A big, filthy man with wild hair motioned for him to roll down his window.

As soon as the glass lowered, the barrel of a high-caliber pistol poked inside. "Give me all your money and I won't hurt you," the man growled.

"Put away that gun and I won't hurt *you*," Xanthus said, his voice low and menacing.

The man didn't seem too impressed. "Yeah man, right. You might notice I'm the one with the..." Before he got the words out, Xanthus had the gun out of the man's hand and pointed back at his face with his windpipe clenched in his fist.

"Hey man, I was just joking," the human choked out.

"Just walk away. And don't come back. If I see your face anywhere near here again, I'll kill you. Do you understand me?"

The man's eyes widened in fear. "Yeah, yeah, I hear you," he said, just before Xanthus released him and he escaped into the darkness.

Xanthus looked toward the little female's apartment building across the street. Could she have found a more dangerous place to live? He placed the gun in the glove compartment. He shouldn't have let the gunman live.

This Dagonian female probably felt at home with these bottom-feeders.

Probably? Aw Hades. He cursed himself and the doubt in his mind. He doubly cursed that he couldn't seem to stop himself from caring about her welfare. He'd be killing her himself, after all. The traitor had to die, regardless of his feelings and no matter how appealing she was. Of course if she died by a human's hands then he wouldn't...

No.

He shook his head at his own idiotic thoughts. If a human killed her, then her body would be taken to the morgue, for the humans to see. He couldn't let that happen. He had to be the one to kill her and carefully dispose of her body. And he would, soon.

Just not tonight.

FIVE

The shrill ringing of the phone was Sara's alarm clock at 6:47 AM. Oh how she wished it had a snooze button.

"Hello," she said, trying to project a smile through the receiver. A trace of scratchiness grated in her voice. She doubted the dolt who called her so early in the morning would notice.

"Sara, I hope I didn't awaken you," a deep, baritone voice hummed in her ear. Ron Hathaway—the guy Gretchen told her she'd been checking out. Well Gretchen was sort of right. Ron was a good-looking guy. Now if he'd just never open his mouth, they'd be a match made in heaven, except for the problem of her deformity. Perfect Ron would take one look at it and scream.

"No, Ron, I've been up for *hours* now. What person in their right mind would want to still be asleep at 6:47 AM?" She always said ridiculous things just to see if he was listening.

"Well beautiful, it's your lucky day." *Nope, not listening.*

"How is it my lucky day, Ron?" Her tone held a sarcastic edge.

"My date cancelled for tonight."

Lucky her.

"So I have in my possession," he said, "an extra ticket to the Indigo Spire concert."

"No," she gasped. Indigo Spire was her favorite band of all time. Darn her for always listening to her MP3 player and for not listening to the radio more often. She hadn't even known they were coming in concert until they were sold out. "You only have one ticket? Gretchen loves them almost as much as me."

"Well, I have one ticket for me and one for you, if you'd like to join me."

"I didn't even know you liked Indigo Spire." Ron seemed more like the take-you-to-the-symphony type of guy.

"Well, actually, I don't care for the loud music, but..."

"Well then, could I buy both tickets from you?"

"Sara, I am trying to ask you on a date."

"Oh." Oh shoot, was more like it. She'd rather stab herself with an ice pick than go on a date with Ron Hathaway. Besides, because of her hideous defect, dating was normally not an option. She and her body were determined to stay out of the public eye. Translation— no relationships, possibly ever. But, Indigo Spire... She just had to go see them. And to see them she had to go on a date... with Ron Hathaway.

Sara groaned.

"If you don't answer me," Ron said, "I'm hanging

up."

"No, no, don't hang up. Um, what were you asking me?"

"I'm asking if you would accompany me to the concert tonight." He enunciated each word in a clipped, annoyed voice. She'd better answer before he changed his mind.

"Yes."

"Well then. Good. I'll pick you up at seven." The dial tone was his goodbye. He and Gretchen must have attended the same etiquette school.

A rumbling in her stomach told her that despite breakfast being an hour away, she was hungry.

She swung her deformity over the edge of the bed and pulled down her long nightgown. She considered her breakfast options as she wheeled into the kitchen. Should she eat Fruit Loops or granola? Did she want to be healthy? Nope. No way. Not after speaking to Ron. She needed comfort food.

A half an hour later, Sara pulled out her laptop. Her phone rang a moment later. Her heart rate picked up in that instant. Now she was excited to hear the phone. Because she had no real friends besides Gretchen, the options of people on the other end were limited. Perhaps it was a new client for her web business. She could sure use the money.

"Hello, this is Sara."

"Hi Sara. This is Steve Rowling. I saw your picture in an advertisement and you look like the kind of girl I'd want to create the web page for my bowling alley."

"Absolutely, Mr. Rowling, What do you have in mind?"

An hour later, Sara started on Mr. Rowling's new web page. She worked long and hard until late in the afternoon. When her eyes began to cross, she thought she should stop working before she became even more disabled than she already was. Besides, she had to get ready for a date.

Ron didn't say anything about dinner so she'd better feed herself before she went. She was ornery enough around Ron—add hunger to the mix and she might just have to kill him.

She ate, showered, primped, applied makeup, and put on her favorite blouse. She exchanged the blanket for a long skirt. She'd have to be lifted from her chair into Ron's car for this date. Spandex wrapped over her defect and worn under her skirt would have to be enough to keep people from seeing it. Spandex had always worked before, but she never felt completely safe with it. It was too darn easy to take it off.

A heavy knock on her door came at 6:59 PM. She opened the door and Ron stepped in. Sara had to admit he looked amazing. His brown, gelled hair looked rumpled, in a very planned and precise way. He was dressed in washed-out jeans. Under his black, fitted t-shirt, his muscles bulged and tapered down to a narrow waist. His blue eyes shone bright against his tanned face.

He stepped up and looked her over. "Is that what you're wearing?" Just when he started to look good to her, he opened his mouth. Too bad the idiot wasn't mute.

"What's wrong with what I'm wearing? This blouse is awesome."

"No, not the blouse, the... wait a minute. You aren't able to wear jeans, are you?"

"Listen, if you're going to hound me about my disability, I think you should just sell me your ticket and we can go separately."

"I don't think so. Your disability is going to turn these tickets into front row seats. This band allows anyone in a wheelchair to sit in front with their dates."

"Really? I've never heard that."

"It's true, according to Donna from the mailroom."

"So is that why you asked me on this date? So I can turn your tickets into front row seats?"

"Don't be ridiculous. I don't even like Indigo Spire. The front row seats are just a perk. No, I asked you because despite your being in a wheelchair, you're beautiful, and I like being with beautiful women." He winked, as if what he said should flatter her.

It didn't flatter her. It infuriated her. *Despite your being in a wheelchair...* Where in the world did he learn to be such an ignorant jerk?

"Well, it's a lucky thing this crippled girl is beautiful enough to be asked out by you." She smiled through gritted teeth.

"Yes, it is." He grinned. "Well, sweetheart, let's

go to this concert."

This night threatened to be a long one.

Half an hour later, Ron wrapped Sara in his arms. Donna was right about the handicapped seating, they were awesome seats. But Ron didn't have handicapped tickets. His tickets were for regular seats fifty rows back. He had to carry Sara up a hundred steps.

They left her beloved chair with security—after she threw a huge fit when Ron tried to leave it at the entrance. She looked at his furrowed and sullen face. He must still be steamed at her for causing a scene. She wouldn't have *had* to cause a scene if he'd been reasonable. That chair was her only way of getting from one place to another.

"Wow, Sara, could you weigh any more?" he asked huffing, sweat beading on his brow.

Her jaw dropped. *He did not just say that.* "I'm sorry, I've been meaning to lose a few pounds. I mean, a hundred and fifteen pounds makes me obese, right?"

"I don't know about obese, but you definitely look lighter than you are."

One, two, three... She counted to ten in her head in an attempt to cool her temper before she opened her mouth.

"You'll be worth the trouble, right?" He raised an eyebrow as he smiled.

She clenched her teeth and smiled back, reining in the venom she so wanted to spew at him. *...Eleven, twelve, thirteen...* She would be counting to a thousand the way things were going.

They reached their seats and Ron plopped her down just as the lights dimmed. A haunting melody billowed through the arena. Everyone around her stood, obscuring her view of the stage below. The music pulsed loud, beautiful, and she wished she could actually see the band. Tall bodies surrounded her, bringing her eye level with several gyrating butts—not what she was hoping to see tonight.

She lasted a full hour before she lowered herself to beg Ron to pick her up so she could see the stage. He smiled as he lifted her out of her seat, his eyes full of mischief. "Sure, but this is going to cost you more, sweetheart." He obviously didn't think she'd heard him. But she did hear the jerk. And if he thought he was going to get anything more than a thank you out of her, he was sorely mistaken.

Sara had decided to tell him to put her back on her seat when she glanced down to the stage and her breath caught. The sight astonished her. Fog covered the stage, lights flashed, and the band looked like beautiful creatures from another world. She loved the song they played. She sang softly, mesmerized by the music. Her body rocked to the beat. Usually, she didn't sing where others might hear, but with the loud music, it seemed pretty safe to sing quietly.

She felt Ron's arms tighten around her and looked up. She immediately stiffened as a jolt of shock-driven adrenaline spiked her blood. Ron was no longer the clueless, fun-loving ignoramus she'd come to know and loathe. His eyes bore down on her and he looked hungry—not like wanting a pizza from the concessions hungry. More like a predator finding a fat juicy meal hungry.

"Ron? Is something wrong?" she asked, never more grateful to be surrounded by thousands of concertgoers.

"You're so beautiful," he said.

"Ron? What is wrong with you? Could you please put me down?" She squirmed as she begged.

He closed his eyes and shook his head like he was trying to shake off a bad dream. "Yes, right. Sorry, this music is giving me a headache."

She sighed as he sat her back down in the grove of pulsating bodies. Still, his eyes kept darting back to her.

When the last song ended, the lights turned up, cueing the concert's end. They sat and waited for the crowd to thin before attempting to leave themselves. Ron fidgeted in his seat.

When he picked her up to leave, he flew down the stairs. In the car, he showed the same energy, driving very fast. His eyes continued to dart toward her. Every time their eyes met, he licked his lips.

"Um," Sara said. "Thanks for taking me to the concert. I had a good time."

"It wasn't so bad," he said. "But I enjoyed the part you sang best of all."

"Oh. You heard that?" Her heart began to pound, the pulsing blood squeezing her chest.

"Oh yes," he answered. "I sure did. Listen, I'm not ready to call it a night yet. Are you hungry?" Ron took a corner fast and Sara slid against the door.

"No, I'm good," she said. She doubted she could eat a bite—not with her stomach attempting to tie itself into a knot. "I'm just tired. I'd like to go home."

"Sure. Okay. But could we stop for a drink first?"

"I don't think so. I'm only twenty. I can't drink yet."

"Don't worry about it. I know a great place and they have fantastic *virgin* drinks." A wide smile spread across his face.

"I appreciate the offer, Ron, but I'm not feeling very well. I'd just like to go home and straight to bed."

"Ooh me too. But let me buy you just one drink."

"Ron..."

"Just one drink and we're out. I promise." He held his hand up in a pledge.

Sara scowled as she turned her head and looked behind them—the direction of her apartment. "Okay. Just one drink and then you take me home."

Ron pulled into a nightclub parking lot. The name "Shockwave" flashed in blue neon lights. He parked, opened his door, and stepped out. Sara chewed her bottom lip and twirled her hair around her finger as she waited for him to get her wheelchair from the trunk. She jumped, startled when he opened her door so soon.

"No use getting your wheelchair when we're going to be in and out so quickly," he said as he picked her up. About a minute later, a man nodded them in at the front door. Bodies packed the room from wall to wall. Lights flashed, music pulsed, and hundreds of people bounced and gyrated to the music. The floral air fresheners didn't quite mask the deep scent of alcohol and a hundred sweating bodies.

Ron's eyes followed two women—a blonde and a brunette—as they strutted by, balancing on five-inch stilettos. Their skirts were so short that if they bent over... Sara grimaced.

"Hey Ron," the brunette said.

"Hello, Kat," Ron answered with an appreciative grin.

"Hi Ron." The blonde gave a little wave.

"Hi Kit," he answered, still smiling.

"Kit and Kat?" Sara said.

"I know. Aren't they cute?"

Cute was not the exact the word she would use for those two.

"Do you come here often?" Sara asked.

"Yeah. This is my usual hunting grounds," he answered, his eyebrow raised.

"Don't you mean stomping grounds?"

A smile spread across his face. "Sure."

Sara began to re-evaluate what she knew about him. She'd always thought he was proper, refined, eloquent, annoying... Now he seemed to be revealing a side of himself she'd never seen before—a creepy side.

A commotion interrupted her thoughts. The women in the club noisily fluttered around someone or something at the front door. Even the stilettos twins ran to join the fray.

"Hey, Ron. I see your taste in women remains impeccable." Sara turned to see a bulging, tattooed man step up to the bar. Ron plopped her down on a stool. She'd never heard such a rough-looking man use the word "impeccable" before. Maybe Ron was rubbing off on him.

"Hello, Thomas," Ron answered with a smile.

Thomas looked her up and down. His eyes lingered on her spandex-covered stump, when they finally returned to her face, his smile widened and eyebrows rose.

"We can't stay long," Ron said. "We just want a quick drink. Sara here will have a virgin blue Hawaiian and I'll have the same—with the alcohol, of course. There's a big tip in it for you if you give her drink a little extra attention to make it just right."

Ron brushed a stray strand of hair away from her eyes, making her skin crawl. Warning bells were going off in her head. *Okay, calm down. Just one drink and I'm on my way home.*

"Sure thing, Ron," Thomas answered. He mixed the drinks. The little extra time didn't amount to much— the drinks were in front of them in about a minute. Ron handed Thomas a bill and Sara could have sworn she saw a fifty on it. Thomas put it in his pocket. She must have been mistaken. These drinks couldn't have cost twenty-five dollars apiece, even with a big tip added on.

She sipped her beverage, surprised at how much she liked it. It tasted fruity, tropical and, within minutes, weariness overwhelmed her. She hadn't even finished her drink when Ron scooped her off the stool.

"I think it's time to leave," he said. "You've definitely had enough."

"But I didn't finish my drink." Her voice sounded funny in her ears—distant and a little slurred. Something felt wrong in all this. A wave of nausea and dizziness washed over her. She grabbed Ron's neck, trying to steady herself. His arms roped around her, but she still felt as if she were falling.

Sara jumped when she heard the car door shut. *How did I get in the car?* She could feel her pulse pounding against her skull. Something told her she needed help, but she couldn't seem to find her voice—or move her arms.

What's wrong with me? Then it hit her. *He drugged me. The creep drugged me!*

She could guess what came next. *Please no!* A nightmare unfolded before her eyes, yet, no matter how upset and frightened she was she couldn't marshal a fight. The powerful drug soon dragged her down into blackness.

SIX

anthus paced around his Harley-Davidson motorcycle and suppressed the urge to hit something. He'd been tracking the Dagonian and her male companion all evening. He shook his head over the name he'd heard the human call her. Sara. In Atlantian, that name meant princess. Right. She was no princess. She was a criminal.

Xanthus growled like a trapped animal as his eyes once again shot over to Sara's building. The adrenaline-rich blood pumping through his body told him something was wrong.

His brain didn't know what to think.

He'd followed Sara most the night. Ron turned out to be full of surprises. After the concert, he'd taken Sara to a club filled with retched humans. Xanthus had barely escaped the place with his shirt on. The human women were so persistent, pressing in on him. He'd barely glimpsed Ron leaving with Sara—nearly losing them as they left. When they'd reached her apartment, Ron carried her into the building as she slept.

Xanthus's instincts had been in overdrive the entire night. Ron's hands had been on her, touching her, holding her, and that had driven Xanthus to the brink of madness. It took a concerted effort not to seize the human by the throat and rip out his windpipe, but that had been the hormones talking. Sara was his target, not Ron. Why couldn't he remember that? He had been consumed with irrational thoughts all evening.

From what he could tell, Sara didn't seem to like Ron. She'd worn a sour expression the entire night, but she'd fallen asleep in his car. She may not like him, but she must trust him enough to sleep in his presence.

Still, human men could be unpredictable.

Ron should have simply put her in bed and left. Xanthus had been waiting for that opportunity. This chance would not slip by him. This honorable soldier had an execution to carry out. He wouldn't hesitate again.

If only the human would leave.

Xanthus glanced at his watch. It'd been five minutes. Ron should have been out by now, shouldn't he? Hades. Xanthus didn't know. Maybe he was overreacting, but as the time ticked on without Ron leaving, Xanthus's animal instincts clawed at him. He took one more glance at his watch. Six minutes. He couldn't wait any longer.

He was going in.

Xanthus stood in front of Sara's apartment door and knocked. Her scent filled his nostrils and his mind. Then he caught another scent—much milder, but it had him nearly blind with rage. A male pheromone. Ron was aroused. Depending on what he found, Xanthus might have to kill the both of them tonight.

He nearly splintered the wood as he pounded his fist on the door.

"Who is it?" Ron asked, clearly annoyed.

"Open the door."

Ron yanked the door open, his eyes burning with fury. "What..." His voice choked off as he saw Xanthus's hulking figure fill the doorway. Xanthus ducked under the doorframe and stepped inside, his eyes searching, trying to catch a glimpse of Sara. Ron stumbling as he stepped back.

"Who do you think you are? You can't just barge in here."

"Where's Sara?" Xanthus said, towering over Ron.

"She's in bed."

"Are you sharing the bed with her?"

"That's none of your business. You're not her father. Sara's an adult. She can have whomever she wants in her apartment and in her bed."

"Your kind is not worthy to be in the same room as her, much less in her bed." Xanthus snarled while he pushed through her bedroom door.

He looked down at her lying across her mattress. His breath caught at the sight of the Dagonian woman this close. She was beautiful, stunning. Black hair haloed around her head and across the pillow. Her shirt lay open, exposing flesh covered with reddened splotches and reeking of Ron's scent. Yet, somehow, she slept peacefully—no, she was unconscious. Xanthus growled at that realization. She was innocent in this situation and it appeared her innocence remained intact. Her wrap and skirt still covered her—untouched. He sighed in relief.

Xanthus heard Ron scrambling through the kitchen in an attempt to make his escape. Less than a second later, Ron yelped as Xanthus seized him by the hair.

"You think you can commit this crime and go on your way?" Xanthus thought of the many ways he would love to hurt this foul creature, but he knew he'd have to answer for his actions. By being here, Sara herself had broken the law. If her secret had been discovered, he would have had nothing restraining him from killing this man, but her secret remained safe. Regretfully, that fact kept Ron safe from permanent arm.

Still, Xanthus could frighten him—give him a reason to fear coming near her again. That *would* be justified.

Fifteen minutes later, Ron was sobbing like an infant and cowering on the linoleum floor in a puddle of urine. Xanthus tired of the stench, more than ready to let the sniveling coward go. "Ron, I'm going to allow you to leave. But if I ever see you near Sara again, even if it's unintentional, you're a dead man. And it won't be quick—I'll make you suffer. Do you understand me?" Xanthus clutched Ron's shirt, twisting it so hard that it cut into his neck.

"I understand," Ron sobbed. "You won't see me again."

Xanthus released him and Ron scrambled out the door.

Xanthus shook his head when he realized the idiocy of his threat. It was pointless. He would be killing Sara in a moment. She would be dead and gone before the night was through.

Xanthus stepped into her bedroom. Light from the kitchen spilled onto her bed, draping across her sleeping form. Her chest rose with every breath. She slept, unaware of the predator stalking her. Xanthus's heart pounded and sweat broke out across his forehead as he looked down on her angelic face.

Now was the time. He had to do it.

Breaking her neck would be the best option. Her death would be quick, painless, and not a drop of blood would spill.

He moved to her side. The swells of her breasts rose and fell in her peaceful sleep. His looked her over and struggled to keep his mind off the fact that she was a helpless woman. Her face, her body, everything about her looked delicate, breakable. Out of all the criminals he'd killed in his lifetime, he'd killed very few females. Especially not lush, beautiful...

Hades, he couldn't kill her... not with her looking like this.

He moved closer and leaned forward. His fingers

fumbled with her buttons. He just needed to close her shirt, and then he'd kill her.

He'd just fastened the last one, when her eyes fluttered and then flew open wide as she gasped. She frantically searched the room and then his face. Her tiny hands clasped around his forearms. "Help me! Please don't let him hurt me. He drugged me. He's going to…" Her words turned into a heart-wrenching sob as she threw her arms around his chest. Xanthus jerked back, startled at her sudden embrace. He sat frozen for just a moment before his arms pulled her trembling body against his. Her quiet whimpers cut through to his heart. "Shh. It's okay," he found himself saying.

"He's going to hurt me," she quietly wailed.

"No, Sara. I won't let him hurt you. It's okay. You're safe." He held her tight, stroking her hair and mumbling words of comfort as she wept against his chest.

Sara's cries soon quieted as drug-laden sleep overtook her again. Still, Xanthus continued to hold her, continued to caress her. He shouldn't have let the filthy human go. He should have broken *his* neck after he stuffed his beating heart down it.

Xanthus lowered Sara's limp, slumbering body onto her bed and pulled a blanket over her. Raking his fingers through his hair, he stood. Tears sparkled on her cheeks. Without a thought, he brushed them away with his thumb.

Several minutes later, Xanthus returned to his

motorcycle. "Well, that didn't exactly go as planned," he said. Now he'd never have the heart to kill her. Perhaps he never had.

He sighed in defeat.

SEVEN

Sara flailed and gulped in seawater. The glow from the surface faded to black as the sea enveloped her. It couldn't be. She'd escaped this nightmare years ago. But here she was, and here she would die, at the bottom of the ocean.

She sucked in a lungful of air and bolted upright in bed. A cool sweat slicked her hair against her head and dripped down her face as she continued to inhale quick gasps.

No matter how many times she'd had the same old nightmare, it always scared the life out of her. She ran her fingers through her damp hair. Her body continued to shake. Looking down, she realized she wore yesterday's clothes.

What had happened last night? She remembered her horrid first date, but she couldn't recall how she had gotten home. Maybe she'd passed out from an overdose of idiocy dealt out by Ron.

It was possible.

Something twisted in her gut and she felt some lingering remnants of fear. She pushed them away. She couldn't deal with forgotten memories right now—

especially unpleasant ones. She just couldn't. Besides, she had other things to worry about, like the $27.00 that wouldn't last the week. She had work to do.

Three hours later, she'd completed several new web pages. Ron briefly passed through her mind. Something told her there would be no second date with him. Thank heavens.

Wheeling over to the refrigerator, Sara grabbed a bottle of water and an apple. As she lifted the apple to her mouth, a knock at the door startled her. The apple slipped from her fingers, bounced once, and then rolled under the kitchen table.

Oh great. That was her last apple. She *had* to go the grocery store today.

Sara wheeled over to the door and leaned toward the peephole Mr. Brown had lowered for her. Good thing he did, she would never answer her door otherwise. Not that she had many visitors—well, except for Gretchen. But her best friend was at school today and Sara wasn't expecting anyone. A girl could never be too careful.

Peeping through the hole, Sara scowled, confused at the inky black on the other side. *Was someone covering the lens?*

She should just pretend not to be home.

"Miss. Taylor, this is Mr. Dimitriou," a deep, muffled voice said. "I'm the new owner of the apartment building. I just wanted to introduce myself to each of my tenants."

New owner? Mr. Brown sold the building?

Maybe she should open the door. She didn't want to offend her new landlord. He might raise her rent or evict her. Of course, if he came in here and murdered her, who cared how much her rent was?

She carefully analyzed the situation. His voice sounded normal—no slurring, stuttering, laughing. His accent though. She couldn't place it. Of course, she was no linguist, but she could make out the usual—Tongan, Samoan, Australian, Japanese...

She tried the peephole again. The stranger moved and she finally got a look at him.

Oh good heavens, he looked like "The Assassin". She remembered he went by Shane Adams now. What would a movie star/pro-wrestler be doing buying a dilapidated apartment building?

Yeah, right. He wouldn't. This man stood massive—very tall, broad in the shoulders, and narrow at the waist. His shirt pulled snug over his chiseled muscles. He wore wide, gold bands around his biceps, like something you'd see on a Roman soldier, except the Romans wore them on their wrists. How odd.

"Miss. Taylor, I heard you in there. If you aren't comfortable opening to me, I could bring a police officer—just to let you know I am who I say. I don't want you to think I'm threatening you in anyway. I know it must be frightening to have a big stranger knock on the door when you live alone."

His voice shook with nervousness.

He didn't *sound* like a murderer. Besides, given

the sheer size of the man, if he wanted to kill her, he could kick her flimsy door in.

Sara sighed and looked heavenward. "Okay, if I die, I die," she said quietly as she lowered her gaze back on the door. She cracked it open and looked out.

She had to wheel back quickly when Mr. Dimitriou reached out and pushed open her door. He stepped in and shut the door behind him. "Hello." He spoke low, his voice as cold as his icy smile. It drove a chill down her spine, raising goose bumps on her back. Letting him in wasn't just a grave mistake, it was *lethal*. The word sliced through her mind.

Sara looked up into his slate black eyes. This wasn't Shane Adams, although there were similarities in his coloring and muscular build. His size was surreal. He towered above her like a giant. Despite his size, his face was boyish and strikingly handsome, much more handsome than the actor she'd mistaken him for. His black hair was short, but long enough to curl around the edges. He looked young for an apartment owner—mid-twenties, maybe.

His undeniable good looks didn't make him any less terrifying. He smiled, showing a nice row of white teeth. For a split second, an image of shark's teeth flashed through her mind.

He looked at her expectantly. Was she supposed to say something? She was too frightened to speak at the moment.

She'd only blinked but, in that split second, she

suddenly found his face inches from hers. "You have blue eyes," he said. It came out sounding like an accusation.

Sara jumped. Then she realized what he'd said. This man was dangerous *and* insane. She struggled to speak, too shaken up to find her voice. She soon gave up and simply nodded.

Where in the world had she put her purse? She would feel so much better with a can of pepper spray in her hand.

His eyes bored into hers. He looked her up and down in a very careful, very thorough inspection as confusion crinkled his brow. The scent coming off him was mildly distracting—warm, musky, like an ocean breeze. Very appealing, unlike his grimace.

His eyes opened wide in shock as he rattled off expletives in whatever language he spoke.

This man belonged in a straightjacket and locked in a padded room.

He paused as if he didn't know what to say. Sara sat very still, in spite of the adrenaline pumping through her veins. She wanted to move, but being confined to a wheelchair, she certainly couldn't move fast enough to escape this hulking man.

"I'm sorry," he said, "but blue eyes are basically nonexistent where I come from. I'm still surprised when I see them."

Their eyes locked and his expression warmed. Soon she felt pretty warm herself. He really was a sight to behold—tall, ripped, with olive skin. The kind of man who could make a woman swoon with just a glance and a smile.

Sara had never before been overly concerned with how she looked, but, at the moment, she was very self-conscience. She wore a simple, fitted, baby blue t-shirt. She'd put on some makeup this morning (thank heavens), and her black hair draped down her back. His warm gaze melted into an intense heat. She found herself overcome with the intensity in his gaze, and didn't know which was stronger, her fear or excitement.

Excitement. Definitely excitement, she decided.

He stiffened, cleared his throat, and shook his head. He muttered a foreign word—she had a feeling it was a swear word.

What was she thinking? She shook herself from her own crazy thoughts. One minute she was terrified for her life and the next she was getting hot over the man who might be her murderer. That just wasn't right, regardless of how insanely hot he was.

He stood silent for several moments as she waited for him to speak. He cleared his throat. "Look," he said, "I need to inform you that now that I own the building, there will be a few changes around here.

"First of all, I've decided I'll be giving notice of eviction to several tenants."

What was he saying? Tenants? Eviction? Could he be her landlord after all? Then his words sank in and her heart dropped. This didn't sound good for her.

"Will I be one of them? Are you evicting me?"

"Oh, no, no." His face softened as he shook his head. "You'll stay. I just don't like the negative element that exists in this building. I have a very good nose for crime and a zero tolerance."

He looked around her apartment, as if to inspect it. She felt a quick surge of pride. She kept her apartment immaculate. He'd approve. There was no way he couldn't. But when he turned back toward her, she had to re-evaluate her opinion. He obviously *didn't* approve of it. He shook his head and glanced her way. If he were her mother, she'd swear his next words would be, "What am I going to do with you?"

He paused for a moment. "I'll be sending workers in to replace your front door and windows, add more secure locks, and install a security system in your apartment."

Sara's jaw dropped. "Um, isn't that awfully expensive? I mean, are you sure you want to go to the trouble? You won't be raising my rent, will you?" Her thoughts jumbled as questions tumbled from her lips. She couldn't afford the apartment as it was. There was no way she could afford more. And she'd live in a tent before she'd go back to her mother.

"No, not at all," he answered. She assumed he was answering her last question.

He smoothly strolled over to the table—so smoothly he practically glided. Maybe his mother had made him practice walking with a book on his head. She almost smiled as she pictured him doing just that.

He bent down, picked her apple up off the floor, and handed it to her. "Thank you," she said, surprised.

"Isn't it difficult for you to prepare your meals in this kitchen?" he asked, placing his hand on the counter.

That question surprised her even more than the apple. "Yes, but I'm used to it. I've never known different."

"You haven't?"

"No. My mother didn't think it worth the lower resale value. Besides, I could manage."

"Wouldn't it be *easier* if your counters were lower?"

"I guess it would." She shrugged. "But you can't think to make such a drastic and expensive change for me."

"I'll have them switched out by next week."

"But sir, wouldn't that make this apartment difficult to rent in the future?"

"Miss Taylor, I own this building and I'll do as I wish. I'd appreciate it if you would stop instructing me."

Was she doing that? Okay, maybe a little. "I'm sorry Mr...." Oh shoot. She'd forgotten his name. It was his fault for having such an unusual name.

"Dimitriou," he said. "Now, you will stop worrying about me raising your rent or evicting you. I will make changes as I see fit and you will remain here as long as you desire, paying the same amount of rent you have been paying all along. Is that clear?"

Boy, what a change from when he'd first stepped

through her door. She'd thought she was staring death in the eye. He was still a force to be reckoned with, but now he seemed to be looking out for her. She didn't know what to think about that. Mr. Dimitriou didn't even know her. What were his motives? She didn't know, but she wasn't about to trust him. Still, she answered him with a clear, "Yes, sir."

EIGHT

"He said that?" Gretchen stood with her eyes wide as her newly sewn satin drapes slid off the curtain rod onto the slate-tile floor.

"Exactly like that," Sara said. "I mean, I'll admit I was out of line telling him what he could and couldn't do with the apartment he owned. But it just doesn't make sense. Why would he pay for all these changes without expecting to raise the rent?"

"I'll tell you why." Gretchen picked the curtain off the floor and slid it back over the rod. "You flashed your baby blues at the man and he fell hopelessly in love with you."

"Yeah, right. That reminds me. He freaked when he saw my eyes *were* blue. I tell you, the man is demented. I think I should be afraid."

"Sweetie, you just worded that wrong. The man freaked when he saw *your* blue eyes. They are an unusual color. I just think he's smitten with you and you can't recognize it because of the giant wall you've built around yourself to keep men out. Well, you can't keep this man out. He owns your apartment. He has a key."

"That's a scary thought." Sara ran red thread through the sewing machine. She'd considered telling Gretchen about her date with Ron to counter her reference to her wall keeping men out, but she didn't say anything. She didn't want to relive the ridiculous night with an ignorant, rude man. She didn't even want to think about that night.

"I think its destiny," Gretchen said. "Now, tell me again what he looks like."

"I already told you. He and Shane Adams could be brothers, except Mr. Dimitriou is younger, much more handsome, and *way* taller. I swear his hair brushed dust streaks on my ceiling. Now, I ask you, how is a girl in a wheelchair supposed to scrub ceilings?" she asked, holding a straight pin in her mouth.

"Your ceilings *are* exceptionally low. But that still puts him at about seven feet tall. Wow."

"Wow—as in scary."

Gretchen climbed the step stool and hung her curtain. After adjusting the fabric, she smiled. "You're in the wrong profession, girl. You should be a seamstress. This looks amazing. Now only one window to go."

"Yeah, yeah. So what do I do about the giant?"

"I think you should plant a big wet one on him next time you see him, but that's just me." Gretchen smiled.

She was not taking this seriously enough. "I don't know why I try to have intelligent conversations with you. Oh shoot. Look at the time. I need to get going if I'm going to be back before dark." Sara wheeled her chair around. She packed her sewing supplies up in a box and scooted it under the table.

"All right, go. You've done your charity work for today. We can finish this tomorrow. Then we can go out and celebrate my new drapes. If you want to invite Shane Adams, I can find a date and we'll double. I'd love to meet him." Gretchen wriggled her eyebrows as she folded the last unfinished curtain panel and placed it in a box.

"It's Mr. Dimitriou, and no, a date with him is completely out of the question. Not only am I broke, but he's my landlord, for heaven's sake."

"Well, don't worry about paying for it. It'll be my payment for the curtains. And some of the best relationships start out between landlord and tenant."

"Yeah, right."

"I'm sorry my car is in the shop," Gretchen said. "It should be ready tomorrow. Do you want me to walk you home?" She pulled the completed curtains closed over the darkening windows, and then smiled in appreciation.

"Oh, sure, and then I could walk you back here," Sara answered. "Then you could walk me home again, and then..."

"I get it." Gretchen dropped her hand on her hip and sighed. "But as strong and independent as you are, a woman in a wheelchair is less able to defend against attackers."

"I know. Believe me, I know, but, not to worry. I have my trusty pepper spray to defend for me," she said, lifting it out of her purse and holding it up.

"Well, keep it handy. I noticed some slimy looking perverts eyeing you the other day." Gretchen grimaced.

Oh, great. Maybe she should have Gretchen walk her home. Yeah and who would protect Gretchen?

Wheeling out the front door of the apartment building, Sara wished she *could* hail a taxi, but she still had to go grocery shopping and she needed what was left of her money to pay for food.

Sara wheeled down the sidewalk. Twilight had painted orange and purple streaks in the sky as she bumped over the curb to cross the intersection of Apohana Drive and Kaniki Way. She passed by a shop called Linens of Hawaii and then passed a corner garage. She paused before wheeling by the gas station. Drivers around here rarely watched for short, wheelchair-bound females.

As Sara approached the first of several apartment buildings, she noticed a tall figure blanketed in the shadows. Through the darkness, she thought she saw the gleam of his teeth for a moment. As he was almost out of sight, she noticed he'd stepped away from the building.

Oh, please, don't let him be following me. She rushed to the end of the block. She took a quick glance over her shoulder. She didn't see him, but that didn't mean he wasn't there behind the dumpster or the mountain of clutter by the road.

Sara's wheels spun over the sidewalk as she hurried. She had lived in this neighborhood for only two months—not enough time for a crippled recluse to meet the people who lived near her. She looked around to find some comfort. All she saw now were rundown apartment buildings with few lighted windows. She knew that if she needed help, she'd be lucky to find it. To survive here, people learned to avoid trouble.

Sara chanced another glance behind her. The same tall figure bounded toward her, half a block away. She wheeled faster. She was going so fast, her arms should have been burning by now. She had to be running on pure adrenaline.

The next block was hers. Her apartment was in the last building on the right, next to a grove of coconut trees riddled with beer cans, cigarette butts, and other discarded trash. Beyond that lay the ocean shore.

She flew across the parking lot to the glass door that led to safety.

What in the world? This wasn't her door. The cracks were gone and the metal was shiny and new.

"What are you doing...?" an angry male voice beat in her ear. Gretchen would have been proud of her knee-jerk reaction. Sara pulled the pepper spray out of her pocket and took aim, spraying the large figure in the face.

"Awwwwww, Gromot." If she thought the voice

had sounded angry before, it was furious now. Funny, she had a flash of déjà vu, as if she'd heard that irate voice before.

Sara fumbled with her keys. After several failed attempts, she finally grabbed the right key and tried to thrust it into the lock. It only went a quarter of the way. "Oh please, oh please, oh please," she chanted as she tried again and again to get her key to work.

"Sara Taylor." The voice calmed, slightly less menacing, and then she recognized it.

"May I ask what I did to deserve getting sprayed in the eyes with acid?" Mr. Dimitriou bent over and pressed hands on his face. He dabbed at his red eyes.

"Oh, Mr. Dimitriou, I'm so sorry. I thought you were... Well I don't know... but I... I thought someone was going to attack me. I didn't know you were here."

"I was about to scold you for being out alone at dusk." He sniffed. "But I see you brought protection and I must say it's quite effective."

He tried to rub his eyes, "Uhg."

"Oh, I'm *so* sorry. I can't believe I did that to you. Come inside and you can rinse your eyes out." She tried once again to unlock the door. "I can't seem to get my key to work."

"I know you can't. This is a new door with a new lock. I was just going to give you your key when you... uh." He sighed. "Well, never mind." He squinted at the lock, slipped in the key, and turned it.

"Oh." She was speechless. Feeling like an idiot

often robbed her of her powers of speech.

Mr. Dimitriou gave the door a gentle shove and it swung open on its own. "This new door should make it easier for you to get in and out of the building."

"Oh, um, thank you." *And why is he spending so much money accommodating my needs?* Mr. Dimitriou followed her down the hall and stopped at her new steel door. It looked like the main door wasn't the only one he'd replaced. Sara remembered her conversation with Gretchen.

Could he be infatuated with her? She looked him over.

No way.

There was no possible way a man who looked like he stepped out of a Gladiator movie could be interested in a little, handicapped woman. She'd always thought Ron Hathaway was good looking, but compared to Mr. Dimitriou? Well, there was no competition. Mr. Dimitriou made Ron look like George McFly.

Mr. Dimitriou took another key out of his pocket, put it in the lock, and held the door open for her. Warning bells rang in her head. He had a key to her apartment. He could come in here whenever he wanted. And she had doubts about this man's sanity. He sure did a lot of things that seemed crazy, and despite his unreal level of hotness, she didn't want to die at the hands of a lunatic.

Sara wheeled past Mr. Dimitriou and was about to bid him farewell when he strolled in and shut the door like he owned the place. Well, technically, he did, but this was her apartment. She paid good money for it.

"Excuse me, Mr. Dimitriou," she began. He took three steps over to her sink, turned on the faucet, and washed out his eyes. Oh right. The eyes she'd sprayed with pepper spray. She *had* invited him in, hadn't she? The man had turned her into an imbecile.

"Listen," he said, "I'm sorry I scared you. It's not easy being nearly seven feet tall. People always think the worst of you. And with you being crippled, it has to be hard living on your own."

"Excuse me? Crippled?" Sara's angst rose. "I know English isn't your native language, so I'd better warn you. People in my condition don't like to be called crippled. It's not politically correct." Sure, she called herself crippled all the time, but that was different.

He cocked an eyebrow. "Oh no? So what's the term I should use?" He leaned against her counter; it creaked under his weight.

"Well, those who don't have the use of their legs are called paraplegic. And those who don't have the use of their arms and legs are called quadriplegic."

"Oh, so you can't move your legs?" He looked suspicious, as if she'd faked her disability. She'd give anything to be able to walk like a normal person.

"No, I can't move my *legs*." She glared at him. Technically, she wasn't lying. Her deformity didn't look anything like legs.

"So, have you been this way since birth?" He

pulled up a chair, straddled it, and made himself at home.

"Do you always ask personal questions that are none of your business?" She narrowed her eyes.

He smiled. "Only of people who spray acid in my eyes."

"It's not acid, it's pepper spray. And it doesn't do any permanent damage." She saw that his eyes were still quite red and so was the skin around them.

Dang, she felt guilty. After all, he'd done quite a bit for her. She glanced at the door and noticed, for the first time, a peephole just her height. Was Gretchen's theory really so farfetched?

"I'm sorry I sprayed you with pepper spray," she said just above a whisper.

His brows furrowed as he flashed a crooked smile. "I'm glad you did."

Okay, maybe he *was* crazy.

"Now I won't be quite so worried about you being out on your own in this neighborhood." He shrugged.

Okay, now that was just sweet.

"Listen, Mr. Dimitriou." She sighed. "How about I try to make amends?"

His brows furrowed. "What do you have in mind?"

"Well, my friend Gretchen invited me to go on a double date with her tomorrow. And I would be happy to treat you to dinner and a show." Did she just say that? What was she doing? There was no way this Greek god would go out with her. She felt her face heat with embarrassment. Great, there goes her confident façade.

"You'd pay to take me to dinner with your friend and her date?"

Actually, Gretchen would be paying, but he didn't need to know that, so she nodded.

"I appreciate the offer." He put his hand on her shoulder.

Darn it. Why did she have to ask him? She should have known he'd refuse.

"But I just wouldn't feel comfortable having you pay for our date. But, if you'd allow me to pay, I'd love to come."

Her eyes widened. "Really?"

His dark eyes sparkled as he smiled. "Yes really."

She brushed her fingers through her hair. Was it hot in here? The shrill ringing of the phone startled her.

"Oh excuse me, it might be a client. I'll be just a minute," she said as she wheeled over to an old, black wall phone. Missing client calls was not an option when one was on the brink of homelessness.

She put on a smile and answered the phone. "Hello, this is Sara."

"Sara, where are you?" Her heart made a splashdown in her stomach. Of all times for *her* to call.

It was her mom.

She held the phone away and covered the earpiece as her mother screeched. It didn't help much. "How could you leave me for so long and not tell me where you would be? You think a few emails telling me you were fine would be enough for me to know you're not dead?"

Sara held the phone back up to her ear and spoke low. She didn't want Mr. Dimitriou to hear this conversation, but with her mom screaming at high decibels through the receiver, it was impossible to have a private conversation.

"How did you get this number?" Sara asked.

"I had to hire a private detective to find you."

"I'm sorry, Mom. I was going to call, but after I moved... "

"Don't lie to me, Sara," her mother said, cutting her off. "You've always been an ungrateful child. I can't believe you neglect me like you do. When I think of all the things I've sacrificed for you, it makes me sick to see how you've turned out. Now I want you to come home right now."

"No, Mom. I'm not coming home. I have a life here. I'm an adult and I need to take care of myself right now."

"You selfish child." Sara felt the vibrations of her mother's voice as she covered the receiver. "You've never cared about anyone but yourself. I shouldn't have come back for you. I should have left you at the bottom of that cliff. I can see why your father never came to get you. You're just like him. You don't care about anyone but yourself. When I think of all I've suffered because of you... I wish you'd never been born."

Sara had heard it all, more times than she could

count. Usually she buckled and apologized, but not this time. This time she said what needed to be said.

"Mom, say what you want. You're just mad because you can't control my life anymore. Get some professional help, and maybe then we can talk."

She carefully hung up the phone, cutting off her mother's tirade midstream.

Sara felt shaken, but still triumphant. She turned toward Mr. Dimitriou and her stomach clenched. His brows furrowed and the corners of his mouth turned down in a frown.

"I'm sorry you had to hear that," she said.

She paused for a long time. What could she say? How could she explain? Her mother was a selfish woman and a nutcase on top of that. There was no way he'd want to date her now. She took a deep breath, and looked down.

"Your mother found you at the bottom of a cliff?"

Her eyes snapped up. "Sort of..." she said. Her cheeks flushed with warmth. "Listen, I know that you agreed to go on a date with me just to be polite. If you'd rather cancel, I'll understand. Really, I will. I invited you on a whim. Honestly, I think it may be best if we just keep things simple. You're my landlord and I'm your tenant. And I like it that way."

Mr. Dimitriou got up, stepped over, and sank to his knee beside her chair as she kept up her explanation. "Don't get me wrong," she said, "it was noble of you to accept my invitation, but I know you couldn't...

possibly...."

Dang. Having his rugged face this close to hers almost made her lose her train of thought. "ever... be interested...."

Xanthus moved in closer, just a breath away. "Hmmm?" He closed his eyes and breathed in deeply. When he opened his eyes and looked at her, the intensity of his gaze bore into her soul.

"...in someone... like me?" Did she just phrase that statement as a question? He raised his hand and pressed his palm to her cheek. His touch was electric. *He's going to kiss me*, was her last coherent thought.

His warm lips pressed down on hers. His mouth moved expertly, coaxing hers into response. And respond she did. A flame ignited a hunger and need she hadn't even realized she possessed. Her hands, of their own accord, rose to his head, her fingers weaving through his hair as she attempted to pull him closer.

This was a new experience for her. She'd never dreamed a kiss could be so amazing. His mouth worked magic with hers, a magic that seemed to have the power to bring her to life in a way she'd never felt alive before. She barely noticed being lifted out of her chair, didn't notice the ties anchoring her blanket rip away. But when she felt the blanket begin to slide, the spell shattered into a million jagged pieces. If the blanket slid any more, he would see her deformity!

Sara attempted to pull away from his iron grip. Somehow, the blanket still covered her, thank goodness.

"Mr. Dimitriou, please stop," she breathed as he trailed hot kisses down her neck.

He didn't seem to hear her as he continued his gentle assault.

"Mr. Dimitriou, stop!"

His body froze.

"Sara," he said through ragged breaths. "I'm so sorry."

"It's okay," she said, breathless herself.

"No. No, it's not. I should have known better than to kiss you in your condition. It was unforgivable of me."

What did that mean? Why should her being in a wheelchair keep him from kissing her? Realization dawned on her as her heart sank. "I was right. I knew you'd never consider me as a real possibility for a relationship." Her lips burned from his kisses and her body cherished his embrace. She wanted him, obviously much more than he wanted her. How dare he toy with her like that? "It's a good thing I'm a crippled girl. At least you have your pity. Would you please put me down?"

"You misunderstand me." He shook his head as he continued to cradle her in his arms.

A single tear trailed down her cheek. "My mother was right about one thing. Guys are pigs." She slapped the tear away.

"Your being paraplegic has nothing to do with it," Xanthus said with ragged breath.

"Oh really? Then what do you mean you couldn't

kiss me in my *condition?*" She slapped her hand against his chest.

He paused for a moment. "You were vulnerable. Your call from your mother upset you and it was wrong of me to take advantage of you in that state."

"Oh. So you weren't talking about my physical condition?"

"Sara, you're beautiful whether you walk on two feet, ride on wheels, or any other possibilities. Nothing changes that fact."

Her heart leapt at the chance that he was telling the truth. Could he accept her the way she was? "But what if my legs are horribly deformed?" She lowered her head and pressed her forehead into his shoulder.

"It doesn't matter. You're beautiful to me." Gently, he lowered her into the wheelchair.

Sara immediately pressed the blanket firmly in place. She noticed Mr. Dimitriou's hair was sticking up in odd places, his shirt was rumpled, and his brows furrowed. He looked incredible.

"Listen, would you do something for me?" he asked.

"Sure."

"Will you promise me you'll be careful? Don't go anywhere alone after dark. Keep that pepper spray handy when you're out even in the daylight. And if you need me, please call me anytime day or night." Xanthus snatched a pad and pen from next to her phone, scribbling out his phone number.

"Do you have a cell?" he asked.

"Well, no, but if my business keeps growing, I'll be able to afford one in a couple of months."

"I'll bring you one tomorrow."

"Listen, I appreciate all you've done, but you can't keep spending money on me. I'm not a child. I can take care of myself," she said with her chin up.

"Please Sara, for my peace of mind. Let me get you a cell phone. Let's just consider it included it in your rent." He tensed, waiting for her answer.

Sara didn't like accepting help. She'd worked hard for her independence. But she knew she would feel safer knowing help was only a phone call away. "Okay Mr. Dimitriou, but I think I'm already paying way below what I should be, considering the amount of upgrades you're putting into my apartment." She immediately regretted what she said. What would she do if he *did* raise her rent?

"You let me worry about the expenses of the building. Your job is simply to pay your rent. And please, call me Xanthus. I think that kiss put us way past calling each other Mr. Dimitriou and Miss Taylor."

He looked at her lips and sighed. "I have to go. Just let me know when to pick you up tomorrow and I'll see you then." He leaned in, pressed a quick kiss to her forehead, and then he was gone.

"Xanthus." Sara whispered his name as she pressed her fingers to her lips and smiled.

Xanthus slung his backpack over his shoulders, climbed on his motorcycle, and started his drive out to the warehouse dock. He raised his face into the light rainfall and breathed in a lungful of clean air.

What had he been thinking? His plan had *never* included kissing her. His control was already in threads. If he wasn't careful, *he'd* be the one hunted down. As it stood now, if he were caught, he was already looking at ten years hard labor. He should walk away—pretend he'd never met Sara.

He just couldn't do it. Not only was she a risk of exposure for Dagonians that he could not leave unguarded, but she was also an innocent, a helpless female who was completely unaware of the axe hanging over her head. Xanthus had always prided himself on his abilities as a warrior. But even *he* didn't know if he could protect Sara from that axe dropping. He was sickened when he thought of what fate awaited her if she were ever discovered.

It was her eyes. They were the dead giveaway to what she was. Those eyes. He shuddered thinking of them. They were beautiful, bewitching—like a sea goddess. But hers weren't the eyes of a goddess, but those of a half-human, half-Dagonian girl.

Xanthus shook himself. Now was not the time to think of beautiful females. He needed to get his mind on tonight's job. Lives depended on the success of tonight's mission.

He pulled up a private road and turned off into an almost indiscernible path through the foliage. He drove his bike in as far as he could, turned off the engine, and hiked into the trees. Being a moonless night, it was black as pitch for a human, but Xanthus saw as well in the darkest of nights as during the daylight. The shoreline came into view as he passed through the palm trees. At the water's edge, he dropped his pack in the sand and stripped out of his clothing. Grabbing his pack, he entered the water and submerged.

He surfaced under the dock and listened for footfalls above. He heard nothing but the chirping of several birds. He took hold of the wooden dock and pulled himself up to peer above. No one was about. He hefted his body out of the warm water into the cool night air. It breezed over him as he lay on the hard, wooden dock.

Several minutes later, his cloaked figure moved on. Light poles above forced him into the shadows. He made his way between several brick buildings to a large warehouse backed up against the shore. He knew that a ship was at the dock, waiting to be loaded before it disembarked. He also knew there were four security guards, armed only with clubs.

With his back against the cement foundation of the large, metal warehouse, Xanthus pulled his pack off his back and removed a small, black disk the size of his palm. He pressed it against the side of the building and pushed a small, red button to activate it.

Xanthus repeated the process on each of the four outside walls of the building. Then he crept across the gangplank and attached another disk against the side of the ship. With the devices in place, it was time to locate the guards.

NINE

"**B**ut I only have a little left to do on your curtains and then they're done." Sara scowled.

Gretchen pushed her through the doors of Macy's Department Store. Perfume floated in the air around them as Gretchen steered her toward the women's clothing section.

"Girl, this is a much more pressing matter. This is your first date since I've known you, and knowing you, it's your first date—*ever.*"

Sara didn't disagree, even though it was no longer true. "So." Sara frowned. "Just because I have a date tonight, I have to buy new clothes?"

"No, you have to buy new clothes because you need something appropriate to wear. Don't get me wrong, your clothes are cute, but we're going to the concert hall. It's an occasion to dress up. Besides, you need something special to wow Shane Adams."

"It's Xanthus," Sara said.

"Xanthus? Sounds Greek. So what's his last name again?"

"Dimitriou."

"Ooo... he *is* Greek. I still can't believe you're dating your landlord. Do you think he'll lower your rent now that you're lip-locking?"

"We are not dating. This is one date. And he is not lowering my rent." She had to put her foot down somewhere.

"No denial of the lip-locking? You kissed him, didn't you?" Gretchen's eyes were wide as she smiled.

"He kissed me actually." Sara felt her face heat. That was a testament to how little experience she had—that she would blush just because someone had kissed her. Gretchen had told many more colorful stories about her love life and she had *never* blushed.

"Oh, wow. We are so getting you a killer dress for tonight. One that shows some skin." Gretchen plowed on through to the women's department.

"No. No showing skin." Sara shook her head.

"How are you going to wow him without showing him some skin?" Gretchen stopped next to a display rack, pulled a yellow, strapless sundress up to her body, and gazed in a nearby mirror.

"Why do I need to wow him?"

"Girl, you have a lot to learn about men." Gretchen held the dress up to Sara. "I don't know. I think this yellow washes you out. Let's see what you look like in blue." She pulled a shiny, navy blue dress off the rack.

"I don't like my blues that dark," Sara said. "Besides, I don't think that style is me."

"You're *so* not going in a muumuu."

"I don't wear muumuus."

"Not technically, but you do tend to cover yourself. It wouldn't hurt you to show a *little* more skin."

"How about I wear a bikini top?"

"No need for sarcasm." Gretchen held up a white, sequined dress with spaghetti straps and a deep V-neck, practically down to the waist. "Oh, look at this dress. If you wear this, you'll have to bring along a crash cart. This'll stop Shane Adams's heart."

"I don't think so. How about we find something with a little more fabric?" Sara suggested and wheeled toward a dress rack.

"Wow, look at this. I *love* this color." Sara pulled a shimmery, aqua blue, wraparound dress off a hanger. "It's sleeveless. Does that show enough skin?" Sara held it up for Gretchen's expert inspection.

"Not as much as I'd like, but the dress is amazing. And I think you like that blue so much because it's the exact color of your eyes."

"Really? I hadn't noticed." Sara wheeled into the general direction of the dressing rooms.

"Just where do you think you're going?" Gretchen propped her hand on her hip.

Sara stopped and wheeled back around. "I was going to try it on. Is there something wrong with that?"

"Girl, you can't try on only *one* thing. Let's find a few more to compare."

"Oh good grief, you always make shopping for clothes a big event."

"It *is* a big event. One you should enjoy more. Now come on. Let's keep looking."

Two hours and four changing sessions later, Sara paid for the blue dress. Gretchen pushed her chair away from the checkout counter. "I sure hate to use this thing." Sara put her credit card back in her purse.

"I'm sure you do. What is your balance on that thing?" Gretchen paused to pick up a sample perfume bottle. She sniffed it, sprayed a little on her fingertips, and dabbed behind her ears.

"Ninety-nine dollars and ninety-eight cents," Sara answered.

Gretchen laughed. "Was this your first purchase on that card? How long have you had it?"

"Yes, it's my first purchase, and I've only had it for six months." Sara sighed. "I shouldn't have used it. It's going to take me forever to pay off the charges."

"Girl, you look amazing in that dress. It's definitely worth it. Maybe you should tell Shane to bring a bib. He's going to be drooling all over himself."

Sara rolled her eyes. "Yeah, right."

"No, really," Gretchen said. "You should show off your curves more often. You have such a tiny waist, and with breasts your size, you look like a Barbie doll. Women pay thousands and thousands of dollars trying to get a figure like yours, and you hide yours under T-shirts. It's practically criminal."

"Where are we going?" Sara realized they were moving past a line of retail stores inside the mall's atrium, when they should have been in the parking lot.

"To get your hair done."

"No. No way. I already spent too much money on the dress. There is no way I'm getting my hair done."

"Sara, I'll pay. Let's just call it payment for my draperies."

"Draperies that aren't even done yet."

"Oh, I trust that you'll finish them. Now I know this hairdresser. He's a legend. And he also happens to be my date for the night, which is why he agreed to do your hair on such short notice. He didn't want to have to look at bad hair all evening."

"Very funny. And I thought all male hairdressers were gay."

"That is *so* not true." Sara looked doubtful.

"Okay," Gretchen said. "Maybe it's true for most, but not Hal. I think he just likes playing with women's hair. Personally, he's completely straight."

"Okay, but no matter what he says, I'm not going short. I like my hair long."

"You like to be able to hide behind your hair. It's like your own personal curtain. But I agree. Your hair is gorgeous long. I think you could use some layers though to give your hair shape."

"Hair has shape? Who knew hair had shape?

"Hair definitely has shape." Gretchen laid Sara's doubts to rest.

"All right, I'll get my stupid hair done. But I'm doing my own makeup tonight."

"No argument there. Your skin is perfect and your makeup always looks fine, when you wear makeup."

"Okay, let's get this over with," Sara said as Gretchen wheeled her through the doors.

A short, sandy blond man with a lanky build and amazing green eyes stepped forward and gave Gretchen a peck on the lips. "Gretchen, you look stunning, as always."

"Hal, you always know how to make a girl feel special."

So this was Hal. He was just a few inches taller than Gretchen's five feet. Sara hoped he wasn't self-conscious about his height. Next to Xanthus, everyone seemed miniature.

Hal looked down at Sara. "Oh, Gretchen, you told me how much potential she had but I had no idea until now."

Sara wasn't sure how to take being talked about in third person when she was sitting right there in front of him.

"You're beautiful, Sara." Okay, maybe she could forgive him for his lack of manners. "With my help, you'll be a goddess." He reached out, lifted her hair, and let it cascade through his fingers.

Sara wasn't sure how to respond to that. "Um... thank you?"

"What kind of products do you use?" Hal continued to run his fingers through her hair. Gretchen was right. He really liked playing with women's hair.

"Um, strawberry-scented VO5 shampoo."

"And?"

"And a hairdryer?"

"You're joking." His eyes brushed over her hair as he inspected it. "Your hair has a softness and natural shine that I've never seen before. You wouldn't believe how much effort it takes to get a shine close to yours. How long has it been since you colored it?"

"Um, I don't color it." She shook her head.

"Amazing. The color is incredible, black as midnight. With the right cut, it'll be stunning. We just have to keep it long. I couldn't bring myself to cut off so much perfection."

He draped a smock over Sara, wheeled her in front of a mirror, pulled out his scissors, and began to snip. Hal's scissors danced over her hair. Like confetti, little clumps of hair began to fall.

Sara closed her eyes and enjoyed the gentle snipping and soft tugs on her hair. In the background, the soft chatter of voices and the sound of the television played for those who actually had to wait for their appointment.

A news program ran and a man's voice hummed in the background, "Famous deep-sea diver, Josh Talbot, has been missing for over twenty-four hours and is presumed dead. He was last seen diving off the coast of Sicily. Searchers have yet to locate his body." Sara shuddered at the thought of him drowning at sea. "We've just received breaking new from the west shore.

Let's go to Amanda, who is on the scene."

Sara opened her eyes, looked at the screen, and saw an inferno. "There has been a massive explosion at Roc Manufacturing on the west shore of Oahu. Firefighters are attempting to contain the inferno, but so far, the winds are fueling the flames. It appears that no one was injured. Four security guards on duty were found unconscious but otherwise unharmed on the south side of the complex. It's not clear what happened to them or what the source of the explosion was. Hopefully, we will have a statement from them soon."

"Wow," Sara said. "That's pretty scary."

Gretchen sat down on a swivel chair next to Sara. Her eyes drifted over the television screen absently. "Yeah, it's really sad. But I'm not going to let anything dampen the mood of your first date, Sara. We are going to have a wonderful time and there's to be no talk of explosions tonight. Speculate all you want tomorrow."

Sara smiled. "Yes, ma'am."

TEN

Triton exploded in a rage. His fists slammed into every sculpture, every wall, and every lifeless marble figure surrounding him. All but one.

He couldn't bring himself to shatter the beautiful face, the image that had put him into this fury. This statue was created by goddess and former friend, Aphrodite, and had been sent to him as a gift. It was another attempt of hers to heal his heart. You'd think she'd have given up after two thousand years.

As young children, Aphrodite had been a special friend of his and had had a tremendous effect on him. She'd woven her magic into his heart and into his life. As cousins, they were very close—as close as any brother or sister. As the goddess of love and procreation, she'd showered him with gifts of attractiveness, charm, and magnetism so powerful that it was the rare human female that was able to resist him.

He'd basked in the attention he got from beautiful women and had fathered many merchildren. The women were a temporary diversion, but the children were never forgotten. At birth, he would steal them away from their mothers and bring them into his kingdom to raise them.

They were his most perfect creations. He loved each one, daughter and son alike, but their petty problems and irresponsibility pushed him to the brink of insanity. It was that irresponsibility that led to their demise.

Because they chose to mock Poseidon, they were the makers of their own destruction. Still, Triton had loved them as much as any father and he'd do anything in order to have his children returned to him.

If only he could snatch them from the clutches of Hades. But Hades did not give up those in his domain without a steep price. Triton had tried bargaining with him countless times. Each time, Hades refused. Now the King of the Underworld wouldn't even agree to see him.

Triton looked up at this latest gift from Aphrodite. It was an especially painful jab—the image of a woman best forgotten. It was a reminder of his one great slip that could have brought him infinitely more pain. Who was he lying to? She *had* brought him more pain. Her memory brought him pain even now.

Triton cursed his own weakness. He had sworn off women, sworn never again to father a child. He would protect his heart at all costs from the painful loss of a father losing his child. The only consolation he found in the situation with this human was the fact that she was barren. If she hadn't been...

"Philotheos," Triton shouted, turning away from the exquisite statue.

"Yes, Master." Triton's faithful servant swam into the room. His many squid tentacles brushed over the piles of broken rubble as he glided across the floor. His wide, bulging eyes surveyed the damage, shocked at the destruction surrounding him.

"Clean this place up," Triton said.

Philotheos jumped, startled at Triton's tone. He rarely spoke to his servants so harshly. Triton forced himself to soften his tone. "Please, I want all traces of this... scene gone. And take that statue somewhere out of my sight." He shrugged over his shoulder, not willing to look at it again.

"Should I destroy it?"

"No," Triton roared, his anger threatening to return. He heard the young squid's heart take off in a sprint. Philotheos was fearful of his master. Triton took several calming breaths before he spoke again. "Do not destroy it. Just put in a location where I will never see it."

"Yes, of course, Sire."

Triton turned his back on his servant and the past as he transported himself to a place where he could be completely alone in his misery—the deepest trench of the Mid-Atlantic ridge.

ELEVEN

Sara should have been exhausted from her shopping trip with Gretchen. But with the prospect of her first date with Xanthus, she was giddy with excitement. She wheeled into her bedroom, laid her dress across the bed, and showered. An hour later, she was primped and ready to go.

Sara marveled at her transformation in the mirror. Her layered hair hung in curls around her face and down her back. She'd put on makeup and her new, pale blue dress. The look was undeniably beautiful. Tonight she felt as pretty as Gretchen always told her she was.

A faint knock on the door woke up the butterflies in her stomach. Sara hadn't seen Xanthus since last night when he'd kissed her. She hoped he'd kiss her again.

When she pulled the door open, Xanthus stepped inside. He was dressed in a crisp, black Armani suit and green, Italian-silk tie. *Wow!* was the only coherent thought she could form in her brain.

"Hello Sara. You look amazing." He smiled and her heart skipped a beat.

Stupidly, all she did was nod. Finally, her brain seemed to catch up and she realized what he'd said. She felt her face flush. "You look pretty good yourself."

"Thanks. I'm not used to wearing clothes... I mean, um, these *kinds* of clothes. I'm sorry. I'll admit I'm a bit nervous tonight."

"It's okay, I'm pretty nervous myself."

"Is everything locked up or do you want me to check the windows?" He lifted the kitchen blinds to inspect the lock.

"It's all right. Everything's locked up. Besides, thanks to you, I have a security system." She grabbed her tiny, silver, coin purse.

"I know, but you can't be too careful. Are you ready?"

She nodded.

Xanthus strolled around behind her and pushed her chair toward the door. "I have to warn you," he said, "it's been a long while since I've been on a date, and I'm not completely brushed up on American dating customs. I hope I won't embarrass you."

Sara punched in her alarm code and Xanthus pushed her out the door.

"Not likely," she said. Just being seen with him would have other women envious. "Why haven't you dated for so long? I'm sorry... I shouldn't have asked that." The cool night air greeted her blushing face as he wheeled her out the front door.

"No, it's fine. I don't know. I guess I was always too busy for relationships." He stopped next to a large, black Porsche SUV. Sara looked at the expensive vehicle and raised her eyebrows. This was a lot higher class than usual for her neighborhood.

He opened the passenger door and lifted her into the seat. The car was warm from the evening sun and smelled of rich leather. She finger-combed her curls as Xanthus folded her chair into the back and came around to climb in himself.

"So, what is it you do?" she asked as he turned the key. The air conditioning switched on and began to fill the cab with cool air.

"Well, I guess you could call me a soldier," he said.

"You don't know?"

"Well, I'm more like a cross between a soldier and a policeman."

She wasn't the least bit surprised. He seemed like the warrior type. "So where are you from?"

"The Mediterranean."

"How long have you been in Hawaii?"

Xanthus sighed. "About a month."

"And you decided to buy an apartment building? You must want to stay a while."

"Not really. I'm here on assignment. I bought the apartment building on an impulse. I'll have to figure out what I'm going to do with it before I have to go back a year from now."

"Oh, so you aren't staying?" Sara asked, disappointed.

He shook his head. "No. I'm needed back home. I

couldn't ever stay here permanently. You'd love it in the Mediterranean. The sea is amazing and full of life."

"More so than in Hawaii?" Sara relaxed against the soft leather. She was comforted, listening to the warm cadences of Xanthus's voice.

"In Hawaii, sea life clings to the shore line. Where I come from, there is marine life that goes on for thousands of miles."

"Well, I don't know much about ocean life. I haven't been near the shore since I was a small child."

"You're joking." Xanthus's surprise was apparent. He glanced over at Sara.

"No, I'm actually terrified of the water. I almost drowned when I was a child and ever since then, I won't go near the ocean."

"Really? What happened?" Xanthus's brows furrowed.

Sara shook her head. "I'm sorry, I'd rather not talk about it."

"It must have been traumatic," he said.

She nodded, but didn't offer more.

Xanthus pushed Sara through the doors of an Italian restaurant across the street from the concert hall. He'd done a search for fine restaurants near the concert. He hoped the food was as good as the reviews said it was. They were seated a few minutes later.

"I love this restaurant," Sara said. "My mom and I used to go to the one on the Big Island all the time." Her eyes were a bright, shimmering blue and her cheeks rosy. She'd never looked more beautiful.

"This is my first time here," Xanthus said. "I don't even know what's good. Do you have any suggestions?"

"The lobster ravioli in tomato sauce is to die for."

Somehow, Xanthus didn't think he'd ever consider dying for *any* kind of human food, but he smiled at her crazy lingo. "I'll take your word for it."

The waiter stepped up to the table. "Welcome to the Orchard...."

Xanthus followed Sara's suggestion and ordered the lobster dish. She didn't follow her own advice, but ordered something called cappelini pescatore. A short time later, Xanthus came face to face with the most terrifying thing he'd ever encountered—human food. What lay before him looked strange, foreign, and smelled horrible—like nothing he'd ever come in contact with before.

He took his first tentative bite and came to the immediate conclusion that it tasted as bad as it smelled. He didn't even have anything to compare it to, but given the taste, texture, and burning hot temperature, the lobster was definitely dead.

Xanthus did his best to look as if he were enjoying the food. Sara's company more than made up for the terrible meal. He was both shocked and delighted to see she was not afraid to speak her mind. It was very different from Dagonian females, who rarely spoke to males—and that was only if directly spoken to. Even when they did, they never voiced an opinion. Hades. If he hadn't been so close to his own mother and sister, he wouldn't have known females even *had* opinions. Sara not only had her own opinions, she spoke them clearly and intelligently.

Resisting her enticing scent was still a trial, but he was finding it easier. She was just so sweet. He couldn't imagine breaching her trust.

Sara smiled, enjoying every minute of her date. Xanthus gently pushed her and her wheelchair across a sidewalk lined with coconut trees. The sun was just beginning to set, bringing a warm radiance to everything it touched and the cool, floral-scented air breezed through her hair like a gentle kiss. The glowing concert hall beckoned ahead.

"Sara," Gretchen squealed the moment Sara and Xanthus stepped through the door. Gretchen hurried over and Hal followed. She beamed at Sara and then looked up at Xanthus. Her eyes went wide and her jaw slack. "Wow," she mouthed, then composed herself and smiled. "Hi, you must be Xanthus. Sara has told me so much about you." Gretchen and Hal both had to crane their necks to look Xanthus in the eye.

"Hello Gretchen," Xanthus said. "And this must

be Hal."

Hal looked taken aback by Xanthus's overwhelming presence. "Nice to meet you," Xanthus said. Hal hesitated a second before he came forward, clasped Xanthus's hand, and shook. He then turned to Sara and his face lit up. He came forward and took her hand in both of his. "Sara, you look stunning." She smiled wide, pleased at his compliment. Then she turned to Xanthus.

Xanthus's eyes were ablaze.

He was jealous. Wow. How he could be jealous of *anyone* else was beyond her, but still she needed to squelch this before it got any worse.

Sara released her hand from Hal's grip and reached out to pull Xanthus in closer. "Xanthus, Hal is my hairdresser."

Xanthus crinkled his brow in confusion.

"He's a hairstylist. He just did my hair today."

"Oh, well he did a wonderful job; you look beautiful." He made an effort to look relaxed, but Sara saw lingering apprehension.

Sara wondered how Gretchen was taking all this talk of her looking so beautiful and glanced her way. She should have known. Gretchen's face was beaming as she smiled and winked at Sara. It was an 'I told you so' wink. Gretchen was always telling her how pretty she was. Sara was forever doubtful and now Gretchen was gloating.

Gretchen came forward, taking Hal's hand.

He melted into her side. "We'd better take our seats," Gretchen said. "Xanthus, you *could* push Sara to her seat but the aisles are so narrow that it might be easier if you just carry her. She's not too heavy for you, is she?"

Sara was mortified.

"This little water lily too heavy for me?" Xanthus asked. "I don't think so." He lifted her out of the wheelchair. Sara was surprised by his quick movement and, for a moment, felt off balance. She threw her arms around his neck to steady herself. He had a smirk on his face and she knew he'd done it on purpose. Her heart beat double time. She wasn't sure if it was from the surprise or the excitement of being held by Xanthus. It was probably from both.

"I'll make sure Sara's chair is taken care of," Gretchen said as she pushed it away.

Moments later, they were seated near the front. Sara looked on in amazement at the concert hall. Plush seats filled the wide hall and even more seats filled the balcony, which seemed to float above the floor. Her excitement built and she had to check herself to keep from bouncing like a toddler in a candy shop. The upcoming performance was a Chinese orchestra with dance performers. It was supposed to be incredible. Sara loved music. It didn't matter the style or genre—if it was good, she adored it.

Xanthus slipped his arm around her shoulders and she practically purred. It just felt so right being here with him. But how would he feel about her deformed legs? It was easy for him to say he'd like her regardless of what her malformed body looked like. He'd never actually seen it. How would he react to seeing it in the flesh?

Sara could still remember the reactions doctors had had when she went in for an appointment after leaving her mom. She'd gone in search of hope, but found only despair. The doctors couldn't have looked more shocked if they'd seen a green alien with squirming tentacles. After days of tests and collaboration, they'd told her the only way she could have any semblance of a normal life was to have it surgically removed. They'd told her there were thousands of people living with no legs and she could go on to have a normal life. But as long as she clung to her deformity, she'd be a freak.

They were crazy, insane. She'd never been back to a doctor since. But, deep in her heart, she wondered if they were right.

She looked over at Xanthus. What would she do if he rejected her? She didn't know if she could take it. And when did she start caring so deeply about him? They'd just met. This was their first date. Who knew if there'd be a second? However, the thought of him rejecting her had her terrified.

"Sara, what's wrong?" Xanthus whispered in her ear.

"What? No, nothing's wrong."

"Is it someone in this hall? Why are you afraid?" He glanced around, looking for the cause of her distress.

This man was too observant. "It's nothing, really."

The lights dimmed and the music swelled. Sara forgot her troubles the moment the music began. Thankfully, Xanthus seemed to relax too. The next hour and a half they were treated to an amazing performance. The music was lively—a beautiful mix of harmonious tunes paired with nimble, energetic dancers. They moved as one with the music, so much so that Sara became convinced that the music and dance couldn't possibly exist without each other.

When the last note had been played, the dancers exited the stage. Sara smiled and sighed. "Wow. That was amazing." She looked at Xanthus.

The smile on his face didn't diminish the intensity of his gaze as he looked into her eyes. "Yes, it was."

In that moment, she felt as if they were the only two people in the concert hall, and she very much wanted to kiss him. From the look he was giving her, he was thinking the same thing. His hand brushed feathery soft against her cheek.

A spike of adrenaline sent icy shoots through Sara's bloodstream. Out of the corner of her eye, she saw a woman stumble on the balcony and sway backward, teetering over the railing high above. Sara turned her head in shock, knowing she was about to see a woman fall to her death.

Xanthus uttered a low oath and raised his hand toward the poor woman just before she fell. Sara felt a concussion of energy coming from him, almost like an intense banging of a large drum, but with no sound. The woman looked as if she were being shoved from behind, which of course was impossible since there was nothing behind her but open air. Still, she pitched forward into the arms of a man who was reaching for her. They both fell into the crowd of spectators.

"How did you do that?" Sara's voice rasped in a low whisper.

"I did nothing," Xanthus said, low and hard, suggesting there would be no argument.

"But I felt..."

"I did nothing, Sara."

She felt tears burning in her eyes. He'd put on a hard mask and she could tell he was furious. She wasn't sure if he was furious with her or himself, but it was there all the same. She held back the tears, not wanting to humiliate herself.

The ride home was miserable. He didn't say a word as tension rolled off him in waves. All she wanted was to get home and in bed so she could vent her hurt and disappointment into her pillow.

Xanthus acted as if he wanted nothing more than to be rid of her. He got her wheelchair from the back and lifted her into it. He strode ahead of her to the front door as she wheeled after him. Xanthus opened the door for her to pass through, which she did. She hurried, knowing the tears were coming. She didn't want to give him the satisfaction of seeing her cry.

"Don't forget to keep your windows and doors

locked. And be sure to set your alarm," he said before closing the door.

Sara couldn't believe him. So that was it? At the end of what started out as the perfect date, she got no goodbye, no kiss, and no I'll call you—just a cold shoulder.

She narrowed her eyes and straightened her spine. "Actually, I think I'll go out," she said to herself as she made her way to her apartment. "Maybe I'll see the night life in my neighborhood. Then perhaps I'll sleep under the stars tonight. I could invite some neighbors, like Slink to join me." She got to her door and fished out her keys. How dare he act as if she had done something wrong! She'd done nothing.

That night was a long one. Sara's mind raced as the moon crept across the night sky. She bounced between anger and hurt. She was also mystified at what exactly had happened at the concert hall. Had Xanthus saved that woman? What kind of person has that power? And if he does, who is he? What is he? Where does someone like him come from?

TWELVE

Xanthus slammed his foot down on the accelerator as the ocean view flew past his window. His self-loathing burned deep inside. He had misused the powers Triton entrusted to him. He had ignored his instructions and had meddled in the life of a human. Not only that, he had risked exposing himself.

Xanthus grunted as he pounded his fist against the steering wheel. He had acted without honor. He had put his own personal feelings above duty. He'd even been neglecting his mission. Oh sure, he'd taken care of the latest cargo of waste that was to be dumped at sea. But then he'd known that the owner and board of directors of Roc enterprises were meeting tonight in response to the bombing of the dock. It would have presented the perfect opportunity to gather them together and send them to Triton to answer for their crimes. Instead, he'd gone to a concert with a criminal.

No, he chided himself. As angry as he was, he couldn't blame Sara, and she was no criminal in his eyes. Still, she was a distraction, and he could not afford distractions. He'd been so worried about her and obsessed with her that he'd lost sight of his mission.

Xanthus needed to take a step away. After all, Sara had lived among the humans her entire life. She could live a few more days without him. He was so close to fulfilling this assignment. He needed to get his head back in the game.

The main office building of Roc was a dark silhouette against the starry sky. The parking lot spread before him, empty. He could smell the remnants of cigarette smoke, perfume, and sweat. They must have left about a half an hour ago. He slammed his fist into the steering wheel again. What would have been an easy round up would end up being a drawn-out hunt. He will have to track down the five members of the inner circle one by one. These five humans had caused the indescribable pain, suffering, and death of thousands of innocent Dagonians.

Xanthus made a mental list of guilty persons. Number one on his list would have to be the Vice president, Trent McDougall. He was due to take a flight in the morning to the mainland, making his capture a time-sensitive matter. He was probably home at this time. He slept alone. His wife had left him when she'd discovered his mistress and his mistress left him when she'd discovered her gym buddy's net worth. Mr. McDougall had yet to find anyone to replace either of them.

Xanthus scaled the side of the McDougall mansion. A large swimming pool lapped just below. He loved coincidences that worked in his favor. He slit a large X in the screen and slipped through the bedroom window. McDougall snored loudly, his large, blubbery body covered in a light blanket. Xanthus moved in close, slapped his hand tightly over the man's mouth, and pinned his arm across his chest.

McDougall's eyes flew open. He attempted to scream but couldn't get out more than a murmur of a sound. Xanthus pulled the squirming man out of bed. He dragged him through his house and out the back door. At the pool's edge, he hissed out the words Triton had instructed him to speak. "I give to you a message from the sea. You have brought death to many of our children. You are now summoned by Triton, King and Guardian of the Sea, to answer for your crimes. You may beg for mercy, you may plead for leniency. You will be given as much compassion as you have shown to those who died an agonizing death at the hands of your poison."

Xanthus removed his hand from the criminal's mouth. The man yelled and cursed, but his eyes were wild and darting around, possibly looking for a miracle to save him. Xanthus reached his hand toward the water's surface and felt power pulse through him. "I send you to Triton to answer for your crimes." He pitched the man headfirst into the pool of water. Bubbles rose as the man sank, his flailing legs disappearing into the churning water. A minute later, the water was calm and Xanthus knew the man was gone.

One down, four more to go.

THIRTEEN

The morning after her date with Xanthus, Sara's temper had settled down and the hurt took up residence in her heart. The next four days were long and agonizing. Xanthus didn't come to see her, didn't call, and didn't even show up in the building to supervise the repairs and upgrades that continued on without him. She kept waiting for the ache in her chest to lessen, but it didn't. If anything, it was getting worse.

Oh, she used every argument she could think of to try to convince herself he wasn't worth the heartache. She told herself she barely knew him. She couldn't possibly care that much about him. She tried to remind herself what a jerk he was, blaming her for something *he* did. She also tried to tell herself it was for the best—he was a deeply disturbed man who regretted saving a woman's life and because of that, she shouldn't be getting involved with him anyway.

Day five proved to be a continuation of the torment she'd been living. Sara put in her ear buds and turned on her MP3 player. She listened to her programmed list of sad songs while she lay in bed. When her stomach started to grumble, she wheeled out into the kitchen to make dinner. A faint, unpleasant odor alerted her that she needed to take out the garbage. She pulled the garbage bag out of the can, tied it off, and headed out.

Sara wheeled her chair out the back door toward the dumpster, the trash bag swinging from her armrest as she listened to a haunting tune and sang softly to herself.

Phantom voices drifted through the trees. "*So beautiful... beautiful...*" The words misted through her soft voice and gentle music, caressing her ears. Sara stopped singing and pulled out her buds to locate the origin of the strange voices.

A moment later, a chilling rumble of laughter broke the entranced mood. "Tane, look who's wandered into our web." A familiar, thin stranger stepped out of the thick trees. His smile stretched across his face, showing crusty, yellow teeth. It was her creepy neighbor, Slink. To his left and right lurked two large strangers.

Sara froze. She was behind her building, completely isolated, and there were three scary-looking men staring at her with wicked grins plastered on their faces. Behind them was a thick, darkening grove of coconut trees. Her trusty pepper spray sat ready in her purse—on the floor next to her living room couch.

"Oh don't stop singing, haole girl," the man on the right said. "Your song is very pretty. Just like you. Don't you think so, Ettie?" He glanced at the large man on Slink's left.

"Oh yeah. That song sure has put *me* into the mood for tonight's activities."

Oh, dear heavens. What had she rolled into? She'd just wanted to take out the trash, not usually a dangerous event. She was in a panic as she stared up at the obvious threat.

"*I have a phone.*" Thank heaven she'd put Xanthus on her speed dial. He may not like her or want to talk to her right now, but she was sure he didn't want her raped and murdered.

Sara yanked out her cell and punched his number. She had just pushed the send button when it was yanked away from her.

"I don't think so, little haole." Ettie walked over to the brick building and slammed the phone against the wall. Small fragments of the phone flew everywhere. Before Sara could react, she was nose to nose with Slink. His rancid breath filled her nostrils, making her gag.

"You should be afraid," she said, trying to take control of the situation. She knew her best bet would be to talk her way out of this. Physically, she didn't stand a chance.

Ettie laughed.

"And why's that, princess?" Slink smirked.

"You obviously haven't seen my boyfriend. He owns this building. He's about seven feet tall, two hundred-fifty pounds of solid muscle, and very protective of me." Lying seemed to be her best option.

"That's what I'm counting on," Slink said. "Your

boyfriend evicted me. He told me he didn't like the way I was looking at you. Well princess, he's *really* not going to like what I have planned for you tonight. But *I'm* sure going to enjoy this. I've wanted to do this for a long time."

"He'll kill you." Sara's eyes darted around, looking for a rescuer.

Slink barked a laugh. "I don't think so. He'll never know what happened to you. No one will. And I'll be long gone before he wonders where you are."

Sara knew it was a futile attempt, but darn it, she had to do something. She tried to make a break for it, turning her wheels hard. Her goal was to reach the front of the building. If she could just get there, maybe someone would see her and help her.

She heard laughter from behind as her chair turned in the opposite direction. Before she knew it, she was bumping along over a dirt path into the trees.

Grabbing onto her wheels didn't seem to do much more than burn her hands. This situation was quickly spiraling out of control. The darkness deepened as they traveled into the foliage. She had to do something. She always told herself that if she was ever in this situation, she would go down fighting.

Not seeing an alternative, Sara pushed herself out of her seat. She landed hard on the ground, her body hitting the metal corner of the footrest.

Slink chuckled, still holding onto the handles of her empty chair. "Nice try, little, crippled haole. Tane, you take her feet, I'll take the head, and Ettie, you take the middle." Slink wrapped his skinny arms around her chest and picked her up off the ground. The other two lifted the rest of her and began carrying her down the path.

Sara fought them with each step—squirming, flailing, and clawing at Slink's hands locked around her. The rumble of the surf interrupted her struggles. It was growing louder. That was their destination. *Oh, please no! Anywhere but there.* But that's exactly where they were taking her, she was sure of it. How better to get rid of her body, than to toss it bleeding into the surf? The sharks would come shortly and get rid of any evidence. She would die in the water, just as she'd always feared she would.

"Please, please no," she begged as she increased her struggle. Maybe if she fought hard enough, they'd murder her now, before they raped her. More importantly, she wouldn't have to go into that ocean alive. Maybe that sounded twisted, but who said phobias made sense? Sara's fear of water by far outweighed her fear of death.

Finally, Sara wriggled out of Tane's grasping hands. Desperate to keep hold of her, Tane clawed, grabbing hold of the spandex wrap. In one smooth slide, the wrap came off, falling in a heap onto the dirt path.

"What the...?" Tane shouted as he jumped back.

"What are you freaking out about?" Slink asked. Sara continued to struggle in his grasp.

"She's a... She's a..." Tane said.

"Stop babbling like an idiot, and pick up her

feet," Slink said.

"She doesn't have any feet."

"Well, she was in a wheelchair. There had to be a rea... son. Stop fighting me, b—hey..." He glared at her as his head bobbed. She was making it difficult for him to hold onto her flailing body. Well, there was no way she was making it easy for him to put her in the water.

"No, man, she don't have feet, she's got..." Tane began.

Just then, Sara swung her body with all her might and smacked Tane across the face, knocking him clear off his feet.

"Whoa." Slink and Ettie dropped her and scrambled away as her body slapped hard against the ground.

"What in the..." Slink's eyes were wide open in shock. He crept forward as he looked carefully at Sara. Even in the fading twilight, he could see her. Her dress was draped over her body, hugging each feature, giving them a clear picture of her shape as it showed pale against the dark sand. "We've kidnapped a... a..."

"Exactly," Tane said, keeping his distance.

"I'm not a mermaid," Sara shouted, turning on her side. Only then did she realize that maybe it would be best for them to think she was a mermaid. Maybe then, they'd think twice about killing her. Of course, they might still kill her, put her in a tank of formaldehyde, and sell her body to the highest bidder. The tabloids would have a field day with her.

"Yeah right. Girl... mermaid... whatever. You just shut up while I think," Slink said. He seemed to be thinking very hard. His eyes narrowed and a slow smile spread across his face.

"Ettie, get the van. We're taking her with us. She has to be worth a fortune. We may have to keep her for a while. We'll just need to find the right buyers. And I know a guy."

A low growl snaked through the trees. It grew louder, driving chills down Sara's spine, and causing the hair on her neck to stand on end.

"What... is... that?" Tane stepped back. Fear was thick in the air. Sara was terrified too, but this time it wasn't the fear of these men that caused it. If a wild animal were loose around here, she was definitely the most helpless of the group. This was turning out to be a very bad night.

The three men stood unmoving, their eyes searching the foliage around them. Darkness blanketed everything and, out of that darkness, an ominous figure emerged. Sara recognized him at once and nearly fainted with relief. Her three kidnappers didn't share her relief. In fact, after looking at Xanthus's fury, they would rather have dealt with a lion than this hulking specter of death.

Xanthus spared Sara only an incidental glance. His focus was on his prey. Sara looked back at Slink and his friends. Slink yanked a gun out from behind his back, making Sara's heart skip a beat. A shadow flew over the ground, distracting her for a moment.

When she looked back to see Xanthus, he was gone.

A rasping, choking sound caught her attention. She turned to see that Xanthus had Slink by the throat. How had he moved twenty feet in a split second? Her eyes darted back and forth, stunned at the impossibility.

Xanthus held Slink high above the ground. The gun dropped as Slink's feet kicked and flailed. Xanthus spoke. His voice was unlike anything Sara had heard before. It was raw, grating, animalistic, and terrifying. "You dare to touch a daughter of Calypso, human?"

"Please don't kill me," Slink said as he clawed at Xanthus's hand around his throat. Ettie and Tane didn't spare their friend a thought as they scrambled into the trees.

"Oh, your fate is sealed. I will do what the law requires."

Xanthus raised a trident. Its three spikes glimmered in the fading light, the razor-sharp points reflecting the moonlight. A slick, metallic sound made Sara shiver as the middle spike retracted, leaving two points forming a U-shape.

Xanthus's movements were quick and fluid. He let go of his grip and speared his trident at Slink's throat. Slink shrieked as the trident came toward him, straddling his neck and pinning him to a tree. His scream choked off as he grasped onto the prongs, struggling to keep his weight off his neck.

Why wasn't he dead? Sara felt sick at the

conclusion she'd reached. Xanthus didn't intend to kill him quickly. One look at Xanthus's face left no doubt that Slink was not getting out of this alive. What kind of monster was Xanthus? Granted these men had intended to kill her, but he was being just as barbaric.

In a flash, Xanthus was gone. A few short moments later, Sara heard torturous screaming in the distance. Then silence.

She didn't know if it was Ettie or Tane, but she knew that whoever had made those terrible cries was now dead.

Slink continued to kick and flail from his perch. "Please. Get me down."

"I can't," Sara said. "I can't reach you." She knew that even if she could, she'd never have the strength to pull the trident out of the tree trunk.

Sara heard another wail, fainter than the first. A few moments later, it cut off. Another one dead.

Xanthus would be coming back. Sara shook, terrified at the prospect. He was a homicidal maniac. What law required him to kill these men? There was no such law in the state of Hawaii. And Xanthus had called her a daughter of Calypso and these men humans? He was completely delusional. She'd be lucky to get out of this alive after all.

Sara's heart was beating out of her chest when he returned. She wanted to tell him not to hurt Slink. Slink may have deserved to spend his worthless life in prison, but she didn't want to lie here and watch

Xanthus kill him. Sara was so terrified that, despite her good intentions, she couldn't speak.

Xanthus walked up to Slink as he flailed about. Grabbing him by the throat, he jerked the trident from the trunk. "Let's take a walk, human."

Xanthus simmered in lethal anger as he held Slink several feet above the ground. He was skinny for a human, and reeked of drugs, alcohol, and body odor. Xanthus forced himself not to crush the human's windpipe. Just the thought of this vile creature putting his hands on Sara had Xanthus feeling murderous.

"Please, don't kill me," Slink said.

"I would love nothing more than to kill you. But I won't. If you had succeeded in your plans tonight, I would have killed you without hesitation. Instead, I'm sending you to a place where you can never harm or threaten another innocent, and if you knew what fate awaited you, you would be pleading for death."

Xanthus stepped to the edge of a rocky overhang and pointed his trident toward the water lapping below. Slowly, he lowered Slink into the water. "I send you to the Panthon Prison human cell block to answer for your crimes." Xanthus knew the prison would accept humans without question.

Small shoots of seaweed sprouted from the sand and slid over Slink's feet. They slithered up and over his skin like a hundred thin, green snakes, cocooning him as they moved up his body. His eyes bulged as he opened his mouth and gave an ear-piercing wail.

Xanthus had also wondered if the screams came more from fear or pain. Triton had explained how the Heitach worked and had given Xanthus the power to command them. They required water to call them forth, and when they came, they not only covered their victims, but also poisoned them, causing an excruciating amount of pain before temporarily shutting down all bodily function. Miraculously, the cocoon would keep the human alive for transport to any place Xanthus commanded.

These were resourceful creatures. They could get through any barrier, travel any distance around the world, and they instinctively knew the exact place you ordered them to go. If he wanted to, Xanthus could send this man to the United States president's oval office and the secret service would be powerless to stop them.

Slink drifted away from shore. His wails were cut off as the Heitach covered his face just before he slipped under the surface.

Xanthus made his way back to the grove of trees. There, encircled in darkness, he found Sara. She was curled up, weeping, her body trembling.

Xanthus felt tormented, guilty. He'd known that she wasn't safe among the humans. But he'd left her anyway, to complete his mission. Well, his mission was nearly complete. Only one guilty person remained to be sent to Triton. Regardless of his duty, Xanthus should never have left Sara unprotected. The humans were dangerous beings. Of course, Xanthus knew she wouldn't be any safer among Dagonians. What in Hades was he to do with her?

What he wanted to do was carry her off to his home and lock her up safe, where no one could hurt her again. In those long moments tonight when he had been unsure whether she was dead or alive, he'd been frantic. Then it struck him.

He loved her.

He loved her with his whole heart, soul, and being. Xanthus knelt down next to her small form on the hard ground. For the first time, he saw with his eyes the evidence of what she really was—a true daughter of Calypso. Her perfect tail fin shone pale against the dark sand.

A whispered breath against Sara's face let her know that someone was very close.

"Sara. You're safe now." Xanthus's voice, so terrifying just a moment ago, was now feathery soft.

Against her better judgment, Sara's fear turned to relief. A sob shook her chest as Xanthus's arms surrounded her. Her hands clawed their way around his neck as she clung to him and cried.

"Shh. It's all right. You're safe." He stroked her

hair.

What was she thinking? This man was dangerous, a murderer. Still, she couldn't seem to help herself. Even though he'd just killed three men, in his arms she felt safe, protected.

Sara was obviously just as crazy as he was.

"Come on. Let's get you out of here." Xanthus slipped his hand underneath her and lifted her off the rocky ground. She kept her arms tight around his neck and tucked her head in the crook of his shoulder.

"I'm so sorry I wasn't here to protect you," he said. "I never should have left you. I won't make that mistake again. Tonight you'll stay at my place and rest. Then I'll decide what's to be done."

"Your place?" Sara's head shot up. "Please, Xanthus, I want to go home. I'd just like to climb under my blankets and try to forget what happened here."

"Sara." Xanthus frowned. "Since I found you, I've spent day and night watching you, worried about you. And if you think I'd take you home and leave you unprotected after you were nearly murdered... Great gods of Olympus. I leave you for a short assignment and look what happened."

"I'm sorry," she said, "but you have to see this from... wait a minute. You went on an assignment? Why didn't you tell me? I thought you were angry with me, that you weren't talking to me."

"You thought I was angry with *you*?"

"Yes. Well, if you weren't angry, why didn't you

call me? Or tell me where you were going?"

"I... I didn't think of it. I'm sorry if you were upset."

"I didn't say I was upset. If you want to leave without a word, it doesn't mean a thing to me. I mean, it's not like we're in a relationship." Sara felt as if she might start crying again.

"Oh Sara, I wasn't angry with you, I was angry with myself. And I'm sorry I didn't call you."

"Wait a minute." She whipped her head around. "We passed my wheelchair."

"I'll come back for it later." He shrugged, heading in the direction of the parking lot.

"Oh, no you won't. I can't leave it out here. Someone will steal it."

Xanthus sighed, turned back, and stepped toward the chair. Blue lights flashed through the trees.

"Is that the police?" Sara asked.

"Looks like it."

"Of all the times for them to show up in this neighborhood. They never have before. Oh no, they're going to arrest you for murder, aren't they? I mean when they find the bodies."

"There *are* no bodies." Xanthus said.

"Then you didn't kill them?"

"No, I didn't." He sighed.

Sara was elated. "Then where are they? Maybe Slink called the police. But that'd be stupid. They were the ones trying to kidnap me."

"Sara, as much as I'd love to continue this conversation, I think we'd better get out of here. I'm supposed to keep a low profile."

Xanthus sat her down in the wheelchair, lifted both her and her chair off the ground, and headed back toward the beach. "Hey, where are we going?"

"We need to get out of here."

"But this path leads to the ocean." Sara's heart started pounding.

"Exactly." Xanthus's eyes focused on her, his voice firm. "I'm a very strong swimmer. And I'm sure you'll find you are too."

"Oh no, I am not. Listen, I don't know what you *think* I am, but I definitely don't swim." Sara looked down at her fin in shock. She curled it under the chair, trying to hide it.

"I know exactly what you are and you are built to swim."

"No, I am not. I have a deformity..."

Xanthus's growl stopped Sara mid-sentence. "Don't ever say that again. You are perfectly formed."

The man was insane. He really was.

Xanthus and Sara reached the shore. Sara's eyes were wide as she gulped in gasps of air. The surf looked like a great beast that threatened to devour her. Xanthus strode toward it, fearless.

FOURTEEN

Sara's chest squeezed the breath right out of her as panic set in. Xanthus lowered her and her chair down to the sand. He stripped out of his clothes and stepped into the lapping water. It was a testament to how terrified she was that she didn't give his amazing body a thought as she sucked in air and tried to wheel through the thick sand, attempting to escape.

The water began to churn and bubble. "You might want to close your eyes. You don't want to see this."

Somewhere in the back of her mind, she heard what he said, but she didn't pay much attention to it. She was too busy trying to get away. All she could think about was the thundering sound of the surf and the giant, threatening waves. Sara started to sob as her chair refused to budge. In desperation, her eyes locked onto Xanthus as she sat, petrified.

Xanthus bent forward, groaning in agony, and squeezed his arms around his chest. His growl increased in volume and then turned into a shriek as the skin on his legs ripped open, peeling back to expose slick, red muscles and white tendons.

Rising

Sara gasped in horror at the grotesque sight, the ocean waves suddenly forgotten. Each of Xanthus's muscles pulsed and throbbed as they grew and morphed. Muscles and tendons snaked around Xanthus's exposed legs, wrapping them from front to back as if they were tying his legs together.

Gray skin rippled down from his waist, covering the exposed flesh all the way to his ankles. Below his ankles, the white bones of his feet had torn through his skin and stretched like skeletal branches. The bones were soon connected with white elongating tendons and then covered by the advancing grey skin forming a great fin.

When the transformation was complete, Xanthus's head flew back as he shouted in triumphant. Shock-driven adrenaline jolted Sara's body. Xanthus looked magnificent and ferocious. It was like coming face to face with a vicious shark.

Sara opened her mouth to scream but the scream choked off when the recognition hit her. She sat frozen, her mouth agape. Xanthus's fin was much like her own deformed legs—the same shape, the same form. The only difference was that hers was flesh colored and his was grey. He must be... a merman? And if that were true, was she really a mermaid?

Sara sat stunned.

She'd never known a merman could look so deadly. Sara's eyes rose to his face. Xanthus looked apprehensive, as if he sensed her alarm. When she saw his trepidation, her fear melted away. This was Xanthus, the man who had been watching over and protecting her since the moment they'd met. He might look lethal, but he would never hurt *her*.

Sara shut her mouth and swallowed. Her eyes, burning with curiosity, brushed over his body in a careful examination. Xanthus was amazing. The skin on his upper body was tanned, muscled, smooth, and hairless. His lower body was dark grey, almost black. His fin looked long and muscular. It fanned out darkly in the sandy surf. He was wearing a wide, gold belt at the waist that matched the gold armbands around his biceps. However incredible his form may have been, what was even more amazing was the fact that he was suspended in the air.

This merman could fly.

"Are you a...?" Sara licked her parched lips.

"Dagonian. We're both Dagonians. Well, you're half. But you're the perfect image of one, except for your blue eyes. Dagonians only have dark brown eyes."

"So I'm not a mermaid?"

"No, you're not. The children of Triton are extinct—killed off two thousand years ago at the command of Poseidon, Triton's own father and King of the Greek sea gods. You're a descendant of the unlikely union of the gods Dagon and Calypso. Dagon is a sea god in the Sumerian pantheon. Calypso is a sea goddess of the Greek pantheon."

"Oh, well that that clears everything up," she

said.

Sara's heart took off in a sprint when Xanthus approached her. She guessed her heart hadn't yet gotten the news that he wasn't a threat to her. Xanthus leaned down, wrapped his arm around her waist, and lifted her out of her chair. Her tail brushed his for a moment. His fin felt rough like sandpaper, where hers was soft, smooth, and no different in texture and color from the rest of her skin.

In one quick move, Xanthus flung her beloved wheelchair a mile out to sea. Okay, maybe it wasn't a mile, but this Dagonian had incredible strength.

"What did you do that for?" Sara asked, breathless.

He put his hand under the backside of her fin and lifted her into a cradle hold. "We can't leave any sign that we were here."

"Xanthus, please. I really can't swim. In fact, I'm terrified of the water." Sara realized where he was about to take her.

"You're going to have to trust me. You can do this." Xanthus's confidence was apparent.

Sara shook her head, tears welling in her eyes. "No, I can't. I really can't go in the water. I'd rather you make me disappear like you did those three men."

"Sara, don't be ridiculous. We don't have far to go."

"Please, don't make me do this," she said, going into full panic mode. Xanthus raised an eyebrow at her protests.

"Can you breathe underwater?" he asked.

"Oh no, please no. It's the most horrible thing imaginable."

Xanthus must have taken that for a yes, because the next thing Sara knew, she was headed straight for the water. Before she could scream, they broke through the water's surface. It washed over her face and body, enveloping her in a black nightmare.

At once, she was fighting him with everything she had. Bubbles churned around them as she struggled, squirmed, clawed, and ran out of air. In one great terrible gulp, she took in a lungful of water.

Then she fought harder.

Xanthus had a tight grip around Sara's waist as she battered his chest and clawed at his face. He responded by releasing one of his arms from around her waist in order to pin her arms down. Now all she had was her fin, which she flailed with all her might, scraping it against his sandpaper skin. She was raw emotion, raw terror.

After a long time of desperate struggles, exhaustion eventually wore her out and Sara was left so weak she couldn't move. Sobs shook her chest as unrecognized tears floated from her eyes into the seawater.

When she'd cried all the tears she had, the haze of fear lifted and she was left feeling drained—emotionally and physically exhausted. Even holding her head in place was too much of an effort and her head bobbed back and forth in time with the strokes of Xanthus's tail. It was a relief when she felt his hand press her cheek into his chest.

It was a long time before the strained breaths of water began to pass more easily in and out of her lungs. Then a miracle occurred. Her fear melted completely away and she relaxed in his arms.

She could hear Xanthus's watery breaths. They were smooth, even, and slow. It was pitiful that as hard as she fought, he wasn't even winded. Or would the correct term be "watered?"

Sara was soothed by the rhythmic stroke of his fin. With her ear at his chest, she heard the steady beating of his heart. Those thump, thump, thumping sounds relaxed her even more. She closed her eyes just to rest them for a moment. Even her eyes were tired.

"Sara?" Underwater, the tones of Xanthus's voice woke her up. She hadn't even realized she'd fallen asleep. How much time had passed? It didn't feel like too long.

"Sara? Are you all right?" He spoke again. His voice hummed in the water and was laced with real concern.

Sara knew he was waiting for a response. Her first instinct was to give him the silent treatment. After what he'd put her through, he didn't deserve an acknowledgement. However, Sara was curious to see what her own voice sounded like underwater. She wasn't going to let him off the hook yet, so she settled on, "I'm not talking to you." Her voice sounded not only weak, but also strange and foreign.

Sara felt his chest shaking and heard a low rumble.

"Oh no, you did not just laugh me." Anger seemed to give her strength. "You heartless beast. You think my situation is funny? You didn't even know if I could breathe underwater, but here we are anyway. I could have died."

"You said that breathing underwater was horrible. That meant you could do it. I would have never..."

"Did I say I could?" Sara interrupted. "You assumed. Thank heaven you assumed right or I would be dead. And I told you I was terrified of the water. I can't believe you pulled me under anyway."

"Sara, I would never have let you drown. I know it was terrifying, but it worked, didn't it? Are you still afraid?"

Sara couldn't think of a thing to say about that. She wasn't about to admit he might be right. Instead, she changed the subject. "Where is your house? It's in the Pacific ocean, isn't it?"

"Actually, it's in the Mediterranean Sea. Remember?"

"What? We aren't swimming there, are we?"

"No, we aren't swimming to the Mediterranean." She heard the smile in his voice and was angry all over again.

"Ouch," he said.

Oh, yeah. She pinched him. Hard too, which was about all she could do. It wasn't her fault he was stronger than she was. Xanthus let the pinch slide without a comment.

"We're going to my houseboat, near Waikiki."

"Waikiki? What is taking us so long? We should have been there hours ago," she said, exaggerating.

"We took the scenic route."

The faint glow of a boat appeared in the distance. As they got closer, Sara made out more boats lined up in a row. "How are we going to get on your boat without anyone seeing us?"

"I have a hatch that opens up from underneath. No one will see us." Xanthus swam up to the boat closest to them and farthest from shore. Underneath, she could make out a dark, round door.

He positioned them below the door, pushed open the hatch, and swam straight up. His head broke the surface of the water a fraction of a second before hers. As she breathed out, ocean water poured from her mouth and down her body. The next breath she took in filled her lungs with warm, humid air. It felt so good to breathe air again.

The room they were in was dark with no windows and a sealed door was just ahead of them. Xanthus closed the lid on the hatch they had passed through and turned a handle to lock it in place. The room was now pitch black, but Xanthus seemed to know exactly where to go. Without hesitation, he moved over to the sealed door and opened it.

He reached down under Sara's fin and once again lifted her up into a cradle hold. In a smooth motion, they were moving through the door. He turned and sealed it shut. They were traveling through what looked to be the main living area, dripping water all along the way. For a houseboat, it was incredibly spacious. Or maybe Sara was just used to her tiny apartment.

It was also very masculine, with dark, knotted, wood-paneled walls. Sconces shaped like old lanterns gave the room a warm glow. The windows were covered with blinds and shut tight. Sparse, oversized furniture was placed randomly throughout the room—a huge leather couch, a large, flat-screen television, a table with two matching chairs. That was about it.

The few items Xanthus had looked expensive and there was not much in the way of a décor theme. It was a typical bachelor pad. Actually, this was the first bachelor pad she'd been in. But it's what she would have expected.

Xanthus sat Sara down on his leather couch. As soon as he moved away, she began to shiver. It felt a little chilly but she guessed her tremors were coming more from shock than the cool air.

"I'll be right back," Xanthus said.

Sara nearly fell off the couch as she leaned forward to get a better look at him as he moved. Her eyes widened in shock. Instead of the vertical walking movements she was used to, he appeared to swim through the air. It looked surreal and amazingly cool.

Xanthus passed through the door of his bedroom and out of sight. She heard a tortured growl. Again, she leaned forward, clutching the arm of the couch. "Xanthus? Are you all right?" He didn't answer right away. For several moments, she was worried. When she was about shout out again, Xanthus walked back in the room wearing a plush red robe. His legs were back. How in the heck did he do that?

Sara sure wished she knew. Her heartbeat picked up as she considered the possibility that he might know how she could grow two normal legs. Could it be possible?

Xanthus had a white robe clutched in his hands. Sara slipped her arms in the oversized sleeves and belted the robe around her waist.

Okay, now that she was clothed and safe, she needed some answers. Sara shot a glare in Xanthus's direction. "All right, Mr. Dimitriou, it's time for you to answer a few questions." She had a million. Her first one was a no-brainer. "How in the world are you able to grow legs?"

"They're a gift from Triton. When I'm on dry land, I have legs. When I enter the ocean, I get my fin back."

"Triton, huh? You don't think he would ever…"

Xanthus frowned and shook his head.

That would be a no. Triton would not be

giving her legs. Well, that stunk, but it wasn't like she knew what she was missing. She'd spent her life in a wheelchair. She guessed she would be staying in one. Still, that one glimmer of hope that had come and gone so quickly was devastating.

Xanthus frowned, pity written across his face. Like he cared anyway, Mr. Nice-one-minute-Jerk-the-next.

"I get it, no legs for me," Sara said. "I do have one question I need to ask you."

She pulled her hair back to keep it from getting the back of her robe wet. "Do you have a towel?"

"A towel? That's your one question?" Xanthus smiled.

"What? No, of course not," Sara answered, feeling foolish.

"Just a minute." Xanthus left and came back with a towel.

"So what is the *one* question you want to ask me?" He looked doubtful. The couch sagged as he sat down next to her.

"Why were you so angry after saving that woman?" Sara saw his eyes darken at that question.

"I was angry with myself," he said. "That night, when I saved that human, I broke one of Triton's most basic rules. I am never to interfere in the lives of humans unless they threaten our way of life or me. I misused the power he granted me. It was a breach of trust." Xanthus paused and sighed. "I just didn't want you to see a woman fall to her death. Then when you asked me how I saved her, it was like having an accusation flung in my face. I was angry with myself. I acted dishonorably."

"Are you sorry you saved her?"

"No. I'm not sorry I saved her. But my personal feelings shouldn't supersede Triton's commands. Was that all you wanted to ask me?" He smiled but the smile didn't quite reach his eyes.

Sara gave half a smile back. "No, there is another." She scrunched her brows in confusion. "How in the world can you fly?"

Xanthus's smile turned genuine. "I don't fly. I hover."

"Fly. Hover. Whatever. How did you do it?"

"See this these bands?" He pulled his sleeve up to show the familiar metal band around his bicep. He also had matching ones on his other bicep and waist.

"Yes." Sara nodded as she looked at the gold band with the strange writing.

"They are maj bands. You humans might call them anti-gravity bands."

"Oh, wow. That's really cool." Sara reached out, touched the metal, and traced the strange writing. "Is that another gift from Triton?"

"No. This one was a gift from Calypso to all her descendants. We've had them for about a hundred years."

"So you grew up with them?" Sara draped the towel around her shoulders.

Xanthus looked away. "Actually, I was around a while before they were gifted to us."

"Excuse me?" Sara's pulled on his arm. "I must have heard you wrong. I thought you've had them for a century."

He cleared his throat and shrugged. "I did."

"How old *are* you?"

"Does it matter?"

"Xanthus..." Sara said.

He paused as if to brace himself for her reaction. "I'm a hundred and sixty-four."

"A hundred and sixty-four? How can you be a hundred and sixty-four? You don't look a day over twenty-five."

"Sara, we Dagonians are immortal. I'll look exactly this way for the rest of my life."

"What do you mean, you're immortal?"

"We don't get old, we don't get ill, and we only die from serious physical trauma."

"So I'm half-Dagonian right? Am I immortal too?"

"I don't know." Xanthus shrugged. "Since you're half-human, you may suffer from human ailments. Have you ever been sick?"

"I had food poisoning when I ate some bad chicken."

Xanthus shook his head. "That doesn't count. That was your body's way of getting rid of rancid food. But you've never had a cold, flu, fever?"

Sara shook her head.

Xanthus sighed in relief. "That's a good sign."

Sara nodded. She was having a hard time accepting what he was saying. Could she really live forever? Was she one of them? Then a thought struck her.

"How did you know I was a Dagonian?" Sara turned, leaned against the corner of the couch, and tucked her fin up underneath her.

Xanthus looked embarrassed at her question, but still he answered. "I could smell you."

"Smell me? Why? Do I stink?" she asked, appalled.

"No, you smell good. Beyond good." The last part he spoke so low she'd almost missed it.

"So, do all Dagonians smell like I do?"

"Only females when they are... fertile. It is a very compelling scent. You actually smell quite different from the typical female, although it's much more appealing to me than any other I've come in contact with. It must be the human in you." Xanthus cleared his throat. He looked uncomfortable with these questions.

"How often are we fertile?" Sara didn't care whether these questions were embarrassing to him. This was her life, darn it.

"Once a year, for about two weeks."

"Oh. That's why I only have a period once a year." Had she just said that out loud? That would go under the heading "TMI" (too much information).

"So, I really am half-Dagonian?" Sara asked. "I actually come from the sea? Oh my gosh, my mom isn't crazy. She really was trying to send me to my father when she tossed me off a cliff."

"She did what?" Xanthus shouted. Sara was embarrassed. She shouldn't have said anything.

"It was years ago," she said, trying to shrug off what had been the most traumatic day of her life.

"Tell me what happened."

Sara was a bit irked at his tone, but she answered anyway. "My mom couldn't handle the pressure of raising me and tried to send me off to live with my father."

"So she tossed you off a cliff into the ocean? How old were you?"

"I'm not sure. I think I was four or five."

"No wonder you were afraid of the water. How long was it before she returned for you?" Xanthus's voice was strained.

"It seemed like a very long time, but it must have been less than a day. I didn't have to spend the night clinging to that rock, thank goodness. To my mom's credit, she did have to climb down some very jagged rocks to retrieve me. We both ended up with quite a few cuts and bruises."

Xanthus growled. "The more I learn about your mother, the less I like that woman."

"Yeah, she's not the sanest person. She is beautiful though, which is probably why she attracted the attention of a Dagonian. I wonder who my father is."

"I have no idea. Most Dagonians avoid humans at all costs. I'm shocked one of us got close enough to father a child. But whoever he is, if he's found out, it will mean a death sentence. Intentional contact with a human is forbidden and carries with it a capital punishment. Procreating with one would be much worse."

"So where does this leave me? What will happen to me if I'm found out?" A worried crease pinched Sara's forehead as she gnawed on her bottom lip.

"Nothing will happen to you," Xanthus said in dark, even tones. Sara heard an unusual popping sound and looked down. Xanthus's fingers were gripping the couch cushion so hard that he'd ripped the fabric at the seam.

"But how can you be sure?" His reaction was scaring her.

"Because, they'd have to kill me first," he said.

Whoa. She hadn't expected that answer.

Sara looked at the large Dagonian, his black hair still wet, curling around his chiseled face, and his broad shoulders framing a formidable physique. Why would he be so protective of her? She wasn't anything special. There must Dagonians that were more appealing. He shouldn't be giving her the time of day.

"Do I look like other Dagonian women?" she whispered.

"No." He shook his head.

She knew it. Judging by how gorgeous he was, Dagonian women would have to be beyond stunning. Sara furrowed her eyebrows, disappointed.

He lifted her chin and raised her face to meet his

eyes. "You're much more beautiful."

Sara's heart fluttered at his words. She thought a stupid grin might have spread across her face, but she wasn't sure. She was too preoccupied with being flabbergasted.

"Really?"

"Yes." Xanthus's mouth turned up in a smile. "Still, you could pass for a Dagonian if it weren't for the eyes. A Dagonian's eyes are only ever dark brown."

Sara began to consider the possibilities. Did they have white picket fences in the ocean? She couldn't ask him that, so instead she asked, "Are there colored contacts I could wear underwater?"

"I don't know. Dagonians don't have a need for them. There's another problem. I doubt you know how to speak Atlantian."

"Oh my gosh. There really is an Atlantis?" Sara leaned forward.

"Yes. It's a bit run down and outdated." Xanthus leaned toward Sara and rested his arm on the back of the couch. "But it still has a sizable population. I'm from the much more modern city of Corin."

"How many Dagonians are out there?" she asked, leaning her head against his arm.

"Total?"

Sara nodded.

"About eight million." Xanthus stroked her damp hair.

"Do they live in all the oceans?" She leaned closer

to absorb his body heat.

"Yes, but most live in the warmer climates of the Atlantic."

"Wait a minute." Sara's head rose. "How did you learn English? Are there a lot of Dagonians here on dry land? And what *are* you doing here?"

"Slow down, Sara." Xanthus draped his arm around her and nudged her back against his side. "I was one of a few Dagonians who studied English as part of my job. To protect ourselves from human discovery, we have to know about them, learn how they think, discover their weaknesses and strengths. It was necessary for me to get to know them and to know them I had to speak their language.

"And I'm the only Dagonian on land. Dagonians as a rule stay far away from humans. I have no idea how your father got close enough to a human to father a child, but obviously he did."

"So what *are* you here for?" She curled up into his side.

"Triton sent me. And you don't need to know more than that."

Sara yawned wide. The evening was catching up to her. Her eyes were feeling heavy. "How in the world could I be tired at a time like this?"

Xanthus chuckled softly. "It's the after-effects of adrenaline." He leaned back, propped against the plush arm of the couch, and pulled her down to lie across his chest.

Sara wrapped her arms around him and laid her cheek against him. Once again, she heard the beating of his heart. She wanted to ask him what he would do if he found out who her father was, but she didn't think she wanted to know the answer.

Sara's breathing deepened and her body sagged, limp against Xanthus's chest. He looked down on this slip of a woman who had effectively woven herself into his heart. Her heart thumped softly against his stomach and her warm breath breezed against his chest.

He leaned forward and pressed a kiss on her head. His heart clenched as he realized how much he loved her.

He would kill for her.

He would even die for her.

At the same time, he was tearing apart at the seams. He was having an identity crisis. He'd lived his entire life ruled by duty and honor, but now, he'd turned his back on those rules—all because of this woman. Truth be told, he began to doubt even before coming here. Even now, the council continued to debate whether to declare all humans who ventured into the sea, free game. That was something he would not be able to accept, regardless of what the council decreed.

Xanthus's belief system was being ripped apart. He'd lived by the system that said laws and rules must be followed, without question. Now he was plagued with doubt and uncertainty. How could you call someone a criminal when they never voluntarily committed a crime? How could being born be a crime? How could he continue enforcing laws when he questioned the rightness of them? Who was he to pick and choose which laws were enforced and which were not?

But if he hadn't questioned, if he'd blindly followed, Sara would be dead right now, and that would be the true crime. Of that, he had no doubt. Then there would be no one to provide justice for her.

Why had he hesitated to kill her in the first place? Was it truly because she had a pretty face? If he'd found a burly, half-human man instead of a delicate woman, would he have completed the execution?

Xanthus had to admit he would have. And wouldn't that have been just as much of a crime as killing Sara would have been?

Yes, it would have been.

So who was the guilty party here?

He was.

Sara sighed. Her face scrunched up as if she were having a bad dream. Xanthus whispered words of comfort to her and stroked her head. Her face relaxed. A small smile tugged at her mouth as she hummed in contentment. Xanthus looked down on her and knew his life would never be the same.

FIFTEEN

A cool breeze brushed Sara's body like a caress. The bed surrounded her in a warm embrace. The glow of daylight seeped through her eyelids. They were especially hard to open this morning. There were no pressing deadlines ahead—they could stay closed for a while.

Wait a minute. Her bed was never this soft.

Sara's eyes flew open.

She lay in the middle of a king-sized bed, centered inside a room with wooden-planked walls and two portal windows. A plush, maroon blanket twisted around the end of her fin and draped off the side of the bed. The robe she wore gapped open. Underneath the robe, her clothes were a wrinkled mess. Sara flicked her tail and the blanket slipped off and fell to the floor.

Sara looked around. Memories from the previous night flooded back into her mind and the surrealism of the situation overwhelmed her. She was in Xanthus's houseboat. He was a Dagonian and she was half-Dagonian. And fairy tales were true—well, at least mythological ones were.

Sara spotted her wheelchair sitting beside the

bed. Her pink sundress and her spandex wrap lay neatly folded on the bedside table. Xanthus must have retrieved them last night. They reminded her of how much her life had changed in one night.

Where should she go from here? Should she go about her life as if nothing had changed? Where would Xanthus go? How long was he going to stay on dry land? He mentioned something about returning in a year.

Sara remembered the thoughts she had had of a white picket fence. In the daylight, they seemed silly. This wasn't a fairy tale story. Xanthus wasn't going to carry her off into the crashing waves where they would swim home to his oceanic castle and live happily ever after.

If she did go home with him, she'd probably get herself executed just for existing. And if any human saw her for what she was, they would be in danger too. Her mom could be in danger, maybe even Gretchen. So here she was, knowing she didn't belong with Xanthus and knowing she didn't belong with humans. Where did she belong?

One thing was certain. She didn't belong in his bed (at least not until they were married). Okay, that was a slip. Sara couldn't possibly marry Xanthus. She didn't belong in his world and she was sure the only reason he'd been paying her so much attention was because she was the only female Dagonian (or half-Dagonian) he'd seen in she didn't know how long. And she was apparently fertile right now, which she guessed caused her to be somewhat appealing to him. She was sure he wouldn't find her attractive any other way.

Now that her head was screwed on straight, maybe she could pull herself out of bed. Reaching over to her wheelchair and using her tail as leverage, she raised herself off the bed and sat down into the seat. She grabbed her clothes, placed them on her lap, and wheeled into the bathroom.

An old-fashioned, claw-foot tub greeted her as she rolled in. A massive spout hung over the tub like a giant, sleepy sunflower. Showering here would be like lying in a downpour. Xanthus must not recognize the advantages of using a sprayer hose to wash. Well, it was an advantage to her. She didn't remember the last time she'd had a bath, but it couldn't be too complicated.

She filled the tub with cool water. Looking down at the rippling water, she smiled when she felt no anxiety. She stripped out of her clothes and locked the brakes on her chair. Putting her weight down on her fin, she lifted herself over to the side of the tub. After lowering her hips into the water, her fin slipped under the surface. When the tub was full, she turned off the spout.

As she laid there with cool water lapping up the side of her neck, she realized the enormity of the situation. She was sitting here, submerged in water, and she wasn't freaking out. Would miracles never cease?

Sara didn't even need Gretchen's psychologist, Dr. What's-his-name. All she needed was to face her fear.

Of course, it helped having a muscle-bound Dagonian force her to do it, but she guessed it was worth it. She closed her eyes and tested herself further by lowering her head under the water. There was a slight flutter in her chest. She couldn't tell whether it was fear or excitement. That was a good thing.

One more test. She took in a lungful of water. The burn was excruciating. Sara began thrashing the moment she realized her mistake, and it wasn't just any mistake. It was a huge mistake. How was she to know that breathing tap water was not like breathing ocean water?

Sara tried to scream but her throat closed off. She flailed her body around in the tub, trying to get a hold of the side. She had to get some air.

Finally, she grasped the side of the tub, pulled herself out of the water, and heaved herself over the side, spilling her body and gallons of water onto the floor.

Through a panic-filled haze, she heard Xanthus pounding on the door. "Sara, what's going on?"

She was desperate for help. *Please, let him come in.* Lying on her back, she clawed at her chest.

More pounding.

"Sara, if you don't answer, I'm breaking down the door."

Sara realized with a shock that she was completely naked. She made a swipe at the nearby towel on the rack and pulled it down to cover herself. Most likely, the towel would be her death shroud.

With a loud crash, Xanthus burst through the door. In an instant, his steel fingers were like vices around her shoulders as he shook her hard. "Sara, breathe." His shouts rang her ears.

She tried to obey, but she couldn't get her throat to loosen. Her eyes were wide and fixed on his face, her fingers scratching and clawing at her throat. Her mouth gaped open, struggling to suck in a breath of air. Xanthus leaned in as if to kiss her. Instead, he pinched her nose, covered her mouth with his, and breathed out hard.

Sara's lungs expanded and felt as if they would burst. Now they were filled with water *and* air. As Xanthus pulled away, a fountain poured out of her mouth, and then gurgling bubbles coughed out from her throat. With great effort, Sara squeezed in a breath of air, whistling it through her swollen windpipe. It felt and sounded as if she were breathing through a tiny straw. Then she coughed out more water and then dragged another howling breath in before her windpipe began to relax.

"Hades, Sara. What were you thinking?" Xanthus pulled her hard against his chest.

Sara didn't answer. She couldn't. She was still sucking air into her lungs and sobbing on top of that.

"If I hadn't been here..." Xanthus said. "I swear, little half-Dagonian, I don't know how you've survived as long as you have. I've been with you a few weeks and have had to save you from death more times than I can count."

That was a big exaggeration. "Just twice," she said between sobs.

"Oh, Moro Mou," he said. "You only die once." Xanthus continued to crush her against his chest, holding her for a long time after she'd calmed down. He seemed to have a more difficult time recovering from this incidence than she did. Finally, he let her go. Mumbling his frustration in Atlantian, he turned to snatch the sundress off the floor. When he looked back at her, he froze. Sara was clutching the drenched towel over her body. He looked at the towel, at the tub, at her drenched hair, and then at the large puddle of water she was sitting in. "Did you cover yourself with a towel *after* pulling yourself out of the water?" he asked, dumbfounded.

Sara's face burned as she nodded.

Shaking his head, Xanthus grabbed another towel off the rack and flung it, along with her dress, over his shoulder. "Of all the insignificant..." he began and then suddenly stopped. Sara looked down in embarrassment.

Xanthus cleared his throat, "Come on, we need to get the chlorine washed out of your lungs and gills." He knelt down, tucked her drenched towel around her, and lifted her off the floor.

Sara wondered how he was going to... "Oh no, please just let me breathe air for now."

"Don't you dare, I did not get beaten to a pulp last night for nothing. You *are* going into the water." And so she did, a few moments later.

If Sara had wanted to push it, she'd have several

legitimate charges of kidnapping against Xanthus, but seeing as how he kept saving her life, she'd let them pass—for now.

Xanthus led her through the water as she swam around the bay. Sara had wondered if swimming was instinctive for a half-Dagonian. Just moments after getting into the water, she realize that no, it definitely wasn't.

On her own, Sara couldn't seem to move in the directions she wanted to. She was sure, to Xanthus, who was full Dagonian and grew up in the water, that she looked ridiculous. Her fin jerked every which way and her hands clawed at the water in an attempt to pull her in the right direction. As she struggled, she ran into several parrotfish, slapped a trumpet fish, and had innumerous scrapes on her hands from grasping the coral and sea urchins.

Sara had to give Xanthus credit. He hadn't laughed, at least not so she could see. There were several times he disappeared for a few moments and came back looking almost *too* serious.

"Are you sure I'm a Dagonian?" Sara asked, feeling out of her element. "I mean, I know I look like one and I know humans can't breathe underwater, but I did a little research myself and did you know that there was an experiment done years ago where rats were found to be able to breathe underwater? And if we look back far enough into the past, each of us is descended from fish. I always thought that maybe..."

"Sara, stop trying to rationalize it. You're a Dagonian. There's no other explanation. You aren't deformed. You aren't an anomaly. You, well, here, let me show you something." Xanthus swam up close to her and brushed his fingers behind her ears. "These are your gills."

Sara marveled at how strange it felt to have his fingers brush at something behind her ears. She hesitated for a moment before she reached back to feel for herself. What she felt shocked her. There were flaps, like the underside of a mushroom.

"Wow, I... I can't believe it," she said.

"Believe it. You're half-Dagonian."

"But how did I miss that? You'd think I would have noticed."

"The gills only open underwater. When you surface, they seal tight. It's a way of protecting them. Gills are very delicate. Now, back to your swimming lessons."

Sara continued to struggle through the water. If not for the beauty around her and the company of Xanthus, she'd be utterly depressed and completely discouraged.

In the daylight, the ocean was very different and so beautiful. The fish were vibrant, the water was clear blue, and the coral bloomed all around, forming mounds and hills.

Not only was the ocean gorgeous, but Xanthus had never looked better, He was definitely in his element. His powerful body glided, twisted, darted, and traveled at inhuman speed through the water. His movement looked like a dance choreographed by the gods. In comparison, Sara felt like a twitching idiot.

It had been close to an hour and Sara still couldn't swim straight. She couldn't imagine ever being able to swim like Xanthus. That Dagonian sure could move, especially when she sort of had a brush with a tiger shark. She was glad Xanthus hadn't had to hurt him. The shark took one look at the big Dagonian and shot away in the opposite direction.

"Sara, you're using the coral as a crutch. You can't crawl across the ocean," Xanthus said, peeling her fingers off the coral.

"I just can't do it. Maybe I'm too human."

"You're doing fine. Just let go and we'll review the proper way to move. Look at me. The movement starts at your head and then travels down your body all the way to your fin. Like a wave. Keep waving and keep your head pointed in the direction you want to move."

Sara did as he explained. Suddenly, her body was gliding through the water. She took a quick glance back at her waving tail. When her head came up, a blowfish was inches from her face. It was gone a moment later, darting away in a flash. She sighed, wishing she could swim that fast. The wall of coral that seemed so far away, swelled in size as she neared its jagged wall. She threw her hands out and curled her tail underneath her, trying to slow her movement.

Xanthus tugged her to a stop. "Good, that's just how to do it. You're doing great. All you need now is more practice."

"What I need is breakfast. I'm starving," Sara said.

Xanthus gestured at the fish around them. "Take your pick. I'll catch it for you."

"Oh no, I don't eat my food live. That is one human thing I must insist on."

"You like sushi, don't you?"

"Well, yes. But it's not swimming when I eat it. It's dead."

While they were having this discussion, a parrotfish swam a little too close to Xanthus. Like a cobra, his hand whipped out and snatched the fish. The next thing Sara knew, he was ripping the fish's head off.

"Here, this one is dead."

"That is disgusting. Besides, it's illegal to kill a parrotfish."

"Not where I come from." He smiled.

"What about the scales and bones? Do you have a knife to fillet it for me?" she asked, expecting him to say no.

Instead, he pulled a knife from his belt. "Parrotfish fillet coming up."

In a few smooth strokes, he peeled off layers of scales. In another stroke, he peeled away a long, thick fillet of meat and handed it over to her. Sara hesitated before she took it.

What was she supposed to do now? She looked at the fillet and felt the soft meat between her fingers. "Okay, I've cooked fillets like this a thousand times, and do I love sushi. I can do this," she said to herself. She made the mistake at glancing over at the head of the dead fish as it floated away and she began to gag. She took several breaths of water and closed her eyes, then lifted the fillet to her mouth and took a nibble.

Sara opened her eyes in surprise. "Mmm, it tastes good."

"Of course it does." He smiled.

After she finished off the fillet, Xanthus offered her the rest of the fish, "Oh, no. I couldn't eat another bite."

"You sure don't eat much," he said just before he finished off her fish.

"I get enough. As big as you are, you must eat enough to feed an entire family." Xanthus proved her right when he ate two more large fish before he was done.

The discarded carcasses were left to smaller fish that huddled in groups to nibble. Sara noticed the tiger shark hadn't returned. "What happened to the shark?"

"Don't worry, Moro Mou." Sara's heart fluttered at the obvious endearment. "Even large sharks stay away from a full-grown Dagonian. I'm surprised that little one came near you. He must have thought you terribly injured."

"Very funny." She glared at him as he smiled.

He was probably right. She punched him hard in the arm and began to float away in the opposite direction. Xanthus moved in so that they were face to face. She kind of liked that about being in the water. He no longer towered over her.

"You know, little half-Dagonian, no one has ever gotten away with striking me as often as you. In fact, *no one* has ever struck me without retribution." What he was saying might have frightened her if it hadn't been for the smirk on his face.

"What do you think I should do about it?" he asked.

Being this close to him gave her a rush and she answered in the best way she could. She kissed him.

His lips were warm, soft, and very willing to kiss her back. When she started to float away, he clutched her face to hold her in place. Sara wrapped her arms around his neck, pulled her body up against him, and wrapped her tail around his. Xanthus's grip tightened just before he growled and broke off the kiss. "That's not a good idea, Mou." His jaw was clenched as he untangled their fins.

"What's wrong?"

Xanthus closed his eyes and blew out a watery breath. His brows furrowed as he straightened his arms, putting distance between them. "You should never wrap your fin around a Dagonian you're kissing, unless you intend to mate with him."

"Oh," she said, embarrassed. "I didn't know."

"Which is why I ended the kiss," he said, taking controlled breaths. He shook his head and whispered something in Atlantian. It sounded like a curse.

Sara felt like a fool. Xanthus looked up into her face, his lips turned up into half a smile. He took another deep breath and gave her a small peck on her pursed lips. "You have a lot to learn, little half-Dagonian. Don't worry. I'll be here to teach you. But right now, we should be heading back. I have movers coming to pack and take my things over to the apartment building. And then later there's a crew coming to replace your counters."

"You're going to be my neighbor?" Sara felt as if a weight had been lifted off her back. Funny, she hadn't realized how threatened she'd felt living alone.

"I don't see how I have much of a choice. You seem determined to get yourself into trouble. I'm just making a preemptive move."

Xanthus pulled her to his chest and swam them toward his houseboat. This situation still seemed surreal to her. She was in the arms of a gorgeous Dagonian, and she wasn't dreaming. Anyone seeing them would think he was a merman and she was a mermaid.

"Xanthus?"

"Yes, Mou?"

"What happened to the mermaids?"

"Why do you ask?" he asked, as if the question surprised him.

"I'm just curious. I've always wondered if I might be a mermaid. Now I know I'm not, but I'm still intrigued by them."

Xanthus looked down. For a moment, he looked guilty. "Well, from what I've been told, the Mer, or sirens as many often call them, were quite different from us. They were lovers of mischief, especially when it came to humans. They saw humans as a source of amusement. They would lure them in with their songs and the humans, unable to resist their voices, would steer their ships toward shallow rocks. The mermaids thought it was hilarious watching the ships crash on the rocks and the men drown in the sea.

"Occasionally, a mermaid would get a human close enough for him to try to steal a kiss. Then she would grab hold of him and pull him underwater to drown him. Still, because of the beauty and mystery of the Mer, the humans were fascinated by them.

"The Mer took their songs and games too far when they choose to mock Poseidon. When Poseidon lost the temple in Athens to Athena, he was furious. He was one of the greater gods, after all. Then a certain Siren began to sing a song about his defeat. It was a disrespectful song that exploded in popularity and, before long, all the Mer were singing it. When Poseidon heard the song, he went into a fit of rage and ordered them killed—every merman and mermaid."

"Wow, that's pretty harsh," Sara said.

"The gods aren't known to be forgiving or tolerant." Xanthus shrugged.

"So how different did the Mer look from

Dagonians?"

"We're similar in body, but differ in temperament. Dagonians are very proud and arrogant. The Mer were very flighty, attractive, but also mischievous. And those humans who thought that someone so beautiful could never harm them died a quick and often painful death. In fact, we Dagonians called the Mer children of the sharks."

"So why don't the humans have any legends about Dagonians?"

"Because Dagonians keep far away from humans. The few humans who have had contact with Dagonians and lived, assumed that the Dagonian was a Mer."

Xanthus adjusted his grip, pulling Sara closer under his chin. She held tight, feeling his muscles ripple under her gripping hands, as he swam. The warm current rushed across her face. It was amazing how fast he could swim, even with a passenger. She wondered if a mermaid could swim as fast. She doubted, from what he was saying, that they ever had Dagonian and Mer races.

"So, I take it Dagonians didn't get along with mermaids."

"We feared the wrath of Triton enough to leave them alone," Xanthus said. "But, Dagonians hated the Mer. You'd be hard-pressed to find a Dagonian that's sorry they are all dead."

"Are you sorry?" She wondered if he was hardened enough to be glad a whole race of merpeople were dead.

"To tell you the truth, I am sorry for what

happened. That was pretty harsh of Poseidon to kill them all, every mermaid and merman. And my mother who is much older than me told me they were not all as bad as so many Dagonians made them out to be."

"How old is your mother?"

"I'm not sure," Xanthus said, surprised. He sounded as if he'd never thought about it before.

"You don't know?"

"She's very old. More than two thousand years."

"You're kidding," Sara said.

"Not at all." She heard the smile in his voice.

"So she might have known some of the Mer," she said.

"I'm sure she did. My own great-grandmother was a mermaid."

"Wow. So you're part Merman?"

"Some," he conceded.

"So has Triton had any more children?"

"No, he hasn't. Losing all his children in such a violent way made him vow that he would never father more."

"If Triton did have more children, what would Poseidon do? Would he kill them too?"

"No, all the guilty have been punished and any new children of Triton would be held guiltless."

An ethereal glow shone through the milky blue water as Xanthus's houseboat came into focus. "Looks like we're home," she said. Her face burned red when she realized what she said. "I mean, it looks like we're at *your* home."

Xanthus chuckled. "Yes, we're home. Well, it's home for now. Would you like to swim from here?"

"Sure, but I'll need help getting in. I don't levitate like you do, Houdini."

"Houdini?"

"He was a famous magician."

"Okay, Mou," he said, "I'll levitate you out of the water."

She took a few stuttered tail swishes forward until she got a smoother rhythm going. "You're doing so much better, Sara. Before you know it, you'll be swimming better than Michael Phelps."

"Oh, thanks." She rolled her eyes and swam toward the surface. "I'll be able to swim better than a human. I can't believe how quickly I've become accustomed to thinking of myself as other than human. I guess I never felt much a part of the human race. So what do you call someone who's half-human, half-Dagonian?"

Xanthus looked away and shrugged.

"You don't know a name for someone like me?"

"Sara, it's been so long since we've had a half-human that we had no need for a name." What he said made sense, but he was acting *way* too strange for her to believe him.

"You *do* know a name for it. You just don't want to tell me."

"Come on, Mou. We're going to be late." Xanthus avoided the subject as he pulled her into his arms. He left her stomach behind as he sped them though the water, up through the hatch, and into his houseboat. He continued on as he raced her into his room, plopped her down on the bed, left, and closed the door behind him. Sara wasted no time peeling off her dress and changing into dry clothes.

A few minutes later, there was a soft knock at the door.

"Come in, I'm decent," she said as she continued to wrap her fin.

Xanthus walked in wearing shorts, a white t-shirt, and flip-flops. His damp curls were still dripping. "It's a shame to cover such a beautiful tail fin, Mou."

Sara scrunched her eyebrows and chuckled. "That still freaks me out, you calling it a tail, although I always knew it *looked* like a tail. I thought just thinking of it that way would mean I was completely insane."

"Here, let me." He took her fin, carefully folded it over, and wrapped it. "I've never seen a tail so flexible."

"It's had years of training." She smirked.

He finished the wrap and lifted her into his arms. "I'm sorry you've had to hide for so long, Moro Mou."

"It's not so bad." She shrugged.

Xanthus looked sad as he gathered her in his arms to leave. A moment later, he carried her outside into the warm, Hawaiian air.

"Hello, Xanthus." A tall, blonde, voluptuous woman waved from the other side of the dock and sauntered over.

"Danielle, I haven't seen you for a while. It's good to know you're back," he said.

"Yes, well, I've had a lot of problems to deal with at work," she said. Xanthus raised an eyebrow.

"This must be your sister, right?" Danielle's eyes were a bit too narrow as they darted down to Sara's spandex-wrapped stump. This woman was jealous. She *hoped* Sara was his sister.

"No, this is Sara. Sara, this is Danielle, a neighbor of mine."

"A very close neighbor," Danielle said. A smile tugged at Danielle's lips when she laid her hand on Xanthus's arm. How close a neighbor was she? Sara's eyes shot over to Xanthus. He was hard to read. He looked a bit bored with the whole exchange, almost too bored. He was hiding something.

"I'm sorry we can't stay and chat, Danielle, but I have some men coming to install counters in Sara's apartment." Sara wondered why he neglected to tell her he was moving.

"Oh," Danielle said with a sigh, obviously relieved. "She's one of your tenants. It's so nice of you to help out someone in her condition."

Danielle put her hand on Sara's arm and spoke to her as if she were a small child. "Sara, you're a beautiful girl. Don't ever let anyone tell you that you won't find love just because you're crippled. You have such a pretty face."

Sara's fingers dug into Xanthus's arm and she had

to clench her jaw to keep herself from saying something she would later regret. Sara waited for Xanthus to tell Danielle *he* cared for her. But he didn't. He wasn't going to tell her. There must be something going on between them and he obviously wasn't willing to end it.

"I'll see you later, Xanthus baby," she called out and strutted away.

Still holding her in his arms, Xanthus strode over to his SUV and placed her in the passenger seat. He pulled out his cell phone and talked while he walked around and got in the driver's seat. "Hello, this is Xanthus Dimitriou. You have some men coming to move my things this afternoon. I was wondering if you could have them come tomorrow instead." He paused. "Yes, I know. Something has come up." He ended the call and snapped his phone back in its holder.

Sara felt as if she'd been punched in the stomach. Was he breaking up with her? Of course, it couldn't really be a breakup—they'd never made being together official. Still, it was obvious that he didn't want to tell Danielle that he was interested in her. Actually, he'd never said he *was* interested in her. Maybe to him, he was just protecting another Dagonian. After all, that's what he did, and a few stolen kisses didn't make him her boyfriend. Sara's stomach was sick when she realized she'd been reading *way* too much into their relationship. She pulled the seat belt across her body and blinked back tears.

Xanthus turned on the SUV. He waited until he

pulled out onto the road before he spoke to her. "Sara, I need to explain."

"You don't need to explain anything, I don't own you." As the words fell from her lips, she made a realization. She may not own him but *he* owned her—both heart and soul. Whether or not she wanted it, her heart belonged to him, but broken heart or not, she still had her pride.

"Sara, please let me explain."

"You don't need to. I understand perfectly."

"No you *don't* understand. Haven't you wondered what kind of assignment I'm here for?"

"Assignment?" She turned, giving him her full attention.

"Yes, assignment." Xanthus sighed. "We've had two Dagonian colonies destroyed due to humans dumping poison into the waters in the South Pacific. I've been tracking down the origin of the poison, and I've traced it to a factory here in Hawaii. I've brought the guilty to judgment. Thank the gods I was able to stop them before more damage was done. There's only one loose end I still have to tie up, then hopefully things back home will calm down enough to avoid an open war."

"So Danielle is part of this?" Sara wrung her fingers together.

"She's right in the middle of it and guilty as sin."

"So is she your loose end?"

"Yes," he said, to her relief.

"What are you going to do to her?" She wondered

if he would punish her himself.

"She'll answer to Triton."

"Wow, Triton?" Sara guessed she shouldn't have felt so jealous of Danielle. She would be terrified to be in her shoes, facing an angry god.

"Yes, and don't ask me what he'll do. I don't know. I only know it won't be pleasant."

"So if the Dagonians decide to retaliate against the humans, how much damage could they do?"

Xanthus sighed. "We could do a lot of damage. About half of the human population lives near the ocean. With massive tsunamis strategically triggered, we could wipe out about three billion."

"Three billion..." Sara felt dizzy. "Hawaii would be gone, everyone would be killed."

"Unless you were lucky enough to be hiking to the top of Mauna Kea. At 13,000 feet, you'd probably survive."

"And this is all because we polluted the waters in the South Pacific and killed... how many?"

"Over three thousand... and for a Dagonian with a lifespan as long as ours, that is astronomical." Xanthus shook his head. "And it's not just that. Humans have been polluting so much of the seas in the last few decades, much of it is unlivable."

"I'm so sorry," she whispered.

"You have nothing to be sorry for. You're not at fault."

"No, but my people are." Sara hoped that Xanthus

could stop this war. But how could one man make a difference?

As Xanthus and Sara pulled into the apartment parking lot, Sara gasped at the sight. It was filled with trucks—Al's construction, Wall-2-Wall Flooring, Water-Works Plumbing, Pest-Assassin Exterminator Service, Bright-Light Electrical, Kinimaka Brothers Painting Service...

"I take it my apartment isn't the only one you're updating," Sara said.

"I'm just doing what any responsible apartment building owner would do. I do have to act the part. Besides, there are small children and old women living in this building!"

"I'm not complaining. Your tenants are going to love you."

"I'm not looking for love from these humans," Xanthus said.

"You may not be looking for it, but you're going to get it."

Xanthus didn't respond, the frown on his face said it all.

That evening, Sara relaxed in Xanthus's arms as one of the *Star Wars* movies played on her little television. She was really too tired to pay much attention to the movie. Watching Xanthus and the other men work was exhausting.

"You really should have let me help today," she said.

"Hm? What?" Xanthus said, distracted by a space battle. Then her words sunk in. "Sara, we went over this. You could get hurt doing manual labor. Besides, that's what I was paying those men for."

Sara rolled her eyes. "You helped."

"They *needed* my help," he said.

Sara bit her lip when she was about to say, *Yeah, right.*

"Humans have quite the imagination." Xanthus said absently.

Sara looked up at him. "George Lucus sure does."

She smiled when she noticed he still had a few lipstick smudges on his face. Like it or not, his tenants now adored him.

"Did you want the last sushi roll?" he asked.

"You can have it," she said as she lay her head down against his chest and closed her eyes. "I'm glad you found some human food you could stomach."

"Barely stomach," he said, correcting her.

Late into the night, Sara awoke in her own bed. She wondered if Xanthus had gone.

She got into her wheelchair, rolled out into her living room, and found him asleep on her couch. At least, half of him was on her couch. His long legs stretched out over the side onto the floor. He didn't look at all comfortable.

Sara sighed. He was so adorable, like an angelic, sleeping giant. And he was willing to forgo comfort to make sure she was safe. She returned to her bed and fell asleep smiling.

SIXTEEN

X anthus swam through the darkened hall toward a secret room located deep inside his father's mansion. He searched for any servants, or worse, his father. He wasn't supposed to be here. He wasn't too nervous—it was long after everyone's bedtime. His father was asleep and wasn't there to tell him that he couldn't go in that room. "It's no place for a child," his father had said. But Xanthus was tough. His father just didn't know him well enough.

Xanthus's tiny hand pushed the heavy door open. He jumped when the lights turned up. He almost fled back to his room. But warriors don't flee from danger, and, someday, he'd be the bravest warrior ever.

When he turned back into the room, his eyes fell on a beautiful sight—the face of a female. Her pale hair haloed her perfect features. Xanthus was about to swim away before she had a chance to see him when he realized something was not right. Her milky white eyes were open, but they couldn't see a thing. She was dead.

Her body floated in a tank—a tank similar to those they kept their fish in at dinner time. But this one stood taller, the water tinted green.

Xanthus wanted to leave, but he had to be brave. What

had happened to the beautiful female? He forced his little body to swim closer. His eyes widened when he saw her chest. Right where her heart should have been was a gaping hole. The sight sickened him. He no longer cared about being brave now. He had to get away from here.

Xanthus turned and swam straight into his father. "Xanthus, what are you doing here?"

"Father," he said. "I was just going back to my room."

"So you think you can just go and I'll forget that you disregarded my order?"

"I'm sorry, Father..."

"No. You wanted to see it. So here, take a good look." His father dragged him over to the tank and pressed his face against the hard glass.

The female's lifeless eyes stared back at Xanthus. He didn't want to see it, but he couldn't resist looking at the gaping, jagged hole rimmed with pale flesh and broken ribs.

"Do you know what she is, son?" his father asked.

Xanthus's brows knitted in confusion. It was obvious she was a female Dagonian. But maybe she wasn't. Why else would his father ask that question? He shook his head.

"It's a pathetic young mermaid. She begged me for her life, but warriors don't listen to sniveling cowards, son. Before I killed her, I cut out her tongue. Then I tore her beating heart from her chest."

Xanthus frowned, his stomach soured. His father was a coward, boasting about killing a weak female. "Why did you kill her?"

"She's a mermaid, that's the best reason," his father said,

with glee in his voice.

"What about King Triton? Why didn't he stop you?"

Xanthus's father glared at him. "Poseidon ordered that we kill all the Mer. The day the last one was killed was a day of celebration for every Dagonian."

Xanthus didn't understand. He'd thought when he became a warrior, he'd be protecting females. Not killing them.

His father snarled and dragged him close so they were nose to nose. "You pity them?" The current of his breath brushed Xanthus's face.

Xanthus was too scared to answer truthfully, so he shook his head.

"You'd better not. The Mer were fouler than humans. I only wish my sons could have joined me in their slaughter."

"Well? Are you coming, son?" his father asked. Xanthus found himself outside dressed in full battle gear. His father floated nearby. "They're this way," his father said. "Be ready. Sirens can be clever. Be sure to put in your earplugs. You don't want to be caught around a Mer without them."

"Yes, Father," Xanthus's deep voice answered as he shoved the wax plugs in his ears. He was now a grown warrior following his father into battle.

Xanthus's eyes darted toward movement in the kelp fields. A figure hid in stalks. His father took off after it. At that moment, Xanthus saw movement from another section of kelp. He shot through the water, snaking around the great stalks of kelp in pursuit. He could see the figure racing as swiftly as it could. But it wasn't fast enough. Xanthus easily overtook it. He grabbed the fin, jerked the fugitive to a stop, and then he yanked on the slate black *hair to turn the mermaid's head to face him.*

His heart stopped.

"Sara?" he whispered in horror as his eyes rested on the terrified face of the woman he loved.

"Good, you caught her, son." His father's muted voice reached his ears as he emerged from the swaying kelp. Blood trailed from his hands, clouding the water. He'd obviously caught his Mer.

"Now make me proud. Let me see you rip her heart from her chest."

Xanthus turned to his father in shock. He couldn't kill her. This was his Sara. He loved her.

"You hesitate? You must never hesitate. Don't forget Poseidon's decree. You must kill her!"

Xanthus turned to Sara. She trembled in his grasp, looking on him with abject terror. She opened her mouth to scream. His father moved like lightning, grabbed her tongue, lifted his knife, and sliced.

Xanthus jolted awake, his heart slamming against his chest wall. What the Hades? He heaved hard breaths as he tried to process what he'd seen.

It was a strange mixture of memories and false dreams. He'd had that same nightmare many times over throughout the years, with no variation. Until now. This time, instead of capturing a nameless mermaid, he'd caught Sara. He felt sick remembering the terror in her eyes—as if she thought he would kill her. Then his father....

Xanthus sat up on Sara's worn couch and dropped his face into his hands. His body shook as he tried to banish the image from his mind.

Thank the gods he wasn't alive when Poseidon gave that foul decree. Xanthus had killed plenty of hardened criminals throughout his years as a warrior but he abhorred killing females. He didn't know what he would have done if he had lived at the time when all Dagonian solders were ordered to kill the Mer. He didn't want to think about it.

Still, why would he be dreaming about killing Sara?

For his peace of mind, Xanthus looked in on her, sleeping peacefully in her room. She was safe. The dream wasn't real. He walked over to her, pressed a kiss to her warm forehead, and inhaled her unique, intoxicating scent.

A moment later, he walked back into the living area and spared the clock a glance. It was 1:14 AM, too early to get up. He lay back on the couch and did his best to reclaim his sleep. But the horror of the nightmare wouldn't leave. He needed to clear his mind. He had planned on waiting until morning to finish his assignment, but now was as good a time as any to tie up the last loose end.

Xanthus left Sara's apartment, making sure everything was locked and the alarm was set. His phone was on and fully charged. He'd had the alarm company link his phone to her system. If Sara's alarm tripped, he'd know immediately.

Back at his houseboat, he showered—he was

surprised to find he enjoyed showering. He loved the spray of the water on his face. Because it was tap water and not seawater, he was able to enjoy it as a human. Being human wasn't as much of a bother as he'd thought it would be, but dressing in clothes was one of his least favorite things. They were scratchy and uncomfortable. Still, they covered his ugly, hairy legs. Even female legs were grotesque to him, but at least they were generally hairless.

Danielle had thought to entice him by wearing short skirts and showing off her long legs. But they just sickened him. He had to hone his acting skills with this assignment. Tonight, he needed to woo her.

Xanthus put on dark swimming trunks, flip-flops, and nothing else. Danielle loved looking at his bare chest. Somehow, tonight, he needed to entice her into taking a late night dip in the ocean. He estimated that would take about two seconds.

As he walked out onto his deck, he saw a couple of young neighbors lounging on their boat, drinking beer and listening to music. That was unfortunate. He'd have to take Danielle somewhere more secluded. He'd hoped to get back to Sara sooner than later. Leaving her alone was making him anxious.

In the darkness, Xanthus strolled down the dock to Danielle's houseboat. He picked up a few pebbles and, one by one, tossed them to her bedroom window, attempting to awaken her.

The curtains fluttered and then were pulled

back. Her glowing face appeared and she opened her window. "I knew you'd come calling." She smirked.

"I was just about to take a late night swim and thought you might like to join me." He raised an eyebrow.

"Sure, sweet thing. Just give me a moment." Danielle walked out her door five minutes later, wearing a bikini top, a tiny, wraparound skirt, and stilettos.

"I know a great place that's just a short drive from here," he said as he walked her to his SUV.

"Babe, with you looking like you do, I'll follow you to the ends of the earth." She raked her eyes over him.

He responded with his own hot once-over. "You don't look so bad yourself."

She smiled and chuckled.

Their destination was just a few miles down the shoreline. He pulled off. Thick foliage lined the road. He squeezed his SUV as close to the trees as possible. "The shore is just a short walk and I've never seen anyone else here. We'll be completely alone. You don't have a problem with that, do you?"

Danielle laughed, deep and throaty. "Oh, you're real funny."

They'd taken a few short steps into the palm tree line when she stumbled, "Oh, my ankle. I've twisted it."

Xanthus knelt down and inspected her injury. "It looks all right to me. Do you want to go back?"

"Oh, no. It just smarts a bit. I'm sure I can swim fine. But walking on it hurts. Do you think you can carry me?" she asked, her big eyes blinking, the corners of her mouth turned down. Pitiful.

He would rather not carry her, but he really looked forward to having the job done. A Dagonian does what he has to do.

"Sure thing, sweetheart." Xanthus swept her up and she giggled, wrapping her arms around his neck. He strode forward, anxious to reach the shoreline. His eyes scanned the trees and he listened for other people in the area. He heard nothing. Danielle was at his mercy and he had a few words to tell this woman before he delivered her to Triton.

"Danielle?"

"Yes, Xanthus?" She smiled and licked her lips.

"How do you live with yourself?" He no longer masked the coldness of his voice.

"What?" she asked, her eyes wide, confused. "What are you talking about?"

"Do you know what harm you've caused with your illegal dumping? Did you and your board of directors just decide one day not to follow the proper procedures of neutralizing and disposing of your waste? Did you think there would be no consequences to destroying whole ecosystems and all life within a thousand square miles?"

"Who are you?" Danielle's eyes narrowed.

"Oh, you'll find out soon enough." Xanthus approached the ebbing surf and stepped into the water. He felt the change coming and was careful not to crush the human woman in his arms during the transformation. His body clenched and Danielle started thrashing around.

"Let me down." She pushed against his chest and then struck him across the face. When the pain of his transformation left him, he tossed her into the shallow water. Danielle scrambled and splashed, trying to get to her feet.

"You can't prove anything. I had..." She looked up to confront him and gasped in horror. "What... are you?" she asked as she stumbled away.

"I am your enemy, Danielle. Now meet your fate." Xanthus reached out his hand toward her and gave her Triton's message. Her eyes widened and her mouth gaped in the terror.

Then he summoned the Heitach. "I send you to Triton to answer for your crimes." Xanthus cringed when he heard her wails. Once she was gone, the relief of having his mission accomplished washed over him. Danielle was no longer his worry, but Triton's. His job was done.

Xanthus returned to Sara's tiny, uncomfortable couch and the rest of the night, he slept in peaceful bliss.

SEVENTEEN

Sara finished washing her hot chocolate mug in her new low sink, placed it in the dish drainer, and pulled the plug. She'd never realized how easy it could be. She could actually see what she was doing and she didn't have any bulky ramp taking up valuable space in her kitchen.

She wiped down the new stainless steel sink and faucets. They sure looked better than the old scratched and stained ones she'd had before. And the granite counters were amazing. She didn't ask how much the upgrades had cost Xanthus, but she could tell they were expensive. Sara felt a twinge of guilt. With the threat of war, she knew being excited about a new kitchen was a pretty frivolous thing.

Sara could hear Xanthus bumping around his apartment as he once again rearranged his furniture. No matter where he put his things, the apartment wasn't going to get any bigger. He was just going to have to deal with the lack of space. She knew that she'd been all for his moving in to the apartment building, but that was before she had a chance to think about how big he was and how small the apartments were. She tried to tell him he didn't need to move in here, that she could take care of herself, but he refused to listen.

Sara wheeled over to her little kitchen table, turned on her laptop, and clicked on the web-creator program. Bills still had to be paid and work needed to be done. She only had a couple of minor changes on the latest web design. This job had taken up the better part of the last several weeks and Sara was so ready to be done.

She smiled as she pulled up the finished web site online and looked. The pages were well organized, the graphics were amazing, and she checked off each requirement given her by Steve Rowling, the owner of Rowling's Bowling and Billiards. She clicked through each page and was more than satisfied with the finished product.

Wow. She may have hit an all-time high. This was her best web site yet. She'd even gotten a bowling ball to roll across the screen, revealing the name of the bowling alley and then, after the ball rolls off the screen, you heard the sound of pins dropping.

Sara shut down her computer and put it in her computer bag. She was ready for her meeting. Mr. Rowling will be bowled over by her design. She chuckled at her own joke.

She rolled by the refrigerator, promising she'd stock it when she got her paycheck. It was just in time, too. Her refrigerator and cupboard were bare. If she'd had to wait one more day, she'd be eating her last can of baked beans for lunch.

Thank goodness, Xanthus had taken her out to eat or caught her dinner this last week, or she'd have run out of food long before now.

She pushed the speed dial on her new cellphone, "Hello Mou, did you get it finished?" Xanthus's warm voice made her smile.

"Yeah, and it looks great. I'm going to start showing this design as an example of my work. I think this will help me get more jobs. I'm sure Mr. Rowling will be happy. I've got an appointment with him in just a few minutes to pick up my check."

"All right, Mou. I'll be right over."

"Xanthus, you don't need to. I mean, I appreciate how concerned you are about me, but this time it's not necessary. Mr. Rowling seems like an okay guy and he owns a successful business. How bad could he be? I'm meeting him at a café just down the street and it's in the middle of the afternoon."

"Sara, just because he's successful doesn't mean he's not trouble. And he's meeting you in a café in *this* neighborhood?" Xanthus didn't need to say more than that. He'd learned many things about the neighborhood in the last couple of weeks—none of them good. Sara knew this because he took it upon himself to inform her, going into great detail about what horrible nightmares awaited her if she ever became careless or complacent.

"Look," he said. "I'll wait in the car. You can go in and work your business mojo and I'll be waiting for you when your meeting is done."

"All right," Sara sighed. "I won't argue, but only because I know it won't do any good."

"Good girl. I'm standing outside your door anyhow."

She keyed in the alarm code and let him in. He had her out of her chair and in his arms the moment he stepped inside. "Hey, you're going to wrinkle my blouse," Sara squealed as she put her arms around his neck.

Xanthus must have not been too concerned about her blouse because he lowered his head for a kiss. She was only too happy to oblige. He kissed the breath out of her and then slowly pulled away. "You taste good." He moaned and gave her one more quick brush of the lips.

"My lip gloss. It's strawberries," she breathed.

"Really? I like it." Xanthus smiled. "Are you ready to go?"

"I was. I need to put on more lip gloss now."

"I'm just going to kiss it off you again."

"You better not. I need to look professional at this meeting. And each time you kiss me, I seem to get all mussed up."

"I like you all mussed up." He nibbled on her ear.

"*You* might." Her voice caught as her heart fluttered. "But I doubt my client will."

"All right." Xanthus pulled away, smirking. "Put your lip gloss back on. I'll kiss it off *after* your meeting."

She smiled, pulled her lip gloss out of her pocket, and slid it over her lips once again. A stray thought struck her. "Do Dagonian's ever wear makeup?"

"You can tell I'm wearing makeup?" Xanthus gaped at her.

"What? No. You?"

Xanthus laughed and Sara relaxed, scowling at her own naivety. "What are you laughing at? I think it's wonderful you're comfortable enough with your femininity to admit you wear makeup."

He chuckled, bringing his lips a hair's width away from hers. Her heart thumped hard in her chest and she felt that familiar tingle she got when he looked at her the way he did. "You do, huh?"

She swallowed the lump in her throat. "I do what?"

His smile widened just before he moved in and kissed her senseless. When he pulled away, she finally remembered where she was and what she was doing. "You weren't supposed to kiss me until *after* my meeting."

"Sorry Mou, I forgot. Don't you think we'd better get going?" Xanthus glanced at the clock.

"Oh shoot. It's getting late. I absolutely *cannot* be late. It's hard enough drumming up business. I can't afford to lose clients for something as stupid as being late."

"Don't worry Mou, you won't be late."

Xanthus had her out the door and in his SUV in less than a minute. Sara was two minutes early when she rolled through the door of the café. A man waved to her from a table in the back. Sara rolled over. He looked taken aback, seeing her in a wheelchair, but soon recovered. He stood and moved a chair aside so she could push her wheelchair under the table.

"Thank you, Mr. Rowling," she said. The way he was looking at her made her a bit nervous.

"Please call me Steve." Mr. Rowling grinned, looked down at her chest, and raised an eyebrow.

Sara glanced down, horrified. She must have had a couple of buttons come loose somewhere along the way. She was showing a lot of cleavage—not the kind of image she wanted to project. She quickly buttoned up. Her face burned red.

She slowly looked up. Mr. Rowling smiled, showing a few too many teeth. She might be young but she was old enough to know when she was being ogled. And for it to be Mr. Rowling, well, that totally creeped her out. He was about fifty years old and had at least fifty extra pounds of fat around the middle. The smell of cigarettes oozed out his pores.

"Well, I saw the website and I have to say... I'm disappointed." He took a gulp of his coffee and shook his head.

Her previous button embarrassment was completely forgotten with that one statement. "What didn't you like about my web design?"

"There are too many things to list. I think it would be easier to say what I *did* like about it. And that would be nothing. I liked nothing about it."

How could she have been so wrong? She had

thought it was brilliant.

Mr. Rowling tapped his fingers against the laminate table. "First of all, I wanted to have a login for members to access certain pages."

"I... Wait a minute. You never mentioned that." Sara pulled out the printout of her notes and turned to the pages listing his instructions. "Mr. Rowling, you never asked for that. Unless you ask for something, you can't be upset that I don't create it for you."

"I remember specifically telling you to do a login page. I can't help it if you don't take good notes."

"My notes are very detailed. You never *asked* for a login." Sara bit off the next words she wanted to say. She needed to calm down. "I understand there must have been a miscommunication. I can have that fixed for you this evening." She sat up straight, willing herself to have a better handle on her emotions.

"That's not the only problem. I wanted a place for people to sign up for bowling leagues *along* with the league schedule."

"I have the schedule but you never asked for a place to sign up. I can do it, but it's sure to take more time and I would need to charge you more."

"Listen, this is very difficult for me. I really wanted to help you out. You're young and new to this business. I took a gamble doing business with you. But I think I should have gone with someone more experienced."

"Listen, Mr. Rowling..."

"Please, call me Steve."

I don't think so. "Mr. Rowling, I need you to look at my notes. I outlined all that you said you needed. I did absolutely *everything* you asked. Now if there are a few problems, I'll fix those with no extra charge, but if you're asking me to redo the entire design, I'll have to charge you for that."

"No Sara, that's where *you're* wrong. You're the one who is going to have to pay for this disaster of a web design. I won't pay you a cent until the whole thing is redone."

"You can't do that. Do you have any idea how many hours I spent on this job?"

"How many hours you spent isn't my concern." He waved her off.

"Mr. Rowling, I did the work you hired me to do. Now I'm going to ask you nicely to pay me the money you owe me and then I'll ask you not to contact me anymore. You can hire someone else to make the changes you want, but I'm through doing business with you." Sara spoke in hard, even tones.

"Hey, not so fast. There's no need to get so upset. I'll pay you the money and no more changes will be necessary."

"You will?" Sara asked, suspicious of the abrupt change.

"I will, *if* you do one teeny, tiny favor for me." He cocked his bushy eyebrow.

"And what would that be?"

He leaned in toward her. "I want just one night,"

he whispered and licked his lips.

"One night for what?" She leaned away, her stomach queasy.

"One night with just you and me, in a hotel room. If you do this for me, I'll pay you your money. I may even give you a big bonus depending on your performance."

Sara's jaw dropped. She couldn't believe she was hearing this. "What? You... you did not just say what I think you said."

"Yes, I did. And I think you'll realize that this is a way we can both get what we want. If you decide against it, you'll never see your money." Mr. Rowling leaned back, folded his arms, and smirked. His gaze drifted behind Sara and all color drained from his face.

"Hello, my love. Are you about done with your meeting?" Xanthus's voice hummed behind her ear. He put his hand on her shoulder, leaned in, and gently kissed her cheek. Mr. Sleaze looked like he was about to cry.

"Actually, sweetheart, Mr. Rowling has refused to pay me." Sara narrowed her eyes at Mr. Rowling.

"Oh? Now I know that can't be right. I'm *sure* Sara must have heard you wrong. As I'm sure *I* was hearing you wrong when I thought I heard you asking my girlfriend for sexual favors in exchange for the money you owe her. A successful businessman like you doesn't get where he is by making those kinds of stupid mistakes. I mean, doing something that idiotic could get a person killed. Am I right, Mr. Rowling?"

Steve Rowling nodded like a bobble-head doll on crack. "Oh yes, it was a complete misunderstanding. I was just about to write her a check." He yanked out his checkbook and began scribbling. "In fact, I liked the website so much I'm giving her a bonus."

"You don't want me to make any changes?" Sara asked—mostly to see his reaction.

"Oh no, no, no. It's perfect. You don't need to do anymore work."

Mr. Rowling's hand shook as he handed her the check. Wow. He must be really scared. The check was for more than twice the amount she had agreed on. "Wait a minute. This is too much. I can't accept this."

"Oh no, keep it. It's how much I would have paid someone with more experience for the work you did." He pulled out a fifty, sat it on the table, and stood.

"I really have to be going, but you and your boyfriend..." He nearly choked on the word boyfriend. "You have whatever you like. It's on me. It's been wonderful doing business with you. Thanks again, Sara. And I'm sorry for the misunderstanding." Mr. Rowling stumbled out the door.

Xanthus pulled up a chair next to Sara. "That son of an eel. He's lucky I didn't break his legs. I sure wanted to."

"Xanthus, my love," Sara said, using the same wording he'd used earlier. "You were supposed to wait in the SUV. I had everything under control." She cupped her hand over his cheek.

"You did, huh?" He smiled. "Then tell me what you'd planned to do about getting your money?"

"I was going to threaten a lawsuit."

"That could have worked if he would have believed you." He picked up her water and took a long sip.

"Oh, he would have believed me. I had a hundred of these business cards made up." Sara pulled one out of her wallet and handed it to Xanthus.

Elaine Hardcastle, Attorney at Law
1-808-555-6592
No One Messes With My Clients.

Xanthus smiled. "That looks like Gretchen's number. I didn't know she's a lawyer."

"You know Gretchen's number?"

Xanthus shrugged. "I know a lot about *everyone* around you."

Sara frowned. "Well, she's not a lawyer yet, but she's great at tough talking. She's gotten more of my clients to pay up than you'd believe."

"You do know it's against the law to impersonate an attorney." He smiled and then finished off her water.

"Xanthus, the people that try to weasel out of paying me aren't looking to draw attention from the police. They pay up. And if they don't," she shrugged. "I just have to eat a lot of macaroni and cheese for a while."

He shook his head. "Sara, you're one in a million."

He leaned in and kissed her. But it was so quick he'd come and gone before she could really enjoy it.

"Let's take a swim out to the reef and I'll treat you to some sea urchin." Xanthus said. He picked up the fifty and handed it to her.

Sara slipped the money and her check into her purse. "Are you sure you don't want to eat here? They have the greasiest food on the island. It's fried in real beef lard, so I've heard." She propped her chin on her hands and fluttered her eyelids.

Xanthus gagged. "I think I'll pass. Human food, especially greasy human food, does bad things to my digestion."

The dulcet tones of Sirena Enbridge's voice floated from Xanthus's cell phone. Sara smiled at his taste in music. He looked to see who was calling. He was somber when he answered. "Hello, this is Xanthus."

He listened to the caller on the other end of the line. "Yes doctor, that's exactly what I want to know. Can you do it?"

Sara's eyes widened. Why was he talking to a doctor?

His face lit up with relief. "You can? That's great. How soon can you do it?"

Sara's hand shook slightly as she poured more water into her glass. She hated doctors.

"You can't do it sooner than that? No, I understand. Okay, yes, we'll plan on it." He ended the call.

Sara narrowed her eyes. "What was that about? You aren't going in for a physical, are you?"

Xanthus smiled, his whole face lit up. "I have great news."

Sara scrunched her brows. Great news from a doctor? Right. She stopped herself before she rolled her eyes. "What is this great news?"

"There's a doctor in California that can perform surgery to change eye color. He is one of the few that can change from blue to brown. Most others only do brown to blue."

"So, you want me to go under the knife to change the color of my eyes?"

Xanthus frowned. "Sara, this procedure is very safe, and it's not like I'm asking you to get a nose job. It's not to satisfy vanity. This procedure can save your life. Don't you understand? Without this, you'll be living your life with the threat of execution over your head, never knowing if you'll get discovered."

A lump formed in Sara's throat when she realized he was right. Darn him. It had been bad enough facing her fear of water, now she had to face her fear of doctors. "You're right, I know you're right. I just haven't had the best experience with doctors."

Xanthus brushed a strand of her hair away from her face. "Sara, I'll be with you every step of the way. You don't need to do this alone. And I won't let anything happen to you."

Sara nodded. "What would you do if they wanted

to cut off my tail?"

Sara jumped at the angry demon that was suddenly looking at her through Xanthus's eyes. "Who threatened such a thing?" he growled. She was seeing the same monster that she'd thought killed Slink and his friends. He looked lethal and terrifying.

"It was a long time ago," she said, afraid to name the doctors.

Xanthus didn't say any more. He didn't need to. She knew the answer to her question. He would kill them.

She tried to change the subject. "So how much longer will I be a blue-eyed girl?"

He sighed and began to relax. "One month. Your appointment is the fifth of next month."

Sara nodded. One more month.

EIGHTEEN

Sara was getting the hang of the whole swimming thing. It only took daily lessons along with a very patient teacher. Swimming proved to be a great way of keeping her mind off the impending surgery. Three weeks away. Sara shuttered at the thought.

Today, Xanthus took her to a large, remote reef several miles out from Kailau Bay. This reef was pocked with holes and tunnels. From a distance, it looked like a giant misshapen block of colorful, fuzzy, Swiss cheese. It presented the perfect place to hone her maneuvering skills. Or so Xanthus said.

Sara swam through a jagged, three-foot wide tunnel in the coral. She snaked her body through and she didn't even add to the many scrapes and scratches on her battered fin. Too bad females didn't have tough grey skin on the lower half of their bodies like the males did. Xanthus said that females didn't need the added protection—they had males to protect them. He simply smiled when she told him that was chauvinistic.

Instead of swimming about in dresses that tended to float up (very embarrassing), Xanthus bought her a whole slew of modified swimsuits that clung to her body. The one she was wearing now shimmered blue. Sara loved how pretty it looked and how wonderfully supportive it felt. It was more comfortable than her normal modified underwear. So she had taken to wearing them under her clothes all the time. It also made it easier when Xanthus decided on impulse that they needed to go for a swim.

Sara twisted her body around and through another gap in the coral. The tip of her tail brushed the coral again. Ouch. She hoped he hadn't seen that.

"Perfect," Xanthus shouted. Nope, he hadn't seen it. "Wait a minute."

Sara followed his eyes to a small swirl of blood coming from the fresh scrape on her tail. Darn it.

"Well, almost perfect." He shrugged.

She thought she might be imagining it, but she suspected there was a perimeter of sharks around them, just out of sight. She could almost see their dark shapes in the distance. Xanthus said they could smell a drop of blood from miles away and she had put more than her share of drops of blood in the water lately. But as long as Xanthus swam near her, the sharks stayed away.

He smiled and pulled her into his arms. "You're a natural, Sara."

"Oh, yeah. That's like telling a human woman she's a natural at walking." She shrugged.

"Only if she's been living her life in the water and has just stepped out onto dry land," he said. "I'd say you're a fast learner. Did I ever tell you how long it took me to learn to walk?"

"You... Oh wow. You had to learn to walk?"

"Yes, and it took me over a month to master it. Just in time to come here. I would still stumble and fall on occasion if I didn't have my maj bands to help me out."

"Really?"

"Yes, I didn't want to tell you. It's pretty embarrassing. I just don't want you to feel like you're not doing well. You're learning to swim much faster than I learned to walk."

Sara smiled and brushed her lips across his. "You sure have a way with words, which is surprising since English isn't your native tongue. By the way, you don't speak Atlantian much, could you say a few words to me?"

"You've already heard a few words, Moro Mou."

"What does Moro Mou mean?"

"It's a term of endearment. Its literal translation means 'my baby'."

"So when you call me Mou, you're calling me baby?"

"Yes, Mou." His lips caressed hers.

"I like that." She smiled.

"Oh, you did? I wasn't even putting much effort into that kiss. I can do much better."

Sara's smile widened. "I know you can. I was talking about you calling me Mou."

Xanthus smiled back. "Sorry. My mistake."

His smile soon melted away. He kept his eyes

on hers as his body inched close. His hands reached out to cradle her cheeks. He looked as if he held the world in his palms and was afraid of dropping it. Sara's chest tightened in response.

"*Sagana po parant poli mi landana, patdrép ma?*" The words rolled off his tongue in a foreign question.

"What did you say?" Her heart thumped against her chest.

He hesitated before he spoke. "I said... I love you more than my life." He paused before continuing. "Will you marry me, Sara?"

"Marry you?" she asked, feeling a bit dizzy. "You want to marry me?"

"Yes, Moro Mou. More than anything."

"I don't understand why you'd want to. I'm not anything special."

"Sara, I don't understand how you could not know how amazing you are. You're sweet, beautiful, frustratingly independent, and the most remarkable woman I've ever met. I love you more than I can say."

"But still... Are you sure you want to be tied to a half-human forever?" she asked.

"I couldn't think of anything better." Xanthus caressed the side of her face.

"But, what if I'm found out? Would you be punished too?" Sara pulled herself in closer.

Xanthus leaned down toward her. "Sara, no one will find out. After your surgery, you'll look just like a full Dagonian. You'll just need to hide out for a while until you learn to speak Atlantian."

"Xanthus, can't we just stay here in Hawaii?" Sara looked around at the beauty and abundant life.

"I'm sorry Mou. We can't. Triton has given me only a year. After that, I have to return to Corin. And Sara, you truly can't stay here. You know that. Can't you see how you have isolated yourself from the humans? Deep down, you know you don't belong with them. You belong here in the sea, with me."

Sara trembled. She loved this Dagonian so much. Could she really go with him, live the rest of her life in the sea, away from her best friend, away from her mother? Okay, that one wouldn't be so hard. But the thought of living without Xanthus nearly choked the life out of her. What choice did she have? She loved him so much.

"Okay," Sara whispered.

"What are you saying okay to, Mou?" He looked hopeful.

"Okay, I'll marry you." Xanthus swept her up in his arms and swirled her around in the water. Sara's laugher bubbled up as she accompanied him on his underwater ride.

"You've made me the happiest Dagonian in the sea, Moro Mou," he exclaimed just before his mouth took possession of hers, making her tail curl.

NINTEEN

"You're positively glowing," Gretchen said as she sipped her guava nectar. She and Sara were sitting under an umbrella outside their favorite outdoor cafe. Gretchen was on another healthy diet—no more Diet Cokes for her.

Sara wasn't ready to break the news to Gretchen yet. Getting married at twenty wasn't something she thought her best friend would understand. How could she? Gretchen couldn't know that they only had so much time before Xanthus had to leave forever. If Sara didn't marry him, she'd be saying goodbye.

"How can you look so amazing this early in the morning?" Gretchen asked.

"It's this new sushi diet I'm on. Xanthus has got me hooked. And I've never felt better." Okay, maybe that was lame compared to marrying her true love, but she had to think of something on short notice.

"Sushi huh? I like sushi. Maybe I'll try it. But I was thinking more along the lines of the love in your life. I'm glad you two got things worked out. Shane Adams is doing wonders for you."

"Would you *please* stop calling him that? I just

know you're going to slip up and I'll be mortified."

"Not to worry, sweetie. I'll behave. You're not going to cancel on me, are you? Hal got us tickets to see the new Steven Spielberg movie tonight."

"No, I won't cancel." And she wouldn't unless she got attacked by another maniac, which since Xanthus had taken up residence in the apartment next to hers, installed a state-of-the-art security system, new windows, new doors, security cameras, replaced her cell phone, insisted on taking out her garbage, and escorting her out in public, she couldn't see how a criminal would have the opportunity. She'd never felt safer.

Sara did some Googling and found out she should be paying much more than she was in rent, considering the updates to her apartment. She tried to bring that up to Xanthus. But he growled at her and told her he couldn't care less whether she paid her rent at all. Whatever happened to Miss Independence? Well, she was about to become Mrs. Dimitriou.

Sara still couldn't wrap her mind around that one.

"Earth to Sara..." Gretchen chimed in.

"What?"

"I've been telling you about Hal and me." Gretchen smiled.

"Oh, sorry."

"I said, I think Hal is the one."

"The one?"

"Yes, my one true love. He hasn't said the words,

I love you, yet, but I think it's just a matter of time." Gretchen's eyes were dreamy.

Sara wondered if that was how she looked when she thought of Xanthus. "That's so wonderful, Gretchen."

"Yeah, he's amazing. And I'm so glad you have a man you love too."

"Am I that obvious?" Sara didn't remember ever telling Gretchen she loved Xanthus.

"It's very obvious. Just look at how much you've changed. You no longer hide under a giant tent. You're wearing bright colors, clothes that show what a great figure you have, and you always seem to have a smile on your face, especially when you're thinking about him. I sure hope he knows how lucky he is."

The waiter stepped up to the table again. "Can I get anything more for you ladies?"

"No, thank you," Sara said. The waiter smiled at her and walked away. "It's amazing he's giving us the time of day, with you sipping nectar and me eating a small muffin with water.

"Yeah," Gretchen said. "He very attentive. To you."

"To me?"

"Girl, he's got eyes for you." Gretchen shook her head. "You really don't know how gorgeous you are, do you?"

"Xanthus once told me I was much more beautiful than the other women from his home town."

"You're more beautiful than pretty much any girl from any town," Gretchen said.

"Yeah, right, although my mom's very beautiful," Sara shrugged. "And I do look quite a bit like her."

"You look almost identical. Thank goodness you don't have her black heart."

"I don't know. I think I'm beginning to understand her better."

"You're not going to reconnect, are you?" Gretchen looked appalled.

"Actually, she called me a little while ago." Sara was surprised she'd forgotten to tell Gretchen.

"Oh no, honey, why didn't you tell me? What happened?"

"It's nothing I haven't heard before. I told her that if she got professional help, we could talk."

"How did she take that?"

"She screamed and hollered, and then I hung up on her."

"Good for you. You're much better off with her out of your life."

"I know you're right. Besides, I've better things to focus on."

Sara felt goose pimples rise across her arms. She looked over toward the street and saw a tall, dark man wearing sunglasses and a black trench coat that dusted the pavement. He lounged against a light pole. A twinge of familiarity tugged at Sara's consciousness, but she couldn't place where she'd seen him before. He removed his dark sunglasses, revealing black eyes filled with hatred. He looked at her and sneered.

"...like a big, strong man who's crazy about you," Gretchen said.

"What?" Sara asked, distracted.

"Better things to focus on. What's wrong?"

"Don't look, but there's a man standing behind you staring at me. And it's not a friendly stare."

"You're kidding?" Gretchen said in surprise. She began to turn her head.

"No, don't look," Sara hissed.

"Do you want to call Xanthus?"

"I'm going to take a taxi back to the apartment anyway. I'll just call ahead and tell him I'm on my way. Besides, I'm sure that man is just grouchy."

"All right, but I'm not leaving until you're in the cab." Gretchen's brows furrowed in concern.

"You're acting like a..." Sara stopped talking when the man began to approach her. Then she made the connection. This man looked and moved just like Xanthus. Although he was shorter and slighter, he was still very tall for a human. Could he be a Dagonian? No... of course, he couldn't be. She was just overreacting.

The man didn't speak a word as he leaned forward, his chin-length black hair swinging forward, brushing a jagged scar on his cheek. She wished his hair covered his eyes too—they were full of revulsion. Sara's heart pounded as the man slipped a folded piece of paper on the table and pushed it toward her.

The menacing parchment beckoned. Sickness clenched Sara's stomach like a giant fist. She really didn't want to read it.

The man didn't wait for her to open it, but stepped around the corner and slipped out of sight.

"You're right," Gretchen said. "He looked like he loathed you. What does the note say?"

Sara's hands shook as she unfolded the paper. Her eyes landed on a scrawled message. The one simple sentence glared at her.

I know what you are.

Sara's heart pounded in her chest as she took in a ragged breath.

She'd been found and now it was over. There couldn't be a happy ending anymore. Her time with Xanthus had been like a fairy tale, but now the story would be over. How could they hide her true identity when it was already known?

Before Sara could stop her, Gretchen grabbed hold of the note.

"I know what you are? What kind of sicko is that?" Gretchen asked, shook her head, and then looked up at her. "Oh Sara, you're really pale. Sweetie, don't let him bother you. I'm sure he's a harmless crack pot."

Gretchen looked her over and apparently didn't like what she saw. "I'm calling Xanthus." She reached for Sara's phone.

"No, no, we can't call him."

"Why not?"

Xanthus had tried so hard to protect her. Sara recalled his reaction when she had asked what would happen if she were ever found out. She had asked him if they would kill her. Xanthus hadn't said no. Instead, he'd said they'd have to kill him first. And that was her answer. If she hung around, she was a dead woman and Xanthus would die first. That was something Sara wouldn't let happen.

"Sara?"

"I'm fine. Really I am." Sara sucked in another deep breath and then plastered on her most convincing smile. If Gretchen called Xanthus, he'd come right away, and she needed time to put some distance between them.

"I'll tell him what happened when I get to his place. There's no need to get so worked up. You're right. That man's simply a crackpot."

Gretchen looked skeptical.

"Listen," Sara said. "I need to get going. Xanthus is expecting me." She tried to sound as nonchalant as she could.

Gretchen's shoulders relaxed. "Okay sweetie. You'll feel better with him around, anyway. Let me know if you don't feel up to going out tonight. You still look pale. It might be best if you stay in."

"To tell you the truth, I don't think I'm up for going out on the town."

"No problem, sweetie." Gretchen wheeled her to the curb and hailed a taxi for her. A yellow cab stopped and a wrinkled, sunbaked man in a Hawaiian shirt got out. He trotted around to help Sara into the back of his taxi.

"Mahalo," Sara said in thanks to him.

"Sure thing, miss."

Sara waved her last goodbye to Gretchen. She wondered when she would ever see her again. *Never*, she told herself. It was not safe for Gretchen to know her. "Where to?" the driver asked as he pulled into traffic.

"To the airport," Sara said, struggling to hold back the tears. She had to pull it together. This was no time to fall apart.

TWENTY

icole Reanne Lamont didn't walk into Hilo International Airport. She waltzed in like a runway model in a fashion show. Men had their eyes on her hips as they swung back and forth. To Sara, they looked like gaping spectators at a tennis match.

Nothing seemed to have changed since Sara had been gone. Everywhere her mom went, she caused a scene. Men ogled, women sneered, and truth be told, Nicole didn't even know that people were watching her. Sara's mom was beautiful, sensual, and super embarrassing to daughter. Sara always looked like a freak beside her.

"Sara, you're home. I missed you so much." Nicole leaned in and gave her a peck on the cheek. Sara inhaled the perfumed scent of plumeria, a native Hawaiian flower. Memories flooded back. Not all of them were unpleasant. Nicole could be sweet when she wasn't being mental.

"Hi, Mom. Listen, I want to warn you that I'm not here to stay. But we need to have a long talk. I have a lot to ask you about."

"Oh yes, dear. Let's get you home and we'll get caught up on what you've been up to."

Nicole pushed Sara toward the baggage claim area, "Um, Mom. I don't have any luggage."

"Okay, baby." Without a second thought, Nicole turned her chair and headed through the crowded airport toward short-term parking.

Oh yeah, that was her mom. Any other mother would be wondering why their daughter came home after disappearing for so long and then showed up with no luggage in hand. But not Nicole. The thought that this was strange didn't even cross her mind.

Nicole wheeled Sara to a Mercedes. Sara looked at the extravagant car and recalled a time when they couldn't afford a wheelchair. Her mom's failed marriages had been good to her over the years.

"Do you want to stop for lunch?" Nicole glanced her way and smiled. Sara noticed she still had flawless skin. Sara didn't think her mother would ever age. At thirty-nine, she was often mistaken as Sara's sister.

"No, thanks Mom. I'd rather just go on to the house right now." Sara leaned her head back and closed her eyes. A headache was building at the base of her skull.

Sara felt the turns in the road and the warm Hawaiian breeze blow through her hair. Xanthus seemed so very far away right now and the hole in her heart grew with each mile. She wondered if he was looking for her. She had texted him just as she was taking off. She'd told him she loved him but she had to leave. She asked him to forget her and go on with his life. Then she'd turned off her phone.

Knowing him, he was busy trying to track her down. Gretchen had to have told him about the note. Sara could imagine how livid he would be. She hoped he's wasn't angry with her. After all, she'd left to protect *him*. Sara hoped he understood that. Maybe once he had time to think about it, he'd realize it was for the best. They'd kill him for just being with her. He had to know he'd be better off without her.

She hoped he could just let her go.

That Dagonian and his stupid note. Where had he come from? Why did he have to show up now, when she finally had a chance at happiness? They could have made it work. She knew they could. Xanthus had no doubt.

How could one simple sentence destroy her world so completely?

"What's wrong, baby? Why are you crying? Aren't you glad to be home?" Oh, great. Her mom had noticed she was crying before she'd even realized it. Nicole was so unobservant. This was epic.

"Mom, I'll tell you everything when we get home. I just need to rest now." Sara rubbed her temples to ease the ache in her head.

"Why not tell me now?"

Because you might freak and I don't want to die in a fiery car crash. Of course, Sara couldn't say that. "I just need to think, Mom. And I just want to get home." That was a lie. Sara hated the fact that she had to come home.

"I knew you'd come back. You love your mother, don't you?"

"Yes Mom, I do." That wasn't a lie. Sara did love her. She just couldn't live with her.

They pulled down the long driveway of her mother's home. Coconut palms lined the sides of the lane and towered over them. The home was a beautiful, canary-yellow, sprawling estate. Its interior was immaculate, but its highest selling feature was the view out the back. There was a thirty-foot, rocky drop to the ocean.

The waves were spectacular, crashing just off shore and against the cliff below. This cliff had given Sara nightmares from the day they'd moved in. The whole time she'd lived in this home, Sara avoided looking out the back windows. Now she could finally appreciate the beauty of it. The whole place was beautiful—the house, its furnishings, and the land around it.

Nicole had bought this house with husband number two and she got to keep it after the divorce, along with a sizable monthly alimony check. Something good had come from being married to that jerk.

Nicole got Sara's wheelchair out of the back. "Let's get inside, I'm starved. I've sure missed your Roman sandwiches."

Great. Just what Sara wanted to do on the worst day of her life—make lunch for her mother. But, Sara really needed money. "Roman sandwiches sound great, Mom. Do we have the ingredients for them?"

"I don't know. The new maid is out for the day, so you'll just have to look around. I'm going to sit down and do some reading. Let me know if you need me to get anything down for you."

"Sure thing. We can have our talk while we eat." Sara looked in the refrigerator and found salami, provolone, onion, sauerkraut, and ham—the most essential parts of a Roman sandwich.

Sara turned on the skillet and began sautéing the onion. A few minutes later, the sandwiches were done. She got out some chips, fresh pineapple, and then plated the food. She wheeled the plates and drinks one at a time to the table. It took several trips to get everything set up. Then she poured some lemonade.

Sara peeked into the living area to see if her mother was still awake. There was nothing Nicole liked less that being woken up from a nap. Thankfully, she was still reading. "Mom, lunch is ready."

"Okay, dear. I'm just going to finish up this chapter."

Oh great. Sara hoped the sandwiches wouldn't get cold.

Ten minutes later, the sandwiches were as cool as the Hawaiian breeze coming through the window. Nicole stepped into the dining room.

"It looks good." Nicole was sure being extra sweet.

Nicole took a bite of the sandwich and surprised Sara when she didn't say a word about the food being cold. Nicole took a deep breath, a sip of lemonade, and said, "So, tell me what you've been up to."

Sara took a few slow breaths before she spoke. "Actually, I wanted to ask you about my father." She spoke low, her shoulders tensed, waiting for her mom's reaction.

Nicole nodded slightly. "I knew you would ask again sooner or later. Are you ready to believe me? I don't want to talk about him if you're just going to dismiss what I say." Her eyes darted in Sara's direction.

"Mom, I'll believe you." Sara heard the sadness in her own voice.

Nicole looked uncertain. "Well, he was the most amazing man I'd ever met—handsome, funny, strong, and so self-assured. We met in a seaside café just outside of Los Angeles. For the next week, we spent every waking moment together.

"I fell hard for him. I was only eighteen and a bit naïve, but I swear he loved me too, but then he told me he couldn't stay with me. You see, his father was a very powerful man. He told me there was no way his father would allow him to stay and he said I couldn't follow him. I was devastated. I was determined to find a way to convince him to stay with me. After all, once you're an adult, you need to make your own path, right? I figured one day he'd have to leave his father and be independent. Why couldn't I be the reason?

Rising

"When it came time for him to leave, he said I had to go on with my life without him. I told him I'd never love anyone like I loved him—and I haven't. Your father is the only man I've ever really loved.

"Still, he left me standing there. But, I couldn't let him leave me, so I followed him. He surprised me when he drove to a beach. I'd thought he'd be headed to the airport, but he parked and walked to the shoreline.

"He stripped out of his clothing and then the most amazing thing happened. He dove into the water and as he swam away, a tail swished out of the water behind him just before he disappeared under the waves. I thought it looked like the tail of a shark and I was very afraid for him.

"When he didn't resurface, I was sure he'd been attacked. I dove out into the water, desperate to find him. I searched for a long time, not finding anything, but I just couldn't stop. I couldn't leave him there. Then on one of my dives, I thought I saw something and followed it down deep. When I ran out of air, I was nowhere near the surface and I blacked out before I could resurface again. The next thing I knew, I was waking up in the hospital.

"My dad stuck by me until he found out I was pregnant. He was furious and demanded I have an abortion. But, I couldn't do it. I couldn't give you up. You were all I had left of the man I loved. Even though you didn't look much like him, you were part of him."

Sara looked down and realized she hadn't

touched any of her food. "What did he look like?" She took a nibble of a potato chip.

"Oh, he was one of a kind. He looked like a Greek god. He was tall, had blond, curly hair, and was very strong. There was one time I was being harassed and manhandled by some drunk men as I was waiting for him after I got off work.

"When your father came and saw what was happening, he let loose on them. They were all unconscious within a few seconds. When he saw the bruises they'd given me, he was angry all over again and kicked their truck, caving in the entire side. The whole thing looked mangled, like it was folded in half."

Sara had seen Xanthus's strength and it was incredible. Still, folding a truck in half with a kick was amazing. And this Dagonian who was her father seemed larger than life.

"Did he know about me?" Sara took a bite of her sandwich, not tasting it. She was too enthralled in the story.

"Oh baby, he never knew I was expecting you. I was told I couldn't have children. Knowing that, we hadn't... you know, well we hadn't used any birth control. I didn't know you could happen, but then you did." Her mother took a sip, her sad eyes watching Sara from over the glass.

"When did you figure out he hadn't drown?"

"It was when you were born. Being alone at nineteen and pregnant, I didn't have much money and

I never had any prenatal care. The hospital staff freaked out when you were born. They'd never seen anyone like you. But I had. I realized I hadn't imagined it. Ty did have a tail."

"Was that his name? Ty?" The sandwich wasn't going down easy and Sara took a sip of lemonade to loosen it from her throat.

"Well, he told me to call him Ty. He said it was short for something else, but he never told me what. I thought maybe he hated his real name, so I didn't press it."

Sara sighed. "I wish I'd met him."

"Me too, sweetheart. You did get *something* from him though."

"I did?" Sara took another sip of lemonade.

"Yes. You may not look much like him, but your eyes are exactly the same shade of blue as his."

Sara was so surprised, she gasped, which was bad considering she had a mouthful of lemonade. She coughed and sputtered, her hand barely making it over her mouth in time to keep from spewing lemonade all over the table.

"Sara, you're supposed to drink—not inhale." Her mother came over to pat her down with a hand towel.

"He had blue eyes?" Sara rasped.

"Yes, he did. Is there something wrong with him having blue eyes?" Sara was having a déjà vu moment. Hadn't she said those exact words to Xanthus when he had freaked about *her* blue eyes? But her father had had blue eyes. How was that possible?

"Are you sure he had blue eyes?"

"Sara, what is this all about? You're scaring me."

"Are you sure?" Sara asked again, her voice rising. Normally, her mother would be upset that Sara had raised her voice, but Nicole was so shocked at Sara's display, she snapped out an answer.

"Sara, I'm very sure. I could never forget his eyes. Now, tell me what you're so upset about."

"I know what I am. At least I thought I did." Sara dragged the towel over her hands and between her fingers to dry the lemonade.

"What are you saying?" Her mother's brows creased.

"I met someone." Sara sighed and dropped the towel down on the table.

"Please tell me you didn't see another doctor." Her mother pressed her fingers into her temple as if the idea gave her an immediate migraine.

Sara shook her head. "No, Mom. I met someone like me."

"What?" Her mother looked stunned. "Who is she? Where did she come from?"

"No, Mom. Xanthus is a he. And he's a Dagonian. He's descended from Dagon and Calypso, Calypso is the daughter of Atlas and Dagon is a sea god in the Sumerian pantheon." Wow. She couldn't believe she'd remembered all that.

"Atlas? Calypso? Like the Greek gods?"

Sara nodded.

"And you say this Xantus..."

"...Xanthus."

"Yes, Xanthus. Is he, does he have a tail like you?"

"Only when he's in the water and then it looks like mine, except his is grey. Xanthus said females have tails just like mine. He said I'm a perfect image of a Dagonian, except for my eyes. He said they *only ever* have brown eyes. So I ask you again, are you sure my dad had blue eyes?"

Nicole's brows knit together as if she wished she could confirm Sara's identity. Instead, she nodded. "I'm sure."

"Does this mean I was right all along, that I'm just a freak? I can't be a Dagonian. So what am I?"

"You're not a freak. You're my Sara, just like you've always been."

Sara sighed, wishing her mother's words made her feel better. But she felt as if the identity that had just been revealed to her had been ripped from her hands. She wasn't anything special. She simply resembled a Dagonian. And her father? Who knew who or what he was?

A heavy pounding at the door made Sara jump. She didn't know how, but she just knew. Xanthus was here. How had he found her so fast?

Sara considered trying to make a break for it out the back door, but she realized she wouldn't get far with no money and more importantly, no way to drive away. Being in a wheelchair was a real handicap sometimes.

"I wonder who that could be," her mother said.

"Just be prepared for a seven-foot-tall, ticked-off Dagonian."

Her mother's eyes widened in fear. "Should I call the police?"

"No, he won't hurt us. Come on, Mom. Let's get this over with." Sara wheeled to the front door.

Saying he was ticked was a big understatement. When Sara opened the door, there was Xanthus towering high above her. He was livid. Still, she saw the relief in his eyes when he saw her. "Sara," he said. "What do you think you're doing? Gretchen told me what happened. Hades, Sara. Why you didn't come to me?"

Xanthus looked a mess, his eyes were shadowed, his hair tousled, and he had a wild look in his eyes. Sara had only been gone two or three hours, but Xanthus looked as if he'd had the scare of his life.

Didn't he know he needed to stay away from her? And how she wished the thought of that didn't make her feel as if she were being ripped apart from the inside out. What was she going to do?

Sara knew what she had to do for his own protection.

"It's over." She began to sob. "Don't you see? Your Dagonians know about me. There's no getting around that. We have no future. And I don't want you to die." Xanthus knelt down beside her and cradled her cheek in his hand. His thumb brushed away her falling tears. He was no longer furious, but his eyes were tender and filled with relief.

"Oh, Moro Mou, don't cry. I'll get this figured out. I don't care what it takes. I won't leave you."

"Why is my daughter afraid, Dagonian?" Nicole's icy voice lashed out.

Xanthus stiffened and he shot a glare toward Nicole. Sara really didn't need this right now.

"Mom, it's not his fault. He's done everything he could to protect me."

Xanthus turned back to her. "Sara, I think it's time we get moving. I can't guarantee that one of us wasn't followed."

"I asked you a question, Dagonian," Nicole shouted. Sara had to admit, her mom had courage. Xanthus looked terrifying as he glared at her.

"Why don't you ask your..." Xanthus glanced in Sara's direction and sighed. "Maybe you should ask Sara's father."

"And how am I supposed to do that? I haven't seen him since before she was born. Now I'm going to ask you one more time, Dagonian. Why is Sara so afraid? Who is threatening her?"

Xanthus sighed. "Contact between humans and Dagonians is strictly forbidden. Because Sara is part human and part Dagonian, she is considered a danger to our society. And now she's apparently been discovered by another Dagonian and I am her only hope if she's to survive."

"Why aren't you turning her in yourself?"

Xanthus glowered and then looked at Sara. Once again, he seemed relieved to see her. "I would never turn her in because I love her and would die before I'd let anyone else touch her."

In a flash, Nicole's demeanor changed from accusing to acceptance. Yeah, her mom was nuts but Sara still loved her. Nicole rushed to an impressionist painting of a waterfall and lifted it off the wall, revealing a safe. "I've got about fifty thousand dollars in cash. I also have a Glock semi-automatic." Nicole spun the combination and pulled the safe open. "I always knew that Sara could be in danger. Truthfully, I thought it was us humans that were the biggest threat. I've always been prepared in case I had protect her from people who would want to exploit her, which is why I went so nuts when she disappeared." Nicole mom was talking so fast, it was difficult to catch everything she was saying.

Nicole rushed forward, holding a black leather bag, opened it, and turned it toward them to show them stacks of bills and a big gun sitting on top. Several boxes of ammunition were tucked inside.

Xanthus looked shocked. "I appreciate the offer, but I have more than enough weapons and money for anything we might be confronted with."

"Sara is my daughter and my responsibility."

"Nicole..." Xanthus looked like he wanted to argue, but then stopped. He grabbed Sara's wheelchair and pushed her toward the door. "We need to leave now." He turned toward Sara's mom. "Nicole, you need to come with us. They'll be after you too."

"But why would they want *me*?" Nicole looked confused.

"You've been with one of us. You've seen him. All of him. And that means prison or death where I come from."

"But he didn't..."

"Let's go," Xanthus growled. As he ripped the door open, Sara came face to face with death.

TWENTY-ONE

The Dagonian's dark, menacing scowl was even more frightening than Sara had remembered. Xanthus opened the door and there the demon stood—the Dagonian from the cafe, the one trying to ruin her life. His black eyes narrowed, burning with hate as he looked straight at her.

The intruder moved inside and shut the door. "Well, little brother. I can't say I'm surprised to see you here with this half-human." He spoke with a heavy accent.

Little brother? The Dagonian that loathed her was Xanthus's brother? Looking at his sneer, she didn't think he'd welcome her to the family.

Xanthus stepped back and growled. "What do you know of her, Gael?"

His brother's grin broadened. "What would you say if I told you *I'm* her father?"

Sara gasped. Xanthus paled and said, "No."

Gael's laughter bellowed. "No, I'm not, but the look on your face almost makes me wish I were."

Xanthus white face flushed red in anger. He stood his ground and waited.

Gael gestured toward Sara. "I must say, this foul creature is easier to look on than your bride was. It's a shame you have to kill her." Sara leaned away as he moved toward her. Lifting a lock of her hair, Gael pressed it to his nose and inhaled. "She smells nice too. Strange though, her scent is not nearly as compelling as a full Dagonian. Perhaps this is how humans smell when they're fertile. I've never mated with a female during her time—didn't want to deal with the consequences." Gael shrugged. "But this half-human won't live long enough for us to worry about that, will she, brother?" He darted a glace toward Xanthus.

"Get away from my daughter!" Nicole scrambled forward and pushed Gael hard in the chest. He moved back, caught off guard. His hand whipped out fast, striking Nicole across her face and sending her into the wall. At that moment, Xanthus was at Sara's ear. "Don't believe a word of what I say next," he whispered.

Before Sara could even blink, Xanthus had grabbed his brother, lifted him by his coat, and slammed him into the wall. "This is my find and my kill, Gael. You will not interfere. I have special plans for them both before they die and you're not part of those plans.

"But you, Gael," Xanthus said. "What is your purpose here? You know wandering off on your own in the human world is strictly forbidden and I've a feeling this is not the first time. The council may turn a blind eye to your other crimes. But not this one. For this, you face death."

The color washed from Gael's face. "You wouldn't. You couldn't want me dead. I'm your brother."

"That didn't mean much to you when you ordered *my* death. And believe me when I say, I'll kill you in a heartbeat if you give me any more reason. Nothing would give me greater pleasure." Xanthus threw Gael to the floor as he issued the warning. Sara was shocked to see a fin peeking from under his long trench coat. Unlike Xanthus, Gael had no human legs.

"Leave now," Xanthus said. "Return to the sea. And if I ever see you on dry land again, I'll kill you on sight."

"I'll leave, little brother, but I warn you." Gael turned and shot a glare at Sara. "If you don't destroy these creatures soon, I'll be back with my army at my side. Then we'll see who destroys who."

Gael rose from the floor, brushed himself off, and strode out the door. He moved like he had legs. Xanthus was right. This couldn't be the first time Gael had been on land. Sara jumped when the door slammed shut. For a moment, she sat gaping at the wooden door. Then, she turned to look at Xanthus. With his feet braced apart, he scowled with barely leashed anger.

Sara searched for something to say to ease his temper. "I heard it might be difficult to get along with in-laws, but I had no idea."

Xanthus turned to her, startled. Then a slow smile crept across his face.

"In-laws?" Sara's mom staggered up to her feet.

"Oh, Mom, don't get up. Xanthus, help her."

"No, stay away from me. I heard what you said. You're going to kill us."

"No, Mom, he didn't mean it." Sara wheeled to face her.

"Sara, you keep out of this. You were always too trusting." Nicole clawed through the bag, spilling money onto the floor in her haste.

Sara's heart dropped when she realized Nicole was looking for the gun.

"It's not there, Nicole." Xanthus held the gun up and released the magazine. It dropped to the floor with a thud. "Sara's right. I have no intention of killing either of you. If there is anyone who should have died here, it would be Gael. I have a feeling I'll regret letting him live."

Sara wheeled to his side. "Xanthus, you can't kill your own brother."

"He's not my brother."

"He's not?"

"Not anymore."

"Enough of this," Nicole screamed and stomped her foot. "I need to know what is going on and I need to know right now. And if I don't like what you say, Dagonian, I'll kill you with my bare hands. And don't you think that I can't." She hurled the bag against the wall. A hundred bullets clattered and rolled across the hardwood floor.

Sara thought her mother's statement about killing Xanthus was ludicrous, but she wouldn't have dreamed of mentioning that with her mother in this state. Truly, if anyone could scream someone to death, it would be Nicole. And she was just on the verge right now.

"Mom, wait. We'll tell you everything. Really we will, won't we, Xanthus?" Sara turned toward him, trying to signal him with her eyes that the situation was desperate and they'd better do as she said.

Xanthus narrowed his eyes and sighed. "Yes, Nicole, we will."

A long while later, Nicole was satisfied with their story, albeit not so happy to hear her twenty-year-old baby daughter was engaged and planned to leave her forever to live somewhere in the Mediterranean Sea.

During Xanthus's lengthy explanation, Sara wheeled to the mess of money and bullets. Maneuvering out of her chair, she sat down on the floor and began to clean up. Xanthus glanced her way and coolly asked, "Nicole, are you going to let your disabled daughter clean up *your* mess?"

Startled, Nicole stood. "Sara, I can get that, baby."

"It's all right, Mom, but I'd appreciate help."

Xanthus and Nicole pitched in and, in no time, it was all cleaned up. Xanthus lifted Sara onto the sofa beside him.

"So let me get this straight," Nicole said. "Your brother Gael hates you and he thought he caught you fraternizing with a half-human girl, which is a capital offense, by the way. So when you told him you planned to kill us, he no longer had any wrongdoing to pin on you. But he broke the law himself, coming up on land. So now that you've threatened him, he wouldn't dare return. Am I right?"

"Right," Xanthus said.

"Okay, I understand." Nicole yawned and stretched. "This has been a really long day and I've had way too much excitement for a woman my age."

"Mom, you're in your thirties."

"Exactly."

Nicole sauntered down the hallway. She paused before stepping into her bedroom. She turned to Xanthus. "Remember Dagonian, my daughter is fertile right now. If you get her pregnant, I'll rip your penis off and feed it to the seagulls." Nicole glared for several long moments, then stepped into her room and pulled the door closed behind her.

Sara's face burned with embarrassment. If only the couch would swallow her whole.

When she chanced a glance toward Xanthus, he looked dumbfounded. "I've never met a more unusual woman." He smiled. "She is like being caught in a whirlpool. She's moody, unreasonable, childish, overprotective, and by the gods, I'm beginning to like her."

"I know how you feel. I love my mom. I just couldn't live with her. She was driving me insane." Sara sighed. "Do you really think it's safe to stay here?"

Xanthus pulled her onto his lap. "It's safe, Mou.

My brother's no match for me."

"He mentioned your bride. Were you married before?" Sara's face felt warm and she knew she was blushing.

Xanthus smiled as he caressed her cheek. "I was engaged many years ago. It didn't work out."

"You don't think Gael can get an army and come back here, do you?" Sara put her hand over his.

"No, I don't. In order to tell anyone about you and your mother, Gael would have to admit that he had traveled among the humans without permission. That action carries a death sentence, even for Gael."

"But you're here." Sara touched his nose.

He took her finger, pressed it to his lips, and then continued. "King Triton granted me permission. And no one argues with him. That is, unless they have a death wish."

"You're sure I'm safe from your brother?"

"Sara, you have to trust me. You're safe from Dagonians for the time being." Xanthus put the tip of her finger into his mouth and suckled. Sara's heartbeat quickened and goose pimples broke out over her arms and down her back.

"Did you love her, the Dagonian woman you wanted to marry?" Sara's voice hitched.

"I thought I did. But my feelings for her don't come close to what I feel for you." Xanthus looked in Sara's eyes just before he lifted her wrist to his lips and began to nibble up her arm. The temperature seemed to rise ten degrees in the last few seconds and she began to tremble.

"You don't think... that maybe, when I'm not fertile anymore... You don't think your feelings about me will change, do you?"

He laid her arm against his chest. "Moro Mou, it's *because* I love you that I put myself through this torture. If I didn't love you, I would keep myself far away from you, away from temptation. I'll tell you this much, our marriage had better come soon. My self-control is being sorely tested."

"It is?" Her voice shook.

"Oh yes," he growled. "But, you can trust me not to shame you. I'll wait until we've spoken our vows. Even then, we should still put off our joining. I want you safe inside my castle before you carry my child."

"Why don't... Wait. You live in a castle?"

"House, fortress, castle... My home is very large and well-protected."

"Oh, wow."

Xanthus smiled, leaned forward, and pressed his lips down on hers for a moment. As he pulled away, he tugged her bottom lip with his teeth and released it with a smile.

"What was that for?"

"I loved the way your lips looked when you said the word 'wow'. I couldn't resist taking a taste."

"Oh, wow," Sara said, drawing out the word.

"Don't push your luck, Moro Mou. You *are* still

fertile."

"Why am I? I thought I was supposed to be for only two weeks. It's been almost four."

Xanthus shrugged. "No female is exactly the same. For some, it lasts a few days and for others, it's over a month. For most, it's two weeks. Lucky is the Dagonian who has a wife whose time is longer." He brushed a kiss across her lips. "Mmm, although right now, it makes things more difficult for me. Keeping my hands off you takes a concerted effort."

"Gael said I didn't smell as compelling as other females."

"He was wrong." Xanthus shook his head and sighed. "To me, you smell ten times, no more like a hundred times as compelling. In fact, I was beginning to think there was something wrong with me. Other males would lose their senses in the presence of a fertile female and I've never had any trouble resisting. Not that they didn't stir me, but you, Moro Mou, are a constant battle for my self-control and you've tested me to my limits."

"I'm sorry." Sara trailed her fingers over his chest. He clasped her hand in his and held it still.

"There's no need to be sorry. There's nothing you can do about it. And once we're married, it'll be a good thing. But right now, I could use a good swim, but I won't leave you and your mother unprotected." Xanthus sighed. "Maybe I'll take one of your human cold showers."

Her human cold shower. That reminded her, she

may not be half-Dagonian after all, but fully human. Actually, she didn't know what she was. All she knew was that her dad had blue eyes. That pretty much ruled out Dagonian, didn't it?

"I've grown to like that contraption," Xanthus said, "and a cold shower is just what I need right now."

"Uh-huh." Sara knew she should tell Xanthus about her dad. Or maybe she shouldn't. Nicole *had* to be wrong. Nicole was probably imagining that Sara's dad had blue eyes because she wanted Sara to have her dad's eyes. Besides that, her dad had legs. Sara didn't know what to think of that. Her mom was crazy. That's what she thought. Sara couldn't believe anything Nicole said.

She refused to think about it anymore. She was a Dagonian and that was all there was to it.

"—Sara, what's wrong?"

"Hm?"

"Sara," Xanthus's voice rumbled, "you haven't heard a word I was saying."

"Oh, I'm sorry. Did I miss anything important?" Sara yawned and feigned sleepiness.

Xanthus raised an eyebrow. He didn't look convinced. "No, nothing terribly important, Mou."

"Oh, okay." She laid her head on his shoulder.

"What's wrong?"

"Nothing's wrong. I'm just tired." Sara wrapped her arms around his neck.

"You know you can tell me anything, right? There's no place for secrets between us."

"I don't have any secrets from you." At least, she hoped not. Please let her mom be wrong. She wanted so much to belong with Xanthus.

"Okay Mou. We'll talk about this tomorrow."

"Mm hm."

"Let's get you to bed." Xanthus cradled her as he stood. She directed him to her bedroom and enjoyed the ride wrapped in his strong arms. Xanthus opened her door, flipped on the switch, and jerked to a stop.

His eyes widened when he found himself surrounded on all sides by teen posters. Movie stars, music bands, and countless baby-faced boys were plastered like wallpaper across her walls.

"Oh, um, this is embarrassing," Sara said. "My mom hung these posters for me *years* ago. I've asked her to take them down over and over again, but she's always been too busy. And they are out of my reach or I'd take them down myself."

Xanthus chuckled. "What have I gotten myself into?" He shook his head.

"I should have just gotten a broom stick and ripped them down."

"Sara..." Xanthus smiled. "So you were a typical teenager. There's nothing wrong with that. But I do need to know one thing."

"What?"

"If I had a poster made of me, would I be on your wall too?"

"Baby, if you had a poster made of you, it'd be

the only one I'd have. Everyone else would look too ugly hanging next to you."

"Good answer." Xanthus's smiling mouth descended on her lips.

He left her room a few minutes later to have his cold shower.

TWENTY-TWO

"Rise and shine, sweetheart," Nicole's voice boomed as she yanked back Sara's bedroom curtains and let in the horrid, beaming sunlight.

"What time is it?" Sara croaked as she pulled the pillow over her head.

"Oh, let me see, it's 5:51. Nothing like an early start and a morning swim, I'll go wake Xanthus." Sara heard her mom trot from her room. At this moment, Sara remembered why she'd left her mother. Her mom had no concept that other people had wants and needs of their own.

Sara heard Xanthus's voice boom from down the hall. "Nicole? What time is it? Get out of my room and let me sleep."

"Okay, grouchy Dagonian, Sara and I will just go without you. We'll be a half a mile down the coast. There's a little beach there and it's always deserted this time in the morning. I can't wait to see my baby swim."

"Sara," Xanthus yelled.

"Huh," she groaned from under her pillow. She was sure he couldn't have heard it, but she was too tired to yell.

"If you go with your mother, I'll fillet you."

"Uh-huh," Sara moaned, with her face sandwiched between her pillow and the mattress.

"You'll do no such thing," her mother challenged.

Sara was hit with a cool blast of air when her blanket was jerked away. "Sara Elizabeth Taylor, don't listen to that fish in the mud. A morning swim is good for you."

"Go away, Mom," Sara said. A moment later, she felt her pillow being tugged away. She held on for dear life.

"Sara, come on. You can't want to go back to sleep on a beautiful morning like this."

"Mom, please, it's too early." Sara felt herself slide across the mattress.

"You know how much I love to swim." Her mom let go of the pillow. A moment later, she had her hands around Sara's fin and began to pull. Sara reached out, grabbed the edge of the mattress, and held on. She knew her mom thought if she succeeded pulling her off the bed, she would relent.

Sara wasn't about to let her win this time. It wasn't a matter of going back to sleep now. She couldn't go back to sleep even if she tried. It was about exerting her independence. She was an adult. Her mom couldn't order her around like a child.

Nicole yanked hard and Sara's fingertips burned but held. The mattress, however, didn't have anything holding it in place and so it slid halfway off the box spring onto the floor.

"What the Hades are you doing to your daughter?" Sara lifted her head and blew her hair out of her eyes. Xanthus stood in her doorway, wearing only a pair of shorts. His hair was tousled and his face had a shadow of whiskers—he looked utterly gorgeous.

Sara was distracted when her mom jerked hard again. This time, Sara's fingers gave way and she slid down the length of the mattress like a playground slide, landing at the bottom. Dang it.

"I'm getting her up," Nicole said, speaking as if this situation was a daily occurrence. "Sara has always been difficult to rouse."

Sara yanked down her nightgown to make sure all her necessary parts were covered.

Xanthus shook his head. A stream of complaints poured from his lips as he strode over, plucked her up off the floor, and carried her into the kitchen. At least Sara thought they were complaints. She couldn't tell because he didn't speak a word of English.

"Xanthus, my daughter shouldn't be eating before going out swimming. She might get a cramp."

Xanthus sat Sara in a chair and dragged his fingers through his hair. "You think Dagonians can't swim after they eat?"

"Well, she's half-human. That may make all the difference."

"Nicole, Sara is not going swimming in the ocean

and neither are you," Xanthus said, exasperated. "Where do you think Gael went after he left? Do you think he's staying in a hotel? No. He's out there, in the ocean. You think he wouldn't jump at the chance to come after you both? If you took Sara out into the water, he'd kill her without hesitation. While you're here with me, he wouldn't dare."

"Oh, well shoot. I really wanted to see my girl swim. I guess we'll just have to take a dip in the swimming pool out back. It won't be as much fun, but I guess it'll do." Nicole snatched up a glass of orange juice and took sip.

"In chlorinated water?" Sara gasped, remembering her experience in the tub. Pool water had to be much worse. "No way, Mom."

"To tell you the truth, I could really use a swim right now." Xanthus crossed his arms over his muscled chest, and eyed her hopefully.

"What?" Sara's voice rose an octave. "You can't be serious."

"Sara, all you need to do is hold your breath," Nicole said. "That's what normal humans do."

"But what if I forget?"

"After what happened in the tub, do you think you could forget?" Xanthus asked.

"Well no, I don't think I'll ever forget. But, doesn't chlorine hurt your eyes?"

"I have goggles, baby," Nicole said as she pranced down the hall toward her bedroom to change into her suit.

"Besides," Xanthus said, "you don't have to put your face in the water if you don't want to."

"Oh, yes she does. I've waited a lifetime to see my baby swim," Nicole yelled from her room.

Sara saw where this was going and she was fed up with it.

She grasped the seat of her chair with her hands, reached her fin out, pressed it down onto the kitchen floor, and lifted her bottom off the chair. Pulling her hips forward, she lowered herself down to floor.

Once she was sitting, she turned over, lay on her belly, and began to soldier crawl toward her room. She'd made it several feet when Xanthus stepped in front of her, squatted down, and silently commanded her attention.

She ignored him and crawled around his feet. "Sara? What are you doing?" he asked. There was a hint of amusement in his voice.

"I'm going back to bed. You and my mom can do what you like, but I refuse to be a part of it."

Sara was grateful that he didn't try to stop her or try to help her to her room. She didn't need either of them telling her what she could and couldn't do. And she could darn well get to her room by herself.

She crawled through her doorway, flicked her fin, and slammed the door shut. She turned her body around, reached up, and locked the doorknob for good measure.

"Where's Sara?" She heard her mother's muffled voice ask.

"She's going back to bed," Xanthus said.

"Oh, no she isn't. I didn't go to all that effort getting her up just to have her go back to sleep. We are going swimming and that's all there is to it."

"Nicole, just let her be," Xanthus said.

"What? It sounds like you're telling me how to raise my own daughter."

"Of course not. She's a grown woman. She has a mind of her own and is determined to use it. And if you don't begin to understand and respect that, she'll just disappear again and I can almost guarantee it'll be longer before you see her again."

Sara sat on the floor next to her skewed mattress and listened.

"But *you* could make her see me. You'll be her husband after all."

"Nicole, Sara does not like to be ordered around. If I ever tried to do that, she'd leave me too, which is not an option for me. I love your daughter and I'd rather lose my tail forever than lose her. If you'd just let her make her own decisions, you wouldn't need to have anyone *make* her see you."

"But you don't understand. I do this all for her own good. When she was little, she wouldn't even come out of her room. She was so afraid of everyone and everything. If I hadn't forced her, she would never have had the courage to leave the house. I did everything for her. I even gave up a perfectly wonderful husband in order to keep her."

"This perfectly wonderful husband wanted you to get rid of your own daughter?"

Oh great, here it comes.

"He knew Sara was unstable and he saw how my life was turned upside down because of her. Charles tried to convince me that I should have her cared for in an institution, but I couldn't bring myself to do it. I had to protect her. It was because of Sara that Charles left me. So can't you see how much I've sacrificed for her? I think I deserve some respect."

A hand clamped down over Sara's mouth. "If I know my brother, this conversation is about to become a lot more heated. Too bad we'll miss it." The next thing Sara knew, Gael's arm was tight around her waist and they were flying across the room. They flew through her open window toward the cliff. Sara's stomach dropped as they dove down toward the water. She tried to scream, but Gael's hand was pressed down too hard against her mouth. She tasted blood.

Sara fought him with everything she had. Gael yanked hard on her head, and squeezed her waist so tightly it was difficult to breathe. "Stop fighting me or I'll break your little neck, filthy cur. Don't mistake me for my brother. I don't have a merciful bone in my body."

Sara stopped struggling. She didn't doubt that Gael would follow through on his threat.

Gael and Sara moved fast through the murky

waters. Sara couldn't see much at first. The water churned with silt and bubbles from the battering waves above. She braced herself for impact just before she slammed into the side of a boulder. The water whooshed out of her lungs and Sara struggled to gulp in some oxygen. Gael turned her around to face him. "I wish I had time to play with you now, but my brother can be a bit unpredictable when it comes to a hunt. And from what I've seen, he'll hunt you to the ends of the earth. That is if I'm lucky."

Gael began to chant. Sara didn't know the words but the cadences were familiar. He was speaking Atlantian. A silver light appeared several feet away. It started small, the size of a pea, and then grew into a large, shimmering circle about six feet in diameter. Sara knew it was some kind of a door. She also knew that if she went through that door with Gael, she'd probably never see Xanthus again.

Sara screamed, wailing high and loud. Gael's eyes flew open wide in shock as he slapped his hands over his ears and roared. Sara continued to shriek as she saw a fist fly toward her. An explosion of pain knocked her head back and darkness engulfed her.

TWENTY-THREE

Where under Olympus was the cab? Xanthus held the blind slat up enough to peer outside the front window.

"Xanthus, I need an outside opinion." Nicole's shout came from her bedroom.

Xanthus narrowed his eyes at the empty street. He sighed, turned away, and tromped down the hall to her bedroom, once again.

Nicole held up two hangers with silky blouses draped off them. Well, this was better than the bikinis she'd shown him last time. Where in Hades was Sara? Shouldn't *she* be helping her mother with her thousand selections?

"You're a man," Nicole said.

Obviously.

"Which one do you think is sexier?" She did a little wiggle and cocked one eyebrow.

"Sexier?" Xanthus cast a glance toward Sara's room.

"Yes, as a man. Which one would you rather see me in?"

"Nicole, don't you think Sara..."

"Oh, Sara *never* gives her opinion," Nicole interrupted. "Besides, she knows next to nothing about fashion."

"And I do?"

"You can tell me which you'd rather see me in."

He sighed. "They both look nice."

"Oh, no. You're not getting off that easy. Choose. I want to know which one you think looks better." One by one, she held them up to her chest.

They were both pretty—silky, bright, feminine. One was yellow and the other green. He liked yellow. It reminded him of the sun. "The yellow one looks nice," he said, venturing a suggestion.

Nicole scrunched up her face. "You're kidding." She held the yellow blouse up to inspect it closer. She turned back to him with an expression that suggested he was insane. "The yellow one? Really? You *have* to be kidding."

Xanthus threw up his hands in defeat. "You asked."

"Well, next time I won't."

Xanthus stomped from the room. "Five minutes, Nicole," he said, "and we're leaving. You'd better pack faster."

"With the help I'm getting, it's probably going to take me an hour."

Xanthus stepped up to Sara's door and knocked. "Sara, it's time we get going. Your mom is nearly done packing. We're heading to the mainland and your mom is going to Maui to visit a friend." He hoped Sara wouldn't argue about leaving with him. He wasn't about to leave her again. Still, he had an important mission to accomplish.

Xanthus waited for Sara to answer. He was met with silence. Why wasn't she answering him?

"Getting the silent treatment, huh?" Nicole asked. "She does that all the time."

She'd never done that to Xanthus before. Uneasiness clenched his gut. What if something was wrong?

He tried the knob. Locked. "Sara, you need to answer me."

He waited for a minute and still there was no response.

"Sara, answer me or I'm breaking down the door."

Still no answer.

Fear seized him. Something was very wrong. Xanthus shoved his shoulder into the door and the frame splintered. Inside the room, he saw the disheveled mess from before, but what he didn't see was worse than a knife to the chest. Sara was gone. The curtains billowed from her open window.

"Sara!" Xanthus's anguished cry rent the air as he raced to the window. He looked out toward the sea. He could still smell her sweet scent but he also smelled the sick odor of his brother.

How could he have been such a fool? He'd thought Gael wouldn't dare touch her while he claimed he‾, but once again, he was wrong about his brother. And Sara might die because of it.

A tremendous pounding in her skull was the first thing Sara was aware of. She felt weightless, almost like she was having an out-of-body experience. She was underwater. Memories flooded her mind. She threw her head back in a panic, slamming it into something hard. Her pounding head now felt like it was about to explode. She reached back to inspect the damage—it felt like she'd split her head open. Her fingers brushed a small lump. Okay, maybe she'd live, for now.

She tried to figure out where she was, but all she could see was pitch blackness.

She couldn't believe what had happened. She'd been kidnapped, taken from her own bedroom, with Xanthus right in the next room. Everything had happened so fast her head was reeling. Or was that just her killer headache?

Sara tried her best to see something, anything at all, as she reached out into the darkness. Her hands bumped into something hard and she lightly touched it. It was a metal bar. She kept searching with her hands and felt more metal bars all around her. She was in some kind of cage.

How would Xanthus ever find her? And would Gael kill her? Should she tell Gael that she and Xanthus were getting married? Would he have second thoughts about killing the fiancée of his brother? No, if that were going to help, Xanthus would have told him yesterday. Instead, he'd told Gael that he was going to kill her.

Telling Gael about her relationship with Xanthus was out of the question. She might die, but Sara didn't want to put Xanthus put on a hit list too.

From the corner of her eyes, a blue glow materialized, illuminating the outline of a jagged entrance to the room she was in. The swelling illumination began to fill the room. As the light increased, she saw that she wasn't in a room at all, but a very large cave.

And she wasn't alone.

There was another cage beside hers. A shadow moved around, circling the cage, a shadow in the shape of a monstrous shark. Sara's heart began to race.

The shadow of the shark got larger and larger until it slammed into the bars. Sara shrieked as the impact threw the side of the cage into her shoulder. The rocking cage pounded against the cave floor. All the while, the light continued to increase. Sara searched her surroundings, rubbing her aching shoulder. Her cage and the shark's were connected. Thank heavens metals bars separated them or she'd be shark food.

Sara moved back, trying to get some distance between herself and the creature. There wasn't much room to work with. Her own tiny cage was about three feet wide and six feet vertical. She remained upright, plastered against the bars. The shark's cage was much bigger than her own, probably about four times as big as her apartment. It allowed the shark to circle around as he stared her down with his black eyes.

"Frightening isn't he, human?" Gael's amused voice came like a mist through the mouth of the cave opening. A moment later, his smiling face appeared. He wore a necklace with an orb that glowed blue, bright enough to illuminate the entire cave. Sara saw that the opening he came through led not to the outside, but to a rocky tunnel.

Sara darted a glance back to the shark. It was the biggest shark she'd ever seen. The colossal shark charged toward Gael. Once again, he hit the metal bars and both their cages shook. Sara's body trembled as she gulped in breaths of water.

Gael's eyes widened in shock as he snarled out a slew of foreign words. Xanthus had taught Sara some Atlantian, but from the sound of it, he wouldn't be teaching her any of these words. She had a feeling they were very foul.

"Amintah is a bit agitated. As well he should be. He hasn't eaten in a very long time. I can see his frustration with having a meal so close and not being able to have even a nibble."

"What are you going to do with me?" Sara did her best to sound brave, but her voice cracked.

"I'm going to have some fun with you, my retched, little cur."

"You aren't going to..." She couldn't say it. She

didn't even want to think it.

"You wish. I put on a good show for my brother yesterday when I said I would like to mate with you. But I'd sooner mate with a sea cow than a filthy human. Not when I have plenty of willing Dagonian females. But I saw what I needed to see. He may have *said* he was going to kill you, but I know my brother. He thought he could fool me, but he's the fool, a fool who is in love with a human.

"And he's given me the means to take him down. Before all this is over, he'll be exposed for the human lover he is. He'll lose everything—his status, his respect, and ultimately his life.

"But first, I must attend to Amintah." He gestured toward the shark. "He's very hungry. Why don't we give him a bite?"

Sara's eyes widened and she clung to the back of her cage. She looked toward the vicious shark. Scars crisscrossed his back. Then she saw two metal rings that looked like handcuffs connected to the bars that kept her separated from the shark. It wasn't hard to figure out what those were used for.

Gael reached out, grabbed her right elbow, and yanked her grip away from the bar. She clawed and twisted with all her might. "Please, no. Please don't do this."

Gael may not have been as big or muscular as Xanthus, but he was still much stronger than she was. Sara was helpless as he put her hand through the metal ring and locked it in place, closing it tightly around her wrist.

"Please, don't do this, Gael. I never did *anything* to you. Why are you doing this to me?"

"I do it for the sheer enjoyment of it," he said with a smile.

Sara yanked and pulled with all her strength, trying to free her hand. The metal cut painfully into her skin. It was no use—her hand was exposed inside the shark's cage. And the shark kept circling.

A few moments later, the shark moved in. Sara sucked in water, closed her eyes, and braced for the attack. Something sandpapery brushed over her knuckles and a jolt of fear nearly stopped her heart. Then she felt nothing. She was shaking hard when she chanced a peek. The shark continued to circle.

She yanked her hand again, trying her best to pull it out.

A moment later, the shark moved in again. Sara closed her eyes and braced herself. Like before, his rough skin scraped over her knuckles.

"Oh Hades, Amintah," Gael said. "Just bite her hand off already." Without warning, the shark turned his attention to Gael, charging him and slamming into the side of the cage. "Amintah, what is wrong with you?" Gael shouted.

The shark turned away and continued to circle. Gael shook his head and scowled. He swam forward and pulled out a knife. "This will get him going." He reached in and slashed the blade across Sara's fingers, cutting deep, bringing instant pain as she cried out. "There's no way he can resist you now."

The shark's gaping mouth appeared in an instant. Gael jerked his arm back just in time to miss the snapping teeth. When the shark couldn't clamp down on Gael's arm, it bit down on a bar. The shark shook the cage violently, jerking Sara's wrist painfully against the band and slamming the metal cage against the rocky floor over and over again. Silt clouded the water.

The shark resumed circling the cage.

Gael gaped at the creature, his eyes following his movement. Once again, Gael looked hopeful when the shark moved in toward Sara. This time she didn't close her eyes, didn't cringe away. Amintah kept his eye on her and for a third time, brushed his body under her outstretched hand. Sara's fear of being exposed to attack had melted away. She was far from being an expert on shark behavior, but she suddenly felt calm. This monstrous shark was not going to hurt her. He was giving her a message. She now understood it perfectly. She had nothing to fear from him.

Gael shouted, enraged.

Sara's ears stung as Gael let loose a string of profanity. She didn't understand a word of it, but it was upsetting nonetheless. He raced over, unlocked her door, and ripped the cage open, cursing at her the entire time.

"I guess I'll just have to take care of you myself." When Gael released her hand, he fisted her hair in his grasp and yanked her out the door. Sara heard the shark slamming into the metal bars as they entered the tunnel. She wished Gael had opened Amintah's door, too.

Sara couldn't believe this Dagonian was Xanthus's brother. She felt her hair being ripped out by the roots. Xanthus and his brother couldn't be more different. Xanthus was a protector, his brother, Gael, was a soulless, evil monster.

"Why are you doing this to me? Why aren't you just killing me?"

"The best things in life are to be savored. And I am going to enjoy watching you die. Triton thinks my brother is a great warrior, but look at him. He didn't have the heart to kill an abomination. By the gods, he fell in love with the abomination.

"The law demands your death regardless of how my brother feels about it. He may think he's above the law, but he's not. And I'm only too happy to rectify the situation. Once it is known what he has done, it will mean his death also."

While he spoke, Gael pulled her through the tunnel's twists and turns, not hesitating a bit when they came to forks in the maze. The light increased as they moved. It was blinding as they entered open waters and Gael swished to a stop.

"Now I'm going to explain what will happen." He pulled Sara up close. She smelled an odor emanating from him and it wasn't pleasant. It made her stomach churn.

"You see, I still can't have anyone think I inflicted injuries on you for my own entertainment, and they can't know I was the one who killed you. They'd never believe that you posed any kind of a physical threat to me, so they'd expect me to bring you in alive. If we were still on the surface, it wouldn't matter what I did to you. But down here, it does. However, if I did bring you in alive, they would rob me of your kill by executing you themselves. I have no intention of letting them have that honor.

"Amintah would have provided the perfect means of killing you with no evidence pointing toward me. But since he decided not to cooperate, I'll have to adjust my plans.

"I still have to produce your body for Xanthus to answer for his actions, and I need to gather evidence to nail my brother for his criminal behavior." Gael smiled a crooked smile.

"Now, I think it's time we got down to business."

An explosion of pain pierced Sara's belly. She looked down and saw Gael pull out a long, curved blade from her stomach. Blood billowed like crimson smoke from her wound. "Maybe we'll have better cooperation from the *other* sharks in this area. Don't be afraid for my safety if you don't see me." He chuckled. "I'll be fine. I'm just going to watch them rip you apart from a distance. I'll be back to chase them off and collect your body when you're dead."

With that said, Gael smiled and left, stirring the

cloud of blood in his wake. Sara was in shock. She could taste the coppery flavor of her own blood as it thickened in the water. She pressed hard on her belly, trying to stem the flow. She didn't know if the wound was fatal, but the way she was bleeding, she feared it could be.

Sara had to get out of here. She jerked forward, her movement unnatural and awkward. She wished she'd had more time to practice swimming. She thought she was getting pretty good at it, but put a knife through her gut and she couldn't swim a lick.

The blood clouded the water, making it difficult to see. She'd closed her eyes for just a moment and felt a bump from behind.

"Who's there?" Sara asked, her voice weak. She pried open her eyes and saw nothing but red haze. Soon, her eyes closed again. There was another bump, this time from underneath. Sara thought it must be the bottom of the ocean because it remained pressed against her body. She still had the strange sense of floating, though. Sara continued to have soft bumps coming from different sides.

Sara tried to swim several times and each time she flicked her tail, there was another bump. Her eyes were too heavy to keep open and she was too weak to call out anymore.

She didn't know how long this lasted, but after a while, she heard a strange humming. It was faint at first. The tones rose and fell like voices but they spoke strange words she couldn't understand. They grew louder and insistent—almost angry. Sara tried to see who spoke, but she couldn't quite get her eyes open.

Then the ground disappeared from under her and she floated. Or maybe she died. Sara wasn't sure. Hands began pulling her, touching her, pressing on her belly. Hadn't she just been doing that? Sara was relieved when the pain began to fade.

TWENTY-FOUR

Warm, sweet-scented water caressed Sara's skin as she floated. Each breath of water brought soothing floral smells and tastes. A hum of music tickled her eardrums and made her smile. It was a strange song. Each note flowed into the next as an odd dance of tone and melody. She'd never heard anything like it.

Sara felt fingers weave through her hair, and then tug in a rhythm that reminded her of when her mother used to braid it. Someone *was* braiding her hair. Who could be doing such a thing?

Maybe it was an angel. She must be dead. Why else would she be feeling such a sense of well-being? She remembered what had happened. Gael had stabbed her, trying to coax the sharks into attacking her. But they hadn't come. She must have bled to death.

Now Xanthus would never find her. How could he ever find her here? She was in heaven, out of reach, even for him. A sob shook her chest and pain shot through her stomach. Wasn't she supposed to feel no pain?

Sara's eyes blinked open. She was in a large,

underwater room. The walls were made of stone. Immense glass windows displayed an incredible view of coral reefs. They seemed to reach up and over the underwater building, cocooning it in a dome. All around the reef swam an array of tropical fish.

She glanced around the room. The ceiling reached over twenty feet high. There were two very large sculptures on either side of the room. They were of dolphins breaching the surface, waves curling up the sides of their bodies.

A beautiful voice lilted in Sara's ears, singing words she didn't understand. She turned to see who was singing. A young Dagonian, about her age, hovered nearby. Black, intricate braids floated in a halo around her head. The Dagonian woman's face was breathtaking. Her eyes were dark, her skin the color of toffee. She held Sara's braided hair in her hands. When their gazes met, the Dagonian woman blinked, and then her eyes widened in horror. Unfamiliar words burst from her mouth just before she let go of Sara's hair and darted out the door. The flowing swish of a blue tail floated out behind her.

Was this a dream? She looked like a mermaid. Her tail was different from Sara's—blue, not flesh colored. And it was much more beautiful. Xanthus was wrong when he said her fin was perfect. It was much too plain.

Sara chided herself. This was not the time to go all self-conscious about her tail. Her stomach was throbbing with pain, letting Sara know she wasn't dead and she wasn't dreaming.

She needed to get out of here.

Sara tried to swim, but she couldn't get her fin to work right. She jerked her way toward the door. Each stroke of her tail brought sharp pains in her belly. She knew she had to hurry—the woman was probably going to get her big husband or maybe the police.

Just as Sara was about to go through the door, she was met by someone frightening—the woman's sister. At least, Sara assumed it was her sister. She was a close likeness to the woman who'd left, except she had cinnamon-brown braids. Now that Sara got a good look at the both of them, she was in awe. They both had tails complete with colorful scales. Their fins were long, flowing, and delicate. To top off their look, fin-shaped bikini tops covered their breasts like colorful butterfly wings. The two Dagonian women were much more beautiful than any image of a mermaid Sara had ever seen.

She almost smiled at the stunning sight. Then she looked the brown-haired woman in the eye and was startled. She was staring Sara down with a hard glare.

Sara braced for what was to come. The brown-haired Dagonian turned to her sister and spoke in clipped tones. She seemed satisfied about something. Maybe satisfied was too strong a word. More like resigned. She probably realized that Sara was not a threat and was completely inept at being in the water.

The brown-haired woman gestured toward

Sara. Her brunette sister hesitated a moment before she slowly approached. They each hooked an arm through Sara's arms and floated her back to where they'd kept her before.

The brown-haired sister spoke to Sara, as if giving her instructions. Sara didn't understand a word of it. She looked at Sara as if expecting an answer.

"I'm sorry. I don't understand."

The Dagonian gasped. "You speak English?"

Sara's eyes widened. From what Xanthus had told her, very few Dagonians spoke English. Who was she?

"You're human?" she whispered.

Sara knew Xanthus wouldn't approve of her telling anyone she was human, but this Dagonian had already most likely figured it out. If the Dagonian knew she spoke English and had the cursed blue eyes, it didn't take a genius to figure it out. Sara hesitated only a moment before she nodded. "Half," she said.

The brown-haired Dagonian barked out foreign words to her sister. Sara could tell they were talking about her. They looked as if they didn't know what to do with her. Sara hoped they would let her go. It couldn't hurt to ask.

"I need to return to the surface." Sara pointed up.

"You live with humans?" the brown-haired Dagonian asked.

"Yes, I do. I keep my fin hidden from them so they don't know what I am. But still, I need to get back."

The woman nodded, apparently relieved. "Yes, you safer there. But you heal first. You died."

Sara assumed she meant she almost died, since Sara clearly wasn't dead now. But she didn't *want* to wait to heal. Xanthus had to be worried sick. If she was gone long, he'd assume she was dead.

"I have to go now. I can't wait."

The brown-haired sister shook her head. "Drink first." She handed Sara what looked like a mermaid's purse with a narrow tube. "You heal faster."

Sara was willing to do anything to appease these Dagonian women and get back to dry land—and a phone. She took it. The bitter-tasting drink didn't go down well. Still, she drank the whole thing and handed it back to her.

"Thank you. So how... Do I..."

Funny, Sara couldn't remember what she was just saying. Her mind felt hazy. A giggle escaped her lips. Now, what was it she needed to do?

"A nap, that's what I need to do. I need to take a nap."

Sara awoke. Her stomach churned and grumbled, hunger twisting it painfully. She needed food. She peeled her eyes open to darkness. Obviously, it was now night. Those deceitful Dagonian women had drugged her. How much time had passed? Xanthus had to be frantic. She needed to get to him.

Looking around, Sara tried to get her bearings. She was still in the same room. It was quite spectacular at night. The walls had a luminescent quality. A faint green glow came from the walls, illuminating the room. There was cloth covering the windows. The sheen of the cloth had the appearance of crushed pearls. They were held in place by rods at the top and the bottom of the windows.

Something covered Sara's body from her tail fin up to her neck. She looked around and realized she was sandwiched in soft, plush fabric stretched across two intricately carved pillars. The cloth brushed her body gently as she swam, easing out of the fabric. This must be the Dagonian version of a bed. They didn't need anything to cushion their sleep; they just needed something to keep from floating about the room.

Sara swam to the open door and peered out into a hallway. She couldn't see anyone out there. She did see that at the end of the hallway, the floor sloped downward. She must be upstairs. She swam out of the room, then down, following the slope. The stone along the slope was carved to resemble interlocking tentacles. This must be a Dagonian version of a staircase.

Sara hurried; she needed to get out. She felt a bit guilty about leaving so abruptly. She hadn't even had a chance to thank them. But she had to get back to dry land. She couldn't waste any more time. If the Dagonians were smart, they'd be glad to be rid of her.

Sara reached the lower level and jerked to a stop

when she heard a voice. "Going somewhere?" The words were clear and well spoken.

Sara turned to see the black-haired sister. "I... Well... I'm sorry. I do have to be going. I thank you for all you and your sister have done for me."

"Sister?" She swam toward Sara and, with a swish of her tail, stopped just in front of her. "Oh, you mean my mother."

"She's your mother? But you both look the same age." The Dagonian smiled at her. "I forget how humans age. We Dagonians don't age after adulthood."

Sara drifted back a bit, nervous at being so close to this Dagonian woman. She was stunning. Her eyes were dark, wide, and full of expression. She seemed to be tall or long, however they described it, and she was wafer thin.

"I'm Adelpha, by the way. And my mother is Chara. She's been the one caring for you." She glanced around, nervously. "She's worried about me being around a half-human." She said this as if Sara should know what she meant. After spending so much time with Xanthus, she kind of did.

"I'm Sara."

"Are you a princess then?" Adelpha's eyebrows rose.

Sara smiled in surprise and shook her head. "No, I'm not. Why would you think I'm a princess?"

"Sara means princess in Atlantian. So you really grew up among them? The humans? Are they as terrible as everyone says? Are humans all murdering, filthy creatures? You look so normal. You must have strong Dagonian genes. But I have to say your eyes are very strange." Adelpha looked at Sara as if she were some supernatural being.

Sara nervously moved to tuck her hair behind her ear, which was pointless underwater. Her fingers brushed over a small, floating braid. Adelpha didn't seem to notice her silly action.

"Humans, for the most part, are loving and caring people," Sara said. "There are some that murder and do other terrible things, but we put them in prisons to keep the rest of us safe."

Adelpha's jaw dropped. "That's just what we do. Are all humans as beautiful as you are? I was told they were vile and ugly. But I must say you would turn quite a few heads down here."

"Well, thank you. And yes, there are many more beautiful women than me. My mother is human and very beautiful. I'm told I'm the exact image of her."

"Wow, it makes me wonder if all the tales I hear about humans are false." Adelpha shook her head, the braids floating around her head waved with the movement.

"I would think most are," Sara said, "but from what I see of you and your sister, Dagonian women are stunning. Just look at your tail fins. Mine is so plain compared to yours."

Adelpha's brows crinkled in confusion and then

her eyes lightened in understanding. She laughed. "These are not our natural fins. They are coverings, something like human clothing. Our true fins look just like yours."

"What beautiful clothing," Sara said.

"Are you not happy with yours? I could get you something else to wear." Adelpha looked Sara up and down.

Sara followed her eyes down and gasped. She was dressed just as beautifully as Adelpha. Her tail seemed to be made of shiny silver scales that reflected rainbow colors and sparkled like magic. The fabric covered her breasts, hugged her waist, and covered her all the way to end of her fin. Her fin fanned out and looked like mist. "Oh, wow," Sara said. She'd never worn anything so amazing.

"I hope you don't mind your stomach being covered. I didn't think you'd wanted anyone to see your wound. If you don't like your covering I could..."

"Oh no, I love it, Adelpha. It's so beautiful."

Adelpha looked pleased with her response.

Sara wished that Xanthus could see her. At that thought, she frowned. "Listen, Adelpha, I appreciate everything you and your mother have done for me. I mean if it weren't for you, I'd be dead. I could never repay you, but I have to get back to the surface. My fiancé has to be worried sick. He probably thinks I'm dead."

"You're getting married to a human? But you can't. Oh dear, I didn't even think of all the complications in your life."

Oh dear was right. How was Sara ever going to explain to Adelpha that she was marrying a Dagonian that was now living on dry land and that he was going to bring her back down here where she didn't belong? She didn't belong anywhere, did she?

"Regardless of how complicated it is," Sara said, "my fiancé loves me for who I am and I love him, too, more than my own life."

Adelpha's face softened and she shrugged. "How can I argue with that? But getting to the surface is not as easy as it seems. If anyone sees you... Well, it wouldn't be good for you. I'm just glad my brothers aren't here. I don't want to scare you, but if either one of them were to find you, they'd arrest you and take you to the counsel. You could even get executed.

"You see, our kind has no tolerance for interbreeding with humans. My mom and I debated whether to keep helping you after we found out you were human. But ultimately, we decided we had no choice. We couldn't just let you die. Besides, you looked so sweet and helpless." She smiled, "To tell you the truth, I'm not sure my youngest brother would take you to be killed. You are such a pretty thing and he may seem tough on the outside, but inside he's quite sweet."

"I have question for you," Sara said. "Where did you learn to speak English so well?"

Adelpha smiled, a sly glimmer in her eyes. "My brother is fascinated with humans. He knows many human languages—funny how humans need more than one. But he said that English is the most universal language, so he taught us. I took to it more quickly than my mother did. She still struggles with it."

"Do many other Dagonians..."

"Adelpha, breakfast please." Sara looked up and saw Adelpha's mother, Chara. She didn't look too pleased with their conversation.

"Yes, Mother," Adelpha said. She swam through a nearby doorway.

"You feel well?" Chara spoke in chopped, halting words.

Sara hadn't even thought about it. Her injury didn't seem to be bothering her anymore. "I feel fine. How long have I been here?"

"Three days," Chara said.

"What? How could I?"

"You sleep."

"Did you drug me the whole time?" Sara asked, incensed.

"Drug?"

"The drink that makes me sleeps."

"Oh no, only yesterday, First two days you sleep. You heal well. Nearly..." she couldn't seem to find the word, "done healing."

Three days. Sara was sick, thinking about how long she had been missing. Still, it wasn't this Dagonian's fault. "Thank you Chara, for your help. But I must be going. I have to get back to the surface."

"You live with humans?"

Here we go again. "Yes, and I need to return."

"Eat first."

Sara's stomach screamed for food, but still she hesitated. She desperately needed to get to Xanthus. However, she would need her strength for the journey ahead. "Okay," she said. "But then I must go."

Chara nodded. "Then you go."

Chara led Sara to a room that she guessed served as the dining area. In the middle of a large, warmly lit room, there sat a very wide, cylinder aquarium with dozens of colorful fish swimming around inside. The top of the case shimmered like there was some sort of force field. When a little blue fish swam at it, it bulged for a moment, but the fish was deflected.

"Sara, I hope these fish are to your liking. I don't know what kind you're used to, so I brought in a wide variety."

Oh my goodness. What was she supposed to do with them? Sara looked at Adelpha and Chara, expectantly. She'd reasoned that she could just watch them and do what they did. But they looked to her as if she needed to go first.

She guessed it would be easiest just to be honest. "I have to tell you that I have no idea how to catch and eat fish."

They both gasped. Adelpha spoke, "Oh, my goodness. Do you eat land animals?" She looked a bit green as she considered the possibility.

"I do eat fish also, but only after someone else

catches them for me." Sara reached out to brush her fingers over the force field. It felt like soft Jell-O.

Adelpha sighed in relief. "Oh. Now that I can do. Which one would you like?"

Sara looked at the variety, but none of the fish looked anything like what she'd gotten in the grocer's case. Sara didn't want Adelpha to feel as if she'd worked for nothing, so she picked one.

Sara pointed to a small, rounded fish with blue stripes. "This one looks good."

"Oh, yes. The blue ring angel fish is one of my favorite too." As the fish swam near Adelpha, she snapped out her hand and snagged it. The fish squirmed in her hand just before she broke its neck, twisted off the head, and placed the severed head back in the tank. The other fish darted over to the floating head and began to nibble. Now she knew where Xanthus got his table manners.

Adelpha handed the headless body to Sara and smiled.

"Thank you," Sara said. Okay, no fillets. She could deal with it. Not wanting to offend them, Sara took a bite into its side. The scales felt strange but as soon as her teeth reached flesh, the delicious flavor exploded in her mouth. This fish tasted much better than anything she'd ever eaten before. Maybe it was because she was so hungry, but Sara couldn't imagine anything could taste so amazing. She had to force herself not to devour the thing like an animal, so she concentrated on chewing slowly.

"This is very good," Sara said after she swallowed.

Adelpha smiled wide. "They are, aren't they? I also love the hermit crabs," she said as she reached deep in the tank and picked up a shell from the bottom, extracting a small crab and popping it whole into her mouth. She threw the empty shell back into the tank.

Sara looked over to Chara and saw her breaking off the head of a small moray eel. Wow, were all Dagonians super strong? Chara was not careful at all as she took large bites out of the side of the eel and chomped on the meat.

"Which one would you like next?" Adelpha took the flesh-stripped carcass from Sara's hands and lowered it into the tank.

"Why don't you let me try to catch one?" Sara asked.

Adelpha smiled. "Sure, but don't be disappointed if you cannot. Our young take several years to master fish catching."

Sara looked around the tank. Let's see, what she needed was an extremely slow fish. Around the other side of the tank, she saw a jellyfish. It moved slowly enough for her. Sara saw Chara move to another side of the tank and snatch a tiny fish. She guessed she didn't need to stay put, so she moved over to the jellyfish.

"Be careful..." Adelpha said.

Before she could finish her warning, Sara reached in and grabbed the slow moving jellyfish around its tentacles. It felt as if she'd grabbed a hot curling iron. She screeched and jerked her hand out of the tank. She held her burning hand close to her chest, careful not to touch the singed flesh.

"Oh, Sara, I'm sorry. I shouldn't have let you... Mom?"

Sara hadn't even realized Chara had left, but as she turned toward her, she saw her swimming back into the room carrying a green blob of jelly in a sheer bag. She looked at Sara as Atlantian rolled off her tongue like an avalanche. Sara had a feeling Chara was saying something about what an idiot she was.

Even so, Chara took Sara's hand and smeared the jelly across her palm. The relief was instantaneous. It felt cool and soothing. "Thank you," she said.

A bump came from the front of the house. It sounded like a door opening. Chara and Adelpha looked at each other with eyes wide and then they looked at Sara.

Chara barked out orders in Atlantian to Adelpha. Adelpha grabbed Sara by the arm and led her toward a small door. She opened it and shoved Sara inside. "Don't say a word," Adelpha whispered. "Keep completely quiet." She eased the door shut. Sara was left inside a small closet. She was only too willing to do as Adelpha asked. The last thing she needed was to end up in prison, or worse, dead.

Sara eased over to the door and pressed her ear against it. She heard another door closing, and then she couldn't hear a thing. She sat in silence, listening to her own watery breaths. Something soft and slimy brushed against her arm. She jumped, knocking into who knows what and making a loud clatter. Oh shoot.

She heard the door to the dining room slam open. "Why are you lying to me? Who are you hiding? I can smell her, Adelpha." Xanthus. It sounded just like Xanthus.

"Come now, brother, it's only a friend of mine who's just left," Adelpha said.

"And pray tell me why a female would be traveling around visiting friends during her time." Could it really be Xanthus? Maybe all Dagonian men sounded like him.

"She didn't know," Adelpha said. "She must not have realized it was her time," Adelpha remarked again, "and you know *we* couldn't have told her. Only males can recognize when it's a female's time."

The door to Sara's closet swished opened and she found herself face to face with an angry, ferocious warrior.

TWENTY-FIVE

Sara was so surprised to see Xanthus, that she sat frozen with her mouth agape. As surprised as she was, he looked a hundred times more shocked.

"Xanthus," Sara said and swam straight toward him.

Xanthus enveloped her into his strong arms. "Sara," he said. "Great gods of Olympus, you're alive."

Sara felt his trembling body surround her and she began to cry.

"Shh, Moro Mou." His voice was low, tormented, and aching for her. "Don't cry, Mou."

As if she could stop. She hadn't let herself truly embrace the reality of her situation until now. It had all been too frightening, too terrifying to face head on, but now that she was safe in his arms, she was overwhelmed with relief. Somewhere deep in the subconscious of her mind, she had believed she would never see him again. Now, tight in Xanthus's embrace, breathing in his warm, masculine in scent, she couldn't hold back the tears. A miracle had occurred and he was here.

Sara found her attention was turned a few minutes later when she couldn't breathe. Xanthus was squeezing the breath out of her. "Xanthus, you're holding me too tight," she gasped. He lessened his grip, allowing her to breathe again.

When Sara was recovered enough to think, she pondered her great fortune. This was his family. She couldn't believe she was here with his family. What were the odds of that?

His sister whispered in Atlantian and Xanthus jerked back. "What? You're injured? Where? Show me."

Sara looked down. There was a barely noticeable seam just below her belly button. She lifted up her shirt at the seam to show her belly and blanched at her own injury. It was long, red, and stitched with many stripes of black thread. "I guess any future of me being a bikini model is gone."

Xanthus was not amused by her jest. He looked enraged. "He did this to you?" he asked. Sara guessed he was talking about Gael, but didn't want to alert his family about his brother's involvement.

"Yes, he was trying to get the sharks to attack me. But they didn't."

"No, they didn't," Adelpha whispered with wonder in her voice. "The sharks brought her to us."

"What?" Xanthus and Sara said together.

Adelpha nodded as her eyes darted back and forth between them, "It's true. It was the most amazing thing I've ever seen. What do you think it means, brother?"

Xanthus looked at Sara, narrowing his eyes as he studied her. Then his eyes flew open wide, as if he'd just had an epiphany. He paused a long time before speaking. "I think I know, but I can't speak of it yet."

Xanthus shook his head as if shaking himself back to reality. "We need to move. Adelpha, Mother, we need to get Sara to the tunnels. It can't be a coincidence that she ended up in *my* home. Others will be coming."

Xanthus towed Sara down the hall to a huge room. It looked to be sleeping quarters. Given the immense size of the room, it had to be the master bedroom. He swam over to a stone picture with a landscape scene of a tropical island. Just below it was a border of scrolled carvings. He pressed down on a raised swirl. Sara felt the soft compression in the water as a section of the wall collapsed in, and then slid open without a sound, revealing a dark tunnel.

"When was this tunnel constructed?" Adelpha asked, surprised. Obviously, she hadn't known about it until just now.

"The same time as the others," Xanthus said. "I just never told anyone about it. Lucky I didn't. I never knew I'd need it to hide someone from my own family."

"Gael?" Adelpha asked.

"He is a soldier. He would be duty-bound to bring her in."

Adelpha nodded, satisfied with his answer.

Xanthus closed the door panel behind them. At first, the difference was so dramatic that Sara thought the tunnel had no light. But as her eyes adjusted, she saw a faint glow from the tunnel walls. It seemed to go on forever, twisting and turning. A door came into view along the way. Xanthus opened it and led the way inside to a chamber.

"Diamo," Xanthus spoke low and the room was filled with light. There was sparse, strange furniture. Sara recognized a sleeping thing-a-ma-jig and there looked to be a wall of bookshelves filled with leathery books strapped inside. She seriously needed to learn Atlantian. Another wall was a giant aquarium. Fish of all shapes and colors swam in this fish tank and the wall shimmered like the surface of the tank in the dining room.

Xanthus turned to face Sara. He cradled her cheeks in his palms in a gentle demand to have her attention. "Now Sara, I'd hoped to prepare for this before bringing you home. But now that you're here, I'll have to make some minor changes in my plan."

Xanthus turned toward Chara, who was looking around the secret room. "Mother, I'm going to need you to bring the priest. Don't go back through my room. Just follow the tunnel through to the exit."

Adelpha turned in surprise. "Why do we need a priest, brother? You can see Sara is not going to die."

"No, but until the priest comes, she's still at risk."

Chara snarled as she rushed forward to Xanthus. He let Sara go and turned to confront his mother. Chara bellowed, shouting at her son, and then she turned a glaring eye at Sara.

What in the world had she done?

Xanthus responded with snarling, brutal words of his own. He also moved in close, towering over Chara as if he were trying to intimidate her.

"I was right," Adelpha whispered in Sara's ear. "My brother wouldn't have turned you over to be executed."

"What are they arguing about?"

"My brother is just reminding my mother that he is the master of this castle and she needs to respect his position."

"But she's his mother. Shouldn't it be the other way around?"

Adelpha smiled. "Of course not. You humans have strange ways. In this case, I agree with Xanthus. Mother is trying to tell him not to marry you."

"Wait. Is that what they are arguing about?"

"Oh yes."

"But why is it so important for him to marry me now? And why is she so against it?"

"He needs to marry you now in order to protect you. You see, a husband is responsible for his wife. And that includes any crime she commits. If a wife commits a crime, the husband serves the sentence."

"That's crazy. So if I am caught, Xanthus would receive my punishment?"

"Yes." Adelpha frowned.

"Well, shoot, if that's the case, I'm never going to marry him."

Adelpha raised an eyebrow. "You speak as if you

have a choice."

"I don't?"

"Well, does your father approve of this marriage?"

"I don't even know who my father is." Sara shrugged.

"What about your grandfather or brother?"

"I don't have a brother and I've never met my grandfather." What was this, the middle ages? Didn't women have a say in something as important as marriage?

"Well then, you don't have any say in the matter," Adelpha said, setting her straight.

Good grief. Dagonians could use some serious women's liberation.

"Don't worry, Sara. My brother is very kind. He'll treat you well."

"It's not me I'm worried about. If I'm caught, he's going to end up in prison or dead. I couldn't live with myself if anything bad happened to him because of me."

"Sara, I think you're worried over nothing. My brother is extremely clever. If anyone can figure out a solution to this problem, my brother can."

Sara glanced back to the heated argument. Chara threw her hands out and shook her head as she looked toward the ceiling. Frustrated words tumbled out of her mouth. Then, with a swish of her tail, she left.

Xanthus swam toward Sara. "Sara, I'm sorry about my mother. She'll come around."

"Is it true that you intend to marry me now in order for you to take the punishment of my crime?"

"Sara..."

"I won't let you do it!"

Xanthus turned to his sister. "Adelpha, would you let us speak in private?"

Adelpha cleared her throat. A smile tugged at her lips. "Sure, brother," she said and left. Sara wondered for a moment where she'd go. To roam the tunnel maybe.

"Sara, we already talked about this. I *will* keep you safe." Xanthus pulled her near and pressed his lips against her forehead.

"You never said that by being my husband that *you* would be the one executed. You could die because of me."

"Sara, you need to trust me. We can make this work."

"No, we can't. I can't gamble your life like that."

"Yet, you thought I would gamble yours when I brought you here? Sara, it goes both ways. Your safety is my top priority, but I'll also tell you this. I have no intention of going to prison. Now, I'm going to ask you again. Sara, will you please be my wife?"

Sara looked up into his handsome face. His dark eyes were filled with love and he was looking at her. It still amazed her that she had captured the heart of such an amazing man—or Dagonian. How could someone so wonderful love a human like her? Wait a minute. She hadn't told him she probably wasn't half-Dagonian after all. Sara didn't want to tell him, but she couldn't enter into a marriage with that kind of lie between them.

"I have to tell you something first. And after I do, you may not want to marry me after all."

Xanthus looked surprised. Well, he was about to be even more surprised. "I'm not a Dagonian. I'm not even half-Dagonian."

"How do you know?" He was calm. He certainly didn't look surprised. Sara didn't know what to think of that.

"My mother told me about my father."

"And what did she say?"

Curiosity burned in his eyes. "She said he had blue eyes. He also had human legs, like you do, when on land. She thinks she saw a fin as he swam away, but she wasn't sure. If she's wrong, I could be all-human. But, even if she's right... You said Triton gave you the ability to change on land. So if my father had blue eyes, legs on land, and a fin in the water, it has to mean something. I don't know what, but I mean... Don't you think it means something?"

"Yes, it does mean something. Sara, I don't want you to repeat what you told me to anyone. I have to straighten a few things out first. So until then, I'm telling you to say nothing about your father—no matter what happens."

"So you understand that I'm not a Dagonian?" Sara asked.

"Yes, I agree you're not a Dagonian." He took her face in his hands and pressed his soft lips to hers. When he pulled away, he looked at her as if he were in awe.

"But you're not human either. You're a mermaid."

"What? But I thought they were extinct?"

"They were. Poseidon ordered them all destroyed."

"But then where did I come from? Who is my father?"

"We spoke of this once before, but I dare not repeat it now until I know the details."

"My father is Triton, isn't he?" She spoke the realization as soon as it came to her mind.

"Shh." He took a quick glance behind him, as if he expected someone to be eavesdropping. He turned back and sighed. "Yes, he is your father. But Sara, it's very important that you keep this to yourself and tell no one. Do you understand?"

"No, I don't understand, but I'll do as you say."

"Good girl."

Anger clouded his features. "Now, I need to know exactly what happened to you after my brother took you from your mother's home."

"Why do you need to know? It's over now," Sara said, not wanting to relive the horror.

"Sara, just tell me."

"Okay, but I'd really rather not talk about it."

Xanthus scowled when Sara hesitated.

"Where do you want to me to begin?" She braced herself for the nightmare.

"Start at the beginning."

So she did. Sara told Xanthus everything that

had happened at her house and about how Gael had knocked her unconscious. She told him that when she awoke, she found herself in a cage next to a shark. Xanthus didn't look too happy with that statement, but he let her continue. When she told him his brother wanted to have some fun with her before he killed her, Xanthus looked appalled.

"Did he touch you?"

"No. He said he'd as soon mate with a sea cow than a human. I guess I should have been insulted, but I was very relieved."

Xanthus seemed to share her relief.

"What he meant was he wanted to torture me."

Xanthus's eyes narrowed. He looked like he was about to explode. But he held his composure and his tongue.

"He wasn't very successful at the torture part though. He took my hand and put it through a metal ring between a shark's cage and mine. He meant for the shark to bite off my hand, I suppose. This is the strange part—the shark did come toward me, but only to brush against my hand. I was very frightened at first, but after he gently brushed my hand several times more, I realized the shark was no threat to me."

"No shark would ever harm a mermaid. Sharks are very loyal to Triton."

"That's good to know. Well, then Gael..." Sara looked toward the door and thought that maybe she shouldn't have used his name. Adelpha might be listening.

"Go on."

"He got angry because the shark refused to attack me, so he tried to entice the shark with my blood. He cut me." She showed Xanthus her hand. A red line streaked across three of her knuckles. The cut was healing nicely. Maybe Chara's drink was healing her hand too.

"When cutting my hand didn't work, he got angry, pulled me out of the cage, and carried me out into open waters where other sharks could get me. And that's about it."

Xanthus shook his head. Sara noticed he looked about a decade older, which was still much younger than his actual age, when you thought about it.

"And how, pray tell, did you get the injury in your stomach?" Xanthus raised an eyebrow.

"Oh, I already told you that one, Gael did it." Sara shrugged.

"Tell me again."

"He just stabbed me. I had no warning. I didn't even see the knife until he was pulling it from my belly. Then he said don't worry about his safety; he was going to watch the sharks rip me apart from a safe place. I think that was his sick attempt at a joke. He said he would retrieve my body when I was dead, and then he swam away. Everything after that was a bit hazy. I don't think I was conscious for very long, and when I woke up, I was here."

Xanthus looked at Sara, conflict raging in his

eyes. He pulled her into his arms. "Sara, as soon as we are wed, I'm going to leave you here for a short time. I will make Gael pay for what he did to you. And, this time, I won't make the mistake of leaving him alive. Then I have business to take care of. But I will be back as soon as I can."

"Business? Right after we're married? But won't we have our honeymoon?" Okay, the thought of the honeymoon scared her a bit, being a virgin and all. But darn it, a woman wanted to feel irresistible and Xanthus seemed to think business was more important. Sara found herself feeling undesirable.

"Yes. We will," he said as he leaned forward. His eyes darkened when he wrapped his arms around her and pulled her hard against his body. Sara gasped. Xanthus took advantage of her open mouth and kissed her, passion driving him. This kiss was a different— more intense, more exiting, and it fairly overwhelmed her. Xanthus had always showed a certain amount of restraint when he touched her, but this time he nearly lost control, bordering on desperation.

Xanthus suddenly froze. He tore his mouth away from hers as he pushed her away, his breathing ragged and his jaw clenched. Sara used every ounce of strength in an attempt to hold him close. It didn't make a bit of difference. He was too strong.

"Do you understand now how much I want you?" he asked.

Sara had a hard time processing what he was

saying. That kiss had rendered her unable to form a coherent thought. When she realized what he'd asked, she nodded, amazed. As much as she wanted their honeymoon, he wanted it more.

"I'm sorry," he said. "I shouldn't have kissed you. The closer we get to our wedding, the harder it is. You're still healing. You need to rest, not be assaulted."

Sara smiled and reached out to take his hand. "I like being assaulted by you."

He answered her with a scowl.

"You didn't hurt me."

"I could have." His eyes were saddened by regret. "You should get some sleep before the priest comes."

Right, the wedding. Sara couldn't believe she was getting married today. "I wish Gretchen and my mother... Oh my gosh, they have to be worried sick. Xanthus, how are we going to let them know I'm all right?"

"Don't worry, Mou. I'll call them while you sleep."

"How can you call from here?" Sara looked around but didn't see anything that resembled a phone.

"I have a dry room with a satellite phone down here. I'll show you where it is and you'll be able to call anyone anytime you like."

"Oh, wow."

The corner of his mouth tugged, almost smiling. "There you go wowing me with your lips again." Then his almost smile turned into a scowl. "You'd better not be fertile when I get back. Now's not the best time to bring a baby into the mix. But so help me, a Dagonian can only wait so long."

Xanthus dimmed the lights for her and left her to sleep before the priest came.

As if she could sleep right before her wedding. Not a chance.

TWENTY-SIX

Xanthus and Sara were married just a few minutes after she awoke.

Sara had to admit, she'd never dreamed that one day she'd get married in a dark tunnel that looked like something out of the *Phantom of the Opera*, wearing a borrowed, mermaid-like costume with a mother-in-law that looked as if she wished her dead. But a girl can't have everything, right?

Her mother-in-law's eyes pinned her with daggers throughout the ceremony. Sara just knew that if Chara could change the past, she would have let her die from her knife wound. The way she was looking at her, Sara didn't doubt Chara now wanted something along the lines of clawing her eyes out.

It was some consolation that Adelpha seemed to be pleased with the marriage. Sara guessed two out of four wasn't bad. Xanthus and Adelpha wanted her. On the other hand, Chara and Gael wanted her dead. That was a bit more extreme than most families.

The priest fidgeted as he stumbled his way through the ceremony. He couldn't bring himself to look Sara in the eye and then he left immediately after. Xanthus told her the priest was honor-bound not to reveal her location to anyone, even the law. He answered to the gods alone. Sara wondered if Xanthus had had to threaten him in order to convince him to marry them. Heavens, she hoped not.

The ceremony passed with Sara in a daze. She had answered "Vei" (the Atlantian version of yes) when Xanthus signaled. He'd then placed a gold ring on her finger, kissed her, and she was a married woman. Or mermaid. Whatever she was, she was a married one.

Sara had no idea what she'd vowed to do in this marriage.

When the wedding was finished, Adelpha and Chara didn't linger, but left immediately, leaving Sara and Xanthus alone.

"So what did I actually agree to?" Sara asked Xanthus. "I don't have to swim naked through the streets of Atlantis now, do I?"

He laughed and pulled her into his arms, "No, thank the gods. Do you have any idea how many men I'd have to kill if you did that?" He smirked. "You simply agreed to see to my every want and need, including scrubbing barnacles from my tail."

Sara was glad to see he was in better spirits now. "Is that something like grooming an old person's gnarly, fungus toenails?" She scrunched up her nose at the thought.

"Something like that." He chuckled. His smiling

lips brushed over hers. "Seriously, you agreed to something on the order of loving, cherishing, obeying, and being faithful to me."

"Oh, that's not so bad. But do I have to obey you? Like everything you say?" Sara thought about how different his culture was from hers, where women didn't have much say in their lives. She was a bit nervous about how much freedom she *would* have.

Xanthus's eyes softened. "Dagonian women are subject to their husbands and must always obey them. But I understand you come from a different culture. I will do my best to ask things of you and not give you orders. You may ask the same of me. Does that ease your mind?"

Sara nodded and looked up into his eyes. Her throat constricted when she realized how lucky she was. She couldn't say her dreams had come true. Sara had never dreamed anything half this good.

She wrapped her arms around Xanthus neck. "I love you."

Xanthus held her tightly against his body and his eyes burned so hot she felt scorched. "I love you too, Sara Dimitriou. I never knew love could be this strong. I swear to you that I will do everything in my power to keep you safe."

His lips lingered over hers.

"Don't you want to kiss me?" she asked, wondering at his hesitation.

"I don't trust myself to merely kiss you. I now

have one less reason for waiting to... to... Hades, I need to leave before I forget my reasons for waiting."

A thunderous crash from beyond the room echoed through the door and interrupted their interlude. Her feelings turned from intense desire to quick fear as she squeaked out a cry.

In that moment, Sara was looking at Xanthus's broad back. "Sara, wait here. I'll be..."

A thunderous voice bellowed in Atlantian. It was a voice of anger, a voice that promised violence to anyone that crossed it.

"Who is it? What do they want?" she asked.

"It's my father," Xanthus said.

TWENTY-SEVEN

"Xanthus, where is the cur? Where is that filthy cur? Your mother sent me a message, telling me what you were trying to do. And we on the counsel cannot allow this. I cannot allow this. Bring her to us now and you will go free. If you try to protect her, you will die."

Xanthus knew Sara couldn't understand a word of what was being said. Still, she had to be terrified. There was no mistaking that kind of anger.

Xanthus rushed to a large trunk, removed an arsenal of weapons, and began strapping them to his body. Sara was frozen, too shocked to move.

"Come, brother," Gael's voice joined his father's. *"I've told them how she seduced you. I've told them of her power. We know you are blameless. Just bring her out to us and you will be spared."*

His father spoke again. *"We understand you tried to marry this human witch. But your mother saved you from that unholy union. The priest was not a true priest. You are not married. You do not have to accept this witch's punishment. You are not bound to her."*

"Xanthus, what are they saying?" Sara asked.

"They're here for me, aren't they? Your mother told them. You need to let me go. Maybe they won't hurt you if you do. We don't have to tell them we are married."

"No," he shouted. "I will not turn you over. You don't have any idea what awaits you."

"Death?" she asked boldly.

"Death is the easy part. What comes before death is the bigger worry."

"*Xanthus,*" his father shouted. "*I have my personal army standing by my side. You will find no friends among them. There is no one to help you here. If you cannot break from this witch's spell, they will not hesitate to kill you, son. You need to try to break from it. You must bring her to us.*"

Xanthus was relieved that he would not have to kill any friends today. He had no respect for his father's soldiers. They were heartless killers, each one. His father was careful when choosing those who fought alongside him.

Xanthus led Sara into the tunnel.

"Sara, I will protect you. But you must do what I say. If I say move, do it without question. If I say stay, don't move. I must know where you are at all times."

"But..."

"Sara, if you don't, you put us both in danger."

"Okay, okay. I'll do it. But I really think you should turn me in."

Xanthus growled. "That's not going to happen. Keep close to me and trust me to protect you. This is what I do."

Xanthus pulled her in for a quick, crushing kiss. "I love you, Sara, never mistake that. And whatever happens, I will do all within my power to make you safe."

"Should I tell them about my father?"

"No," Xanthus snapped. "Whatever you do, don't do that. Your life would be worth nothing. No, just keep quiet and if worse comes to worst, I will figure out a way to get word to your father. Now follow me."

Xanthus moved as quickly as he dared. Sara still wasn't a very strong swimmer. His tail brushed against her outstretched hands while they swam through the tunnel. The light grew brighter as they neared the exit. He knew that the bulk of the army would be meeting them there. His mother would have told them where the exit was. She'd obviously let his father and the others into his castle. He couldn't chance going through it. He'd made it nearly impenetrable, but that also meant that getting out would be a problem.

So the place of battle would be amongst the coral.

Xanthus smelled the soldiers before he saw them. There were three of them ahead in the tunnel. He drew his weapon. It was a butterfly dart gun that could shoot two dozen tiny, poison-tipped darts. The moment they were in range, he fired. He heard cries and grunts from the Dagonians.

Xanthus and Sara swam toward the exit of the tunnel, passing by the floating corpses of the three Dagonians. He slowed his approach, grabbed Sara's hand, and pulled her against his body as they hugged the side of the tunnel.

The light was blinding as they reached the mouth of the cave. Xanthus tucked Sara behind his back. He could feel her jump when the army sounded a battle cry.

Sara focused on breathing steadily and not panicking. The last thing Xanthus needed right now was her falling to pieces.

"Stay here," he ordered, and then he was gone. She heard the clanking of metal as she felt currents of water pushing her from one side to the other, and from above. As her eyes adjusted to the light, Sara saw Xanthus flying like a ghost through the water. He clashed with Dagonian after Dagonian as they came at him one after the other. Each warrior's face was contorted with rage, anger, and bloodlust.

Xanthus clutched a trident in one hand and a sword in the other. He met and deflected each strike, each spear, even each harpoon that was being shot from a distance. Sara had no idea how skilled a warrior Xanthus was until now. Countless soldiers surrounded him, yet they couldn't land one strike against him. But every blow delivered by Xanthus met its mark, slashing flesh, and dismembering limbs.

Sara was sickened when Xanthus took the head off one soldier and then in the same swipe, the armed hand of another. Red, billowing clouds filled the water.

Rising

Out of the clouds, Sara saw a spear come straight for her head. She screamed—fear and horror driving her wailing cry. Xanthus deflected the spear at the last second.

A moment later, the sounds of battle ceased. Sara continued to scream as she felt an arm clamp around her waist and a hand slap over her mouth.

Then there was silence.

The fighting must have been over, given the stony silence. That could only mean one thing—Xanthus was dead.

TWENTY-EIGHT

"Greetings, brother." Xanthus barely heard Gael's shout over the ringing in his ears. He emerged from the crimson cloud to find his brother with a small spear gun pointed at Sara's temple. Xanthus caught Sara's eye. The relief that came over her face was overwhelming. He had no idea why she was relieved, given the fact that he'd failed her.

"Her scream packs a punch down here, doesn't it?" Gael said. "It's deafening, literally. I should have known what she was the moment I heard her scream before, but it wasn't until I saw her with the sharks that I knew. And then those beasts wouldn't let me near her."

Xanthus shook his head. The ringing in his ears was deafening. He could barely catch what his brother was saying. But his hearing was the least of his worries. Sara's life hung precariously in the balance. One false move and he knew his brother wouldn't hesitate to kill her. It would be the last thing his brother ever did, but that would be little consolation to Xanthus if Sara were dead.

"The last time she screamed like that," Gael said, "it took me a full two hours before the ringing stopped and my hearing returned. Thank the gods I have some ear plugs this time or I'd be having the same problem again."

The coppery taste of blood was thick in the water. The limbs and bodies of three dozen dead soldiers floated around them in a haze of red. Xanthus had killed nearly all of them. Sara's high, wailing scream had driven the rest of them off. But that didn't make any difference in the end. Xanthus had no choice but to submit to his brother. His mind was working hard to figure out how to get her out of this. Right now, nothing was coming to mind.

If the counsel were honorable, he could tell them what and who Sara was. Honor would demand they turn her over to her father. But the counsel was less than honorable when it came to the Mer. Their hatred ran deep. Telling them Sara was a mermaid would end very badly. The council would be safe from Triton's wrath if he and Sara were both dead. Dead men tell no tales. Yet, if he held his tongue, they would be sent to Panthon Prison to await execution. It would be hell, but at least they would be alive. And while he lived, there was always a chance of escape. Xanthus had never thought so before, but then he'd never been so highly motivated.

"Lead. Brother, you..." Gael spoke too softly for Xanthus to catch every word.

Xanthus shook his head in confusion.

"Oh for the love of..." Gael shouted, "P-a-n-t-h-o-n P-r-i-s-o-n." He enunciated both words loudly and gestured in the direction of the prison. Xanthus understood and nodded. With a lump in his throat, he led them on to their doom. Gael followed, dragging Sara along, his hand clamped over her mouth and the point of the harpoon digging into her temple.

Gael didn't give Xanthus any window of opportunity for escape. Gael was very careful not to loosen his grip or turn his attention from his prisoner. Xanthus knew as long as his brother kept her in close peril, he would have no choice but submit.

On their way to the prison, they were met by other soldiers who surrounded them. One look at Sara's blue eyes and the shouts of outrage began. Xanthus looked up and saw Kyros among the men. His friend was white with shock. Xanthus saw him speak with a guard, who was snarling in anger. Kyros shook his head in disbelief. He gave Xanthus a desperate look. He didn't move for several long minutes. With a sigh, he swam towards Xanthus's home.

If only Xanthus could have given Kyros a message. But they were not alone. He couldn't chance it.

The scene unfolded in horror before him. Word spread quickly that a half-human had been captured. Crowds gathered, lining the road to Panthon Prison. The Dagonians shouted, taunted, and hurled out threats. It took all of Xanthus's control not to retaliate. The only thing he could be thankful for in this situation was the fact that Sara didn't understand the sick and horrific threats they were shouting. But she could see the anger, and she looked terrified.

Sara kept darting desperate glances over to him. He was her only hope. And he couldn't help her. Despair slammed into him and he could scarcely breathe.

Sara smelled the prison long before she saw it. The stench overwhelmed her. The only thing she could compare it to would be the carnival latrines she'd seen as a child. Add to that oozing, rotted meat and multiply it times a thousand and it might come close to the smell.

Sara's eyes widened when she saw the prison. It was enormous, dark, and foreboding. She'd never seen such a stark structure in her life. Wooden spikes stuck out of the ground like porcupine quills surrounding the outer perimeter of the prison. Skulls balanced on many of the sharp points. One of them was obscured by frenzied fish. Sara was sure that she wouldn't want to see what was in the midst of the ravaging fish. She doubted it would be pretty.

"Scary, isn't it? Just wait 'til you get inside." Gael's whispered voice chilled her as they approached the terrifying prison.

"Sara, when I remove my hand from your mouth, you will not scream. If you do, Xanthus will die. If you try to contact anyone outside of the prison, try to escape the prison, or do anything at all to displease me, Xanthus dies. Do you understand? His life is in your hands. You decide if his head is the next one impaled on these spikes."

Sara began to tremble as the full weight of their situation sunk in. She kept her eyes on Xanthus. He looked calm, like he had everything under control. Maybe he had a plan for their escape. She just hoped the plan didn't end up getting him killed.

The guards moved to open the heavy entrance doors. Inside, the dark hallway gaped open like the entrance to hell. Sara sobbed as they entered. She could see Xanthus's calm façade burn away. He struggled against the guards when they led him away from her. He snarled angry, desperate words.

A guard answered with his own rage as he struck him across the face and shouted at him.

Sara gasped as the cruel guard slammed the blunt handle of his spear into Xanthus's back. She wanted to scream at the guard to tell them not to hurt Xanthus. But she remembered, all too well, what Gael had threatened and held her tongue.

"I wouldn't cause any trouble, if I were you." Gael sneered as he spoke to Xanthus. "If you give them any difficulty at all, or if there happens to be any commotion anywhere around you, the guards will alert the warden and he'll kill the half-human immediately."

Sara felt the last shreds of hope peel away with those words.

As soon as Xanthus was gone, Gael pulled Sara up so they were nose to nose. "Enjoy your last day alive, human. Mark my words. You will die soon and I will be the one to deliver the fatal blow. You will yet die by my hand, mermaid," Gael said, and then shoved her into the hands of the guard.

Sara's mind flickered to a thought. Wasn't Xanthus supposed to take her punishment? She clenched her mouth shut, unwilling to remind them and risk Xanthus receiving her punishment. He would probably die anyway for all the soldiers he killed today. And if he died, she wouldn't want to live. She'd welcome death.

A moaning cry escaped her lips as she trembled in fear. Xanthus had told her of the danger she'd face if she were found. But she'd never really thought it possible. Things like this just didn't happen to good, American girls. But here she was, living a reality worse than her most terrifying nightmares.

Sara looked around at the dark, rocky hallway. Green algae swayed like dead, rotting fingers pointing her toward her death.

The guard pulled her along, avoiding her gaze. She had no idea where she was going or what would happen to her. Were they going to torture her before she was executed? She hoped not. She hoped she lived long enough to escape, and even more, she hoped they wouldn't harm Xanthus. Of all the things they could do, that would be the worst.

They snaked their way through winding hallways. The guard stopped as he came upon a door guarded by one small soldier. Well, he was small for a Dagonian. The guard holding her arm spoke to the other guard, who nodded, left for a moment, and then brought back a chain with shackles. He snapped one of the shackles around her fin and then pushed her through the door. A blast of putrid air hit her face as she fell. Her body hit the dry, silted ground several feet below. She coughed as she breathed in the dust her fall had stirred.

The guard remained within the wall of water as his hand reached inside to clamp the other end of the shackle to an iron ring mounted to the wall. Then he shut the door. Sara was chained to the wall inside a dry cell. She lifted her hands off the floor to see them caked with mud. A giggle escaped her lips. So this is the torture they had planned for her? Tears streamed down her face as her giggles turned to sobs.

A familiar voice called out from within the room. "Well, look who's come to join us."

TWENTY-NINE

anthus's blood pulsed in his throat as the guards led him deep into Panthon Prison. The water seemed to thicken and darken. The cells were packed with inmates. Each wore the same expression—a mixture of shock and elation. Half of the criminals here had been brought in by Xanthus. He'd never dreamed he would one day be a prisoner alongside them.

"Oran... Ry..." His voice growled low. "The female is not what she seems. I am giving you fair warning. If you find yourself on the wrong side of this, you will assure your death. And it won't be delivered by me, but by someone infinitely more powerful. But if you help me, you will not go unrewarded."

"Shut up, prisoner," Ry said, poking the point of his harpoon at Xanthus's back, drawing blood.

Rage and despair nearly overcame Xanthus when they reached the deepest prison cells or 'the belly of the beast' as they called it. The cells here were small, so small that a Dagonian couldn't swim, couldn't even move. Each cell was a living coffin. Whether you were put in head first or tail first would determine how much you suffered here.

Tail first—you would still be able to catch the occasional fish that swam close to the bars of your cell. Head first—you had no chance. You'd waste away and die a slow death. Some of the Dagonians down here were nothing more than skin and bones. Their near immortality allowed them to live quite a long while despite their emaciated conditions, but each moment was wrought with a hunger so fierce they were soon driven mad.

Xanthus heard the wailing of other prisoners. He'd always hated this part of the prison. The endless suffering, the way each Dagonian, no matter how strong-willed, succumbed to the misery here was difficult to witness. No one who had been here for any length of time could escape the madness. He knew Sara's only hope was for him to convince one of the guards to help them.

"I will give you one final warning, honorable guards." Xanthus spoke low. "Don't listen to my father, brother, or the counsel on this one. They are wrong, clinging to twisted beliefs. In this case, it will lead to a great number of deaths and suffering for us Dagonians. You don't know who it is you hold in this prison. Help her and you'll find protection, but harm her in any way and there will be no mercy."

Oran turned to Ry. "Maybe we should listen to him. Xanthus has always proven honorable before."

"Are you siding with a cur lover?" Ry shouted

and curled his lips in disgust.

"But he said she isn't what she seems. I think we should believe him."

"Well, I think you may need to be taken before the counsel yourself. You know the punishment for disobeying a counsel order."

Oh yeah. Oran's life as a soldier would be over.

"You're right," Oran relented. "He's got to be lying."

"I know I'm right. This pathetic Dagonian has decided to side with the human murderers. He deserves our worst."

Xanthus didn't like the sound of that. But he'd reached Oran on some level. It might not take much to push the soldier into helping him.

Ry opened a cell that had recently had its bars replaced. They looked shiny and strong. There would be no breaking out of this.

Xanthus resisted the urge to try to reason more with the guards. He didn't want to appear desperate, despite feeling just that. Instead, he narrowed his eyes and gave them a hard look that promised retribution. Oran took one look at his face and quickly turned away.

"In the cell," Ry said.

Xanthus began to back his way in.

"No. You go in head first."

"You really want to do that?" Xanthus sneered. "The counsel might be angry if I'm not alive to answer for the many soldiers I killed this day. But hey, it's your life."

Doubt clouded Ry's eyes for a brief moment and then it was gone. "If you're that important to them, they'll ask for you long before your life expires. Now move."

Xanthus inched his way into the dark, stony cell. He felt as if he were entering his own coffin. Perhaps he was. His mind raced. Should he have continued to fight after Sara was captured, regardless of whether or not they survived? Death may have been a better option. He hoped not, but at this moment, he had serious doubts. As bad as he found his own situation, he was tormented not knowing what was happening to her. The guards were not known for their gentleness, but so help him, if they laid a hand on her, he'd send them all to Tartarus to answer to Hades, or better yet, he'd send them to her father.

With that thought, a light switched on in Xanthus's head. A smile spread across his face. There was hope after all. Once the guards were gone, he spoke the words that would bring him unimaginable pain.

T HIRTY

Sara's eyes widened as they rose from the ground and rested on the last person she expected to see deep under the ocean's surface.

Slink.

He was flanked once again by Ettie and Tane. "No," she said in surprise. "What are *you* doing here?"

"Dreams do come true." Slink ignored her question. His smile widened, showing blackened teeth. His body looked more emaciated than ever.

"How's your boyfriend?" Slink chuckled. "It looks like he's doing a great job protecting you."

"Shut up, Slink." The deep, baritone voice caught her attention. She looked toward the opposite end of the long, narrow cell. A blond, tanned man strode toward them. His skin was dusted with white (salt maybe). Her defenses rose. There was something familiar about this man.

He sauntered over to her. "Sorry about Slink. I think his mother dropped him on his head when he was a baby."

The stranger put his hand out to shake hers. She kept her hand to herself, not willing to trust this prisoner yet.

"Don't worry, I won't bite. I can't vouch for those three." His head jerked back towards Slink, Ettie, and Tane. "My name's Josh, Josh Talbot."

Sara's jaw dropped. "You're the famous deep sea diver. The one that was lost in a diving accident."

Josh barked out a laugh. "You heard about that? It was no accident. I made the greatest discovery of this century, this millennium, probably of all time. Too bad you merpeople don't want to be discovered. Nice to meet one that speaks English."

"They aren't merpeople. They call themselves Dagonians."

Josh raised his eyebrow. "They?"

She ignored his question and looked around, inspecting the cell. It was not overly large, about ten feet wide and twenty feet long. The stone walls were layered in algae. Iron rings were bolted in the wall about every six feet. The floor was bare silt, except for a few rocks, a bowl of dirty water, and a couple of fish bones. The opposite wall was not made of stone, but was a wall of water. Sara couldn't see much except blue water, grey silt, and a school of silver fish.

"Who cares what they call themselves," Slink said. "They're all worthless. They think they can keep us down here. We're Americans. We have rights. These things don't feed us. They give us dirty water to drink; there are no beds, no bathroom, and no hope of leaving. And she's one of them. She's the reason we're here in the first place. I say we rip off her arms and have ourselves some seafood. What do you think, Ettie? Tane? You think you're strong enough to do it?"

Ettie moved forward. "Oh, yeah. I could do it."

"No one touches her without going through me," Josh said.

"Back off, Talbot. She has it coming," Slink said.

"You idiots don't realize." Josh shook his head. "She's not like us. She can escape if we help her. Then, if we do, then just maybe she'll help us get out of here too. Dudes, there are hundreds of feet of water between freedom and us. And as good a swimmer as I am, there's no way I could make it to the surface. I'm not seeing any better option, are you?"

"I can't leave," Sara said.

Josh turned to her. "Sure you can. That lock doesn't look too complicated. I know I could spring it."

"You don't understand. They have my husband here. If I escape, they'll kill him."

"Well, shoot." Josh plopped down, cross-legged in the sand. "You know, keeping my famously optimistic attitude has not been easy down here."

"Join the club," Sara said, eying Slink and his friends. They had strolled away and were whispering enthusiastically amongst themselves, planning something. Slink put his arm around Tane's shoulder. It was then she noticed Slink's hand was shaking. Drug withdrawals. That wouldn't put him into a very reasonable frame of mind.

"Okay." Slink slipped his arm away from Tane and strolled over to Josh.

Josh stood and Slink sneered at him. "Now that we know she won't help us, we're back to my original plan. And don't try to stop us, Talbot. We out number..." Josh's elbow slammed against Slink's nose. Blood exploded from his face as he bent forward. "Augh. What's wrong with you?"

Ettie and Tane came at Josh from opposite sides. Josh stepped back and Tane's fist hit Ettie in the forehead. From there, it was an all-out brawl between the three of them. Fists flew, kicks landed, and spittled grunts peppered the sand with blood.

What Sara didn't see until it was too late, was Slink coming up behind Josh with a rock in his hand. She shouted out just in time for Josh to turn around and get slammed in the face with it. He fell unconscious to the floor, blood running from a gash in his forehead.

"Whoa, that's a good one, Slink. Now what do we do with him?" Ettie took his jaw and moved it around, as if trying to work out the pain and stiffness from being punched.

"I say we put his head in the water and keep it there." Slink kicked Josh hard as he lay prone on the sandy floor. "What better way for a deep sea diver to die than by drowning?"

"No," Sara shouted. "He can't hurt you now. Just leave him alone."

"Oh look," Slink said. "It's the filthy little

mermaid begging for his life. I'd say that gives us more reason to kill him."

"But won't the guards be angry with you?" she asked.

"The guards? Like they care. Talbot here already killed two other people just this last week and the guards didn't bat an eye at it."

"He killed two men?" Sara didn't know why that bothered her. She'd seen Xanthus kill dozens of Dagonians earlier today. Maybe it was because Josh was a human, and humans weren't supposed to kill other humans.

"Oh, yeah. He was thinking he was all tough," Slink said. "Said he'd been a Navy Seal. The two guys who were here before us weren't impressed and decided they wanted to play around with Talbot. Talbot didn't like the games they played and later that night, he killed them while they were sleeping. Yeah, this Talbot is a real winner, killing people in their sleep. He's a coward, that's what he is.

"Come on, Ettie, Tane. Let's put his head in the water and see how long this diver can hold his breath."

"No, please, just leave him alone," Sara shouted as they shoved Josh's head into the wall of water. Josh jerked awake and thrashed around. Sara scooted along the floor and grabbed Tane's ankle. Tane responded by kicking her arm away.

She grabbed again. "Please stop."

Tane growled and slapped her hard across the

face. Sara felt as if her cheek had exploded. Through the spots of floating lights, she saw Josh flailing as Ettie and Slink held his head in the water.

She covered her face with her arms and began to cry. "Please let him go. Please let him go. Please let him go." Sara tried to block out the horrifying images. She'd thought she'd gotten over her fear of drowning, but it was all coming back to her. She continued to plead in a tormented rhythm that came from deep inside her. Eventually Josh's thrashing stopped and still, she continued to plead. "Please let him go."

Silence surrounded her. The only sound left now was her small keening and low chanting. Josh must be dead. She didn't know him well, but the short time she had, he'd been kind to her. Her heart broke a little at the terrible way he'd left the world.

Somewhere inside this torment, a part of her expected at any moment to be accosted. Almost without thinking, she wrapped the chain around her fingers, leaving a long loop she could swing if necessary. She knew when it came to physical strength, she didn't stand a chance against them, but she'd go down fighting.

When a few moments passed without an attack, she took a chance and glanced up. There they were—all of them, including Josh Talbot—staring at her. She squealed in surprise.

"You let him go," she said in total shock.

Slink eyes blinked, confused. "Of course. You asked us to. Why did we? What in the... Ettie, why did you let Talbot go?" he asked as he shoved him.

"I don't know. She asked us to? You let him go, too." Ettie shoved back.

"It was her voice," Tane said. "She was singing, you know... mermaids... sirens... they can hypnotize people with their voices."

Sara thought that was the most ridiculous thing she'd ever heard. But then again, come to think of it, people did seem to lose their minds every time she sang a tune. That was why she never, ever sang around other people. As a child, the attention she got had frightened her. Even Ron had lost his mind when she sang at the concert. Maybe Tane was right.

Sara felt like an idiot knowing what she was about to do, but hey, at this point, anything was worth a try.

Her melodious voice rang out and, to her surprise, it had a greater effect than she ever thought possible.

THIRTY-ONE

From within a dry, air-filled dungeon deep under Triton's palace, a voice was pleading for mercy. "Please, I just want to go home," the human woman cried. Her sobs caused her nose to drip mucus and her makeup-smudged eyes to swell red—definitely not becoming on her.

"Now Danielle," Triton said. "We've gone over this. You and your friends are responsible for killing over three thousand Dagonians. If I let you go, where is the justice in that?"

"But I didn't even know that Dagonians existed," she shouted, grating on his nerves. If the human couldn't show him more respect, he'd forget his intention of leaving her alive and turn her into sea foam, so help him.

Triton marched over and bent down, staring at her nose to nose. "I warned you. Do not raise your voice to me."

Her eyes widened. "I'm sorry. I was upset."

"I know you were. You're not the only one upset about this situation. Here, let me show you another example of what you've done."

"Please, no."

Rising

Triton raised his trident and manifested the body of a Dagonian infant lying pale against the sand, his black, glassy eyes open. Triton ignored Danielle's wails.

"This child was the firstborn son of a married couple named Ata and Hera. They had waited years for a child and were finally rewarded for their patience with his birth. They'd smothered him with love and affection for only two weeks. When he was merely fifteen days old, they were in their home enjoying a peaceful evening, unsuspecting that danger lurked from above. Hera had the babe at her breast when the poison descended on their home. The effects of the poison were felt immediately. It burned like acid, eating away at them, as they breathed it through their gills. They suffered for over an hour, clinging to one another until they finally died."

"I didn't know. Don't you think I would do things differently if only I'd known?" Danielle collapsed on the sandy floor and sobbed.

Without warning, several feet away, the floor swelled. It continued to grow until the sand vomited a large form covered in Heitach. "Well, it looks like your good friend, Xanthus, has sent me another guilty party. Shall we see who it is? Perhaps it's a friend of yours."

Triton raised his trident and the Heitach slithered off the body, which collapsed onto the ground. Triton recognized him at once.

"What is this?" He slammed his trident against the floor. "Xanthus Dimitriou, what is the meaning of this?"

Xanthus groaned and pushed his aching body away from the sandy ground. "Majesty," he said, his voice raspy. "I have important news for you, Sire."

Triton glared. His mouth twitched, almost smiling as he thought about the pain Xanthus had voluntarily endured. The Dagonian was a glutton for punishment. "And you couldn't come to me in the normal way? You know there are better ways to travel than by Heitach."

"Yes sir, but it was the only way I could think to get out of Panthon Prison."

Triton was dumbfounded. "And just what were you doing in Panthon Prison? I was under the impression you were still on land."

"I was imprisoned, along with Sara, my intended wife."

"I was not aware you were engaged. So you came down here to save your bride from prison? You know once she is in Panthon, there is no hope for her."

"That is usually true, but I was hoping you could help me," Xanthus said.

Triton was annoyed. Anytime a mortal got close to a god, it was only a matter of time before they start asking for favors. "What crime did she commit?"

"Her only crime was being born, Majesty. She was born on the surface. She has hidden among the humans since her birth twenty years ago."

A lump formed in Triton's throat and he felt as if

a stone had been placed on his chest. He knew that there was only one likely answer to his next question. Still, he hoped beyond hope that he was wrong. "And pray tell me, who is this prisoner's mother?"

"Her name is Nicole."

Xanthus and Danielle were blown back hard against the stone wall as Triton erupted in a roar. Xanthus landed on the floor. He pushed himself up to confront Triton. The sea god had transformed, exploding into a twenty-foot tall figure with gaping jaws of sharp, serrated teeth and burning red eyes. He looked like a demon. His deafening roar filled the dungeon with retching torment.

"I have a daughter? How could I not know?" He screamed in anguish. His head whipped around as accusing eyes pierced Xanthus. "Now your Dagonian's have her in prison. How dare they put a daughter of Triton in Panthon Prison! I will kill them all. They will writhe in pain and agony while their flesh is slowly eaten away. So help me, if they harm one hair on her head, they will all die this day." He moved in close, his towering figure bent over Xanthus as his voice roared like a beast.

Xanthus was struck with fear at the awesome power and fury of an angry god. Still, he was somehow able to find his voice. He hoped Triton would hear him out before striking him down.

"They don't know she's your daughter."

Triton moved closer, and snarled. "But you knew, didn't you? Why would you not tell them?"

"Sara and I were the only ones who knew the truth. You don't know the hatred my father and the counsel had for your merchildren. She does not as yet bear your mark of protection. If they had known the truth, they would have had both of us killed and our bodies destroyed before you could learn of her existence. I knew it was safer for them to think she was half-human, half-Dagonian. At least until we could come to you."

Triton narrowed his eyes, perhaps deciding whether or not to blow Xanthus into oblivion. Danielle stirred and began to whimper. Triton turned his trident on her and in a flash of light, she was gone.

Xanthus had to ask. "Is she...?"

"...back with the humans." Triton's answer was dismissive. He paused, deep in thought. "I'll need you to come with me to the prison. Maybe you can keep me from killing every Dagonian I lay eyes on."

Triton sighed. "Somehow I don't think that would endear my daughter to me, at our first meeting, to see her father kill everyone in sight."

"Yes sir. I *must* go regardless. It is killing me not knowing whether she is being mistreated. If that is the case, I may join you in your killing spree."

"Well, let's hope it doesn't come to that."

Xanthus had no warning when a flash of light blinded his vision. When he could see again, he found himself at the doors of Panthon Prison. Triton was back to his normal form. Xanthus hoped he wouldn't ever have to see him in his angry god form again.

There were two large guards stationed on each side of the door. The larger and meaner looking of the two swam forward. "Xanthus Dimitriou, I don't know how you escaped from your cell, but it's good of you to turn yourself in."

"Let us pass," Triton said.

The guard turned to him in disgust. "I don't know who you are, but no one..."

Triton raised his trident and the guard began to shake. He thrashed around, wailing as his body shriveled up around his bones and, a moment later, his skeletal form floated away lifeless, carried by the gentle current.

Xanthus turned to the other guard, whose eyes were wide in horror, his face white as sea foam. "You might want to let King Triton pass."

"Yes, of course, Majesty." The guard shook himself out of his stupor, yanked open the door, and let them in.

As soon as they passed through the doors, guards rushed in and surrounded them. Before there were more misunderstandings, Xanthus shouted. "King Triton is here for his daughter."

The group erupted in a confusion of voices and questions. "There is no mermaid being held here."

"A daughter of Triton, here?"

"I thought they were all dead." The questions

came at them from all sides at once.

"Enough," Triton shouted. The building rumbled at his voice and cracks branched out from the foundation and up the stone walls. "Where is the half-human prisoner, called Sara?"

A small guard inched forward. "She was put into the human cell."

This was not where Xanthus expected her to be. He'd expected her to be put into a cell by herself. When he thought of those who would be with her, he exploded in anger. "Take us there now!"

The guard flinched back. "Yes, of course." As they rushed away, Xanthus heard the other guards flee the building.

Triton and Xanthus raced through the maze of hallways into the more rough tunnels of a crumbling part of the prison.

They approached an old, beat-up door. Xanthus was surprised to find no guard there.

"Where did the guard go?" The small guard asked, echoing Xanthus's concern.

"Let me pass," Triton demanded. The guard moved aside. Triton grabbed the door and ripped it off its hinges. As he passed through to the air pocket, his transformation from merman to human was smooth and flawless. Xanthus immediately followed along with his not-so-smooth conversion as he turned human.

"Well, hello there," a deep, cheerful voice greeted them.

Xanthus looked around, afraid of what he might find. He had sent Slink and his pathetic sidekicks to this cell himself. He'd had no idea that Sara would have *ever* been put in here with them. He was sick with worry about what they might have done to her. But what he found was a cheerful human sitting amongst the three unconscious, bleeding forms of Sara's old neighbors. Sara was nowhere to be found.

"Where's Sara?" Xanthus asked.

"The little Dagonian? Oh, she sang her way out of here."

"She what?" Xanthus was confused at the answer.

"Do you know where she was headed?" Triton asked the human.

"She was going to save her husband."

Triton turned to Xanthus. "Where were you being held?"

"In the belly of the beast."

"You Dagonians are so dramatic." Triton shook his head. "Why is she calling you her husband?"

"I tried to marry her. She thinks we are married, but I found out the priest was not a true priest. I decided it was best for her not to know we aren't actually married. She was ready to turn herself in to save me."

"Your Dagonian laws are ridiculous. Why a man should have to pay for his wife's crime is beyond me. Still, a daughter of mine was willing to make that kind of sacrifice? That *is* surprising."

"Your daughter is an amazing woman."

"So, if you aren't married, why were you imprisoned also?"

"I killed about three dozen soldiers when they came to take her," Xanthus said, unregretful.

"I would expect no less of any husband of my daughter."

Xanthus and Triton moved quickly through the tunnels. As they moved further in, darkness enveloped them. The stifling gloom and stench of rot increased as they neared the dungeon area that held the most heinous criminals.

"They really must not have liked what you did to put you down here," Triton remarked.

"You could say..." Xanthus heard a faint singing voice that brought him to a stop. It was beyond beautiful. It was the most amazing...

Triton lifted his trident; a beam of light shot out and struck Xanthus like a slap in the face. "What did you do that for?" Xanthus asked.

"I think it's best, if you're to be my daughter's husband, that she not have that kind of power over you."

Triton and Xanthus once again rushed forward. As they neared, the sound of Sara's voice became clearer. She really did have a lovely voice, but her lyrics and cadence left a lot to be desired. Xanthus gave that a fleeting thought as he hurried toward her. From what he heard, she seemed to be instructing a guard in song to keep looking for him.

They came around a corner and her tiny, frantic

figure came into view.

Triton gasped. "She looks just like her mother."

THIRTY-TWO

Sara's frustration grew with every passing moment. Locating her husband had been much more difficult than she'd expected. Half of the effort she'd exerted in her search had been used to keep the guard on task. He hadn't been able to keep his stupid, groping hands off her. She worked a few words of exasperation into her tune, as she once again slapped him away.

With each passing moment, she'd grown more and more anxious until now, she was about to panic. A couple of times she'd stopped singing to call out to her husband, only to find the guard snapping out of his trance and making a grab for her. A few desperate screeches of a melody was all she needed to be safe again.

"Moro Mou." A familiar voice came from down the passageway. Sara turned and found Xanthus and another Dagonian swimming toward her.

"Xanthus," she cried as she swam at him so fast that she nearly knocked the wind out of herself when they collided. His arms encircled her. His warm embrace had never felt so good.

"I was so worried," she said. "We've been through

these cells three times, now. And I couldn't find you. This guard insisted you were here. Well, I don't know if insisted is the right word. He said it in his I'm-under-your-spell-and-will-do-your-bidding voice."

Xanthus shook his head. "And here I thought I'd be the one saving you, Mou. But it looks like you've saved yourself. How could I have forgotten the siren's song? So you hypnotized them with your voice?"

Sara nodded. "I guess you could say that. I just found out I could. It was cool at first, but now it's just annoying. This Dagonian keeps touching me. But still, I was able to get out and find you. By the way, how did you get out of your cell?"

"Hello Sara." The Dagonian stranger inched forward.

"Hold it right there." The guard raised his spear.

"Oh, not again," she said and then opened her mouth wide to continue her stupid song.

The stranger lifted a trident and froze the guard on the spot.

"I... uh..." Sara's song ended in startled surprise. The guard's statue-like form floated down to the floor. She turned to Xanthus and whispered, "Can all Dagonians do that?"

Xanthus smiled and shook his head.

Sara turned back to the stranger. He looked like any other Dagonian, maybe a bit larger and more muscular. About Xanthus's size actually. But his eyes, they had the same blue luminescence as hers own! "Are you Triton?" she asked, suddenly timid.

Triton nodded. He looked unsure.

"Are you my dad?" she asked, hopefully.

He gave a tentative smile. "Yes, I am."

"Majesty," Xanthus said, "may I suggest we take this reunion to a more appropriate place?"

Sara could hear the wailing of prisoners in the background. Xanthus was right. This was not the best place for a family reunion. Light blinded her for a moment and then her vision came into focus in the most beautiful seascape gardens she could have ever imagined. There were huge, colorful anemones, giant clams, coral the size of palm trees, hundreds of colorful fish, and towering sculptures all set in front of the most amazing castle she'd ever seen.

"Sara," Triton said. "I don't know what I can say or do to make up for not being there for you. Living as a mermaid amongst the humans must have been very difficult for you. I'm truly sorry."

Sara shrugged. "You can't help what you didn't know. I don't blame you for anything. Besides, I think I did all right."

"You ended up in Panthon Prison." Triton's voice was thick with regret.

"I was there for a few hours." She shrugged. "I'm just glad Xanthus found me. My husband is an amazing Dagonian, don't you think?"

Xanthus cleared his throat. "Well, actually, we're not really married, Mou."

"What?" Sara asked.

"The priest was a fake." Xanthus cocked one eyebrow and shrugged.

"He was? When did you find out?"

Xanthus shrugged.

Sara's eyes widened. "You knew all along, didn't you? And just *when* were you going to let me know?" Sara pushed him away.

"Um, I just told you," Xanthus said.

"You should have told me as soon as you found out. There was no reason that we both needed to end up in prison. Oh, that reminds me. Josh Talbot. We need to go back to the prison. He needs our help."

"Who's Josh Talbot?" Triton asked.

"He's a human, a deep sea diver. He was in the cell with me. He protected me from Slink and his friends. It almost cost Josh his life. I hope he's okay. I couldn't figure out how to take him with me. And I couldn't bring myself to have Slink and his friends drown themselves. I hope my rash decision didn't end his life."

"Don't worry, Sara," Triton said. "We saw him when we went to find you. He looked like he had things under control. And anyone that saves a daughter of mine will be well rewarded.

"Now, I think it's time I hear who took you prisoner. I want names. I want details and don't leave anything out." Triton looked Sara in the eye.

"I'll let Xanthus tell you. He knows more than I do. The situation was hard for me to understand since *no one* spoke English. I would like to know what was said, too." Sara put her hands on her hips and fixed Xanthus with accusing eyes. He responded by pulling her into his arms. She didn't resist. Instead, she wrapped her own arms around his waist and laid her head against his chest.

Xanthus related the entire story to her father. Sara's tightened her grip at the more shocking or horrendous accountings he told. He related to Triton every detail of what had happened. He even told Triton about his father's epic hatred of the Mer and how, even now, he kept the body of a mermaid in his home. It was obvious why Xanthus had chosen not to tell his father about her true identity. In the end, he had laid all his family secrets out for the god to inspect.

Her father's response was surprisingly mild. "Very well, Xanthus. I can hear the anger and your wish for retribution in your voice. But I would rather you forget all that happened. Focus on taking care of my daughter and making her happy. I will see that all the guilty are punished and you'll think no more on it.

"Furthermore, I know you have your heart set on convincing the humans of the error of their ways and cooling the feelings of hatred your Dagonians have for them. Although I think it's an impossible task, I understand your desire. I also know that in order for you to accomplish your goal, you must mingle with your enemy and live among them for a time. I will grant you as much time as you feel you need.

"I also know that you love my daughter and wish to marry her. Here's where the conflict in me lies. I have a desire to get to know this daughter of mine and I don't trust the human's at all. They are a selfish and self-serving people. But I can also see the great love my daughter has for you and I doubt she'll want to live apart from you. So here's my compromise—I will allow her to return to the surface with you under certain conditions. First, that she is guarded at all times, either by you or by other soldiers you trust to keep her safe. My protection does not extend into my uncle Zeus's domain, so you'll have to take special precautions. Then she must take at least three months out of each year to visit me, so that we may get to know one another as father and daughter."

"But..." Xanthus sounded like he was about to protest, but stopped himself.

Her father gave a knowing smile. "You may accompany her on her visits if you wish."

"Thank you, Sire."

"Um, Father... I was wondering. I mean, if I'm going to be on land for a while. Do you think you could...?" She paused, losing her nerve to ask for her greatest desire.

"Yes? What would you ask of me, daughter?" Triton looked confused at her hesitation.

"Sire," Xanthus said, "I believe she would like to know if you could gift her with human legs."

Sara braced for his response. He couldn't possibly say no, could he? Maybe there was more to it than waving a wand or casting a spell. Perhaps there were rules against giving a mermaid legs.

Triton didn't answer. He simply slammed his trident against the sandy sea floor. The water around them drained as if someone had pulled a plug. As the water receded, Sara found herself on the beach of a beautiful tropical island. As the last of the water withdrew from around them, she could hear Xanthus growling in pain. Then a strange new sensation distracted her. When she realized what it was, she gasped, amazed beyond words. She looked down and found herself standing on legs.

Xanthus rushed over in a panic. "Sara, are you all right?"

"Yes, I'm fine." She beamed.

He grabbed her, horrified. "Are you sure? You're not hurt?"

Sara shook her head.

"You think I would cause my daughter pain?" Triton bellowed.

Xanthus turned toward her father. "But why do I have to..."

"Your type of change uses less of my power." Triton shrugged. "Besides, you can handle it. In fact, I'm considering having you travel by Heitach and report to me monthly."

Xanthus paled.

Triton laughed. "That was a joke, Dagonian."

Xanthus breathed out a sigh of relief.

Sara smiled as she pranced around, enjoying the

sensation of the sand beneath her feet. Then she began to skip. It was all so amazing, a beautiful feeling. Her legs felt as if they'd always been a part of her. She could walk, run, skip.... She felt nimble, as if she could dance and twirl, maybe even cartwheel. She stopped herself before she tried that. She'd hate to break these new legs.

She turned to Xanthus, who was talking to her father.

"She looks like she's been on human feet her whole life," Xanthus remarked, amazed. "I don't understand—it took me months to learn to walk."

"Get used to it, Dagonian," her father replied. "She's my daughter. I'm willing to use more of my power on her than I would on you."

Sara sprinted to her father. She wrapped her arms around him and pressed her face into his wide chest. "Thank you, Dad." Her heart swelled to near bursting.

Sara looked up to see the Guardian of the Sea with a tear in his eye when he responded. "You're welcome, baby."

Sara felt a sharp tingle trace along and around her cheekbone in some unseen design. "What was that?" She touched her fingertip along the path.

"It is my mark. To warn all who see it that you're under my protection. No Dagonian or any other creature of the sea would dare harm you while you carry that mark. Just remember, it's only seen in the water. On land you're still vulnerable."

Sara stepped away from her father's embrace.

"Now," Triton said, "one more question before the evening falls. Do you want me to marry you both now or do you want to wait for a big wedding fit for the daughter of a sea king?"

"Well, I don't know." Sara turned and approached Xanthus. He reached out and took her hand. "Would it be better to wait until after—you know. When I'm not fertile?" Sara whispered the last word so that only Xanthus heard her. She could feel her face burn.

"We already did." Xanthus smiled. "And I can't tell you what a relief it is."

"So what is your answer, daughter?" Triton raised an eyebrow.

She and Xanthus stepped into each other's arms and answered in unison. "Now."

EPILOGUE

Triton should have dropped Gael and his father on a sand dune in the middle of the Sahara Desert, but Sara made him swear to her that he wouldn't kill them. And even though technically, it would have been the heat and baking sun that killed them, Triton knew his daughter wouldn't see it that way, so he did the next best thing. He turned them into humans and left them stark naked on the Kansas plains, surrounded by hundreds of miles of dry, golden wheat fields.

They deserved much worse, but a guilty conscience can make a god do things out of character. Actually, a guilty conscience *was* out of character for a god and lately, he seemed to have more than his ungodly share.

Triton's heart clenched as he thought of the tragic story that was his life. He could no longer blame his father and the Dagonians, although he'd tried for over two thousand years. Now he acknowledged that any other god would have done the same thing his father had done if they had been so severely disrespected and humiliated. And the Dagonians... Well, they were just following orders.

The destruction of his children had been his own fault. It had been his fault for not teaching them respect, for not giving them boundaries, for overindulging them. He'd seen how Sara had turned out—so selfless, humble, and kind. Under Nicole's mothering, his daughter had flourished.

Triton fisted his fingers in his hair and crumpled into himself at the pain that was still there when he thought of Nicole. It had been twenty years, but he could still taste her on his lips, feel the shape of her body in his arms. She was the beauty that nearly crushed a god into oblivion—the most amazing, exquisite, and perfectly maddening woman he'd ever met.

Triton had blamed Aphrodite for his lapse in judgment, but if it *were* her magic that had caused the torrid love affair, why was he *still* tormented by the memory of the human girl? The magic should have faded long ago.

Regardless of where his feelings came from, he could no longer bury himself from the memory of them or the pain. Nicole was his daughter's mother, the mother who had raised her. He could not continue to hide. He would have to confront her.

He wished for a moment that he'd had the courage to ask Sara if her mother had found happiness with another man, but he couldn't bear to ask. Some all-powerful god he was.

He had to see her. He had to see if she was happy,

see if she had found love. He dared not hope she could ever learn to love him again, learn to trust him again.

It took all the courage Triton could muster to flash himself to Nicole's home. He took in the view of her bright, yellow house and his heart sped up double time. Before he lost his courage, he stepped up to her front door. He was terrified. He remembered every detail of the day he had left, the day she had shredded his heart with her pleas that he not leave.

Now that he was back, what kind of welcome would he receive? A loving one would be too much to ask. An angry reception would be what he deserved. A dispassionately civil one would be too much to bear.

By the gods, he was over-analyzing this. With his heart pulsing under his ribs and his chest trembling with nervousness, he raised his fist and rapped on the door.

ABOUT THE AUTHOR

    I'm a mom who writes books in her spare time: translation—I hide in the bathroom with my laptop and lock the door while the kids destroy the house and smear peanut butter on the walls. ;) I was born in Utah but lived in Salina, Kansas until I was 13 and in Garland, Texas until I was 18. I'm now back in Utah—"happy valley". I'm married to a wonderful husband, James, and we are currently raising 6 rambunctious children. My interests are reading, writing (of course), martial arts, visual arts, and spending time with family.

Clean Teen Publishing